DATE			

© THE BAKER & TAYLOR CO.

MURDER AT
MT. FUJI

MURDER AT MT. FUJI

Shizuko
Natsuki

St. Martin's Press
New York

MURDER AT MT. FUJI. Copyright © 1984 by Shizuko Natsuki. Translated by Robert B. Rohmer. All rights reserved. Printed in the United States of America. No part of this book may be used or reproduced in any manner whatsoever without written permission except in the case of brief quotations embodied in critical articles or reviews. For information, address St. Martin's Press, 175 Fifth Avenue, New York, N.Y. 10010.

Design by Lee Wade

Library of Congress Cataloging in Publication Data

Natsuki, Shizuko, 1938-
    Murder at Mt. Fuji.

    Translation of: W no higeki.
    I. Title.
PL857.A85W213 1984   895.6'35   83-24458
ISBN 0-312-55287-4

First Edition
10 9 8 7 6 5 4 3 2 1

MURDER AT
MT. FUJI

1

The House
by the Lake

The special express to Gotemba departed at noon from the northwest terminal of Tokyo's Shinjuku Station. Most of the seats were occupied as the train pulled out of the station, the passengers returning home after having paid their New Year's respects at the Meiji shrine. More than half of them got off at the next station down the line. Gotemba, the train's final destination, was the jumping off place for excursions in the Mt. Fuji region; from there one could go to the mountain itself, or to the nearby Fuji Five Lakes district. Winter, however, was the off season in that area and by the time the train approached its final stop, fewer than twenty percent of the seats were still occupied.

In Tokyo the weather was dry and clear, but as they approached the mountains, the sky grew overcast with dark, snow-laden clouds, and when the train finally reached Gotemba at two o'clock, light snow was falling.

Jane Prescott descended from the empty coach. Hunching her shoulders, she buried her chin in her muffler for protection against the icy wind. She looked about at the melancholy scene, her gaze taking in the shabby roof and pillars of the station building. It reminded her of the rural train stations back home in Oregon. As she passed through the ticket-taker's gate, the old-fashioned clock in the gable of the building indicated 2:03.

Light snow was swirling and dancing around the seedy plaza in front of the station. A row of real estate offices and small inns lined the far side of the plaza. Sacred straw ropes marking the holiday season hung looped beneath the eaves of the inns and fluttered indifferently in the cold wind. Within moments all the passengers had dispersed. Perhaps because it was still early in the season, the

1

Shizuko Natsuki

crowds of young skiers and skaters one might have expected to find there were absent.

Several taxis and private cars moved about the plaza. An empty taxi cruised to a halt beside Jane, but she shook her head and began walking. A sign directed her toward the bus stop where a clutter of signs indicated which buses went where. Several buses were waiting, clouds of white smoke rising from their exhaust pipes.

Jane's destination was a villa in the country, where Chiyo Wada was anticipating her arrival. She had been instructed to take the bus to Asahi Hills, an exclusive vacation community on the shores of Lake Yamanaka. Jane had promised to telephone Chiyo before she got on the bus so her friend could meet her when she arrived.

Consulting the posted schedule, Jane learned that there were three buses every two hours, and that the next bus departed at 2:30. She rummaged through her shoulder bag for a small notebook and coin purse and looked around for a public telephone. Her view was obstructed by a large man sauntering toward her.

"Are you going to Lake Kawaguchi?" he asked in fluent English. He spoke pleasantly in a deep, somewhat husky voice. He had thick lips and rough-hewn features and appeared to be in his mid-thirties, maybe a bit older. A short, black raincoat was draped over his massive shoulders.

"No," replied Jane, also in English. "I'm only going as far as Lake Yamanaka."

"What part of Lake Yamanaka?" he asked with an innocent smile, but Jane had the feeling she was being carefully appraised. She wore a fur-lined Burberry coat and tan Indian boots, and carried a shoulder bag and a small overnight case. No doubt she appeared to be one of those typical foreign women who enjoyed traveling alone.

"Well, actually, I'm going to Asahi Hills."

"Oh, well so am I. If you like, I'll give you a lift in my car." He indicated a silver sports car parked at the edge of the plaza. It was a Mercedes-Benz hardtop with Tokyo license plates.

Jane looked at the car, then back at the man. This sort of invitation was really not so unusual. Particularly when one traveled alone in rural areas one often encountered someone who offered a

2

ride out of the goodness of his heart. Knowing this the traveler could accept a ride with little to fear. The practice may have derived from the American custom of hitchhiking, but it was certainly much safer to accept a ride from a stranger in Japan.

Jane paused to take a breath before replying. "Thank you, I appreciate your offer, but I've already arranged to have a friend meet me at the bus stop."

The man's gaze took in the coin purse and the notebook in Jane's hand. "Have you already made arrangements, then?"

"I'm just on my way to call now."

"Wouldn't it be easier if I simply took you to your friend's house and dropped you off?"

"Well, perhaps, but . . ." Jane decided that on the bus she would have a chance to make inquiries about what the villas around here were like. "I guess I'll take the bus after all."

"All right, if that's the way you want it." The man looked disappointed as he turned and walked away.

After watching him walk to his car and drive off, Jane retraced her steps to the station, where she had noticed a yellow pay phone located beside a bare Ginko tree.

I wonder, she thought, if it would have been dangerous to accept a ride from that stranger?

She went to the telephone booth and dialed the number of the villa. The phone rang three times before a young woman's voice answered, "Hello, Wada residence." It was not Chiyo's voice, so Jane assumed it was one of the maids who had come from Tokyo to help with the housework. Jane dropped a hundred-yen coin in the telephone slot and said in fluent Japanese, "Hello. My name is Jane Prescott. Is Chiyo in?"

"Yes. Just a moment please."

Two or three minutes passed before a woman's soft voice answered, "Hello." Jane immediately recognized it as Chiyo's.

"Chiyo, is that you? I'm at Gotemba Station. I just arrived."

"Oh, you're here. I've been waiting for you." Chiyo's voice was vibrant with sincere delight. "It's late. I was worried that something might have happened."

"I'm sorry to have worried you. Last night the members of my foreign student club went out to play mah jong and I'm afraid I slept in this morning. How is your work coming along? I hope you're making progress?"

"Yes, I suppose I am, but it's hard without having you here to help me."

Jane explained that she would be taking the 2:30 bus, and Chiyo said she would be waiting at the Asahi Hills bus stop. It was a forty-minute bus trip.

"I suppose the others have already arrived by now," said Jane, hearing people's voices in the background.

"The rest of us have been here since yesterday. The chief accountant for the company and a couple of the maids are still around, but after they leave, it looks like there'll only be about eight of us here this year."

"They're all members of the family then?"

"Yes, that's right."

"I'm afraid I'll be intruding on a family affair."

"No. No, not at all. We consider it an honor that you came all this way just to be with us for the New Year's holiday. Mother said I was most unreasonable to ask you to come here in the first place. But anyway, I'm so pleased you've come, really I am."

Hearing this put Jane's mind at ease. "Well then, I'll just barge right in and make myself at home." With this parting comment she hung up the phone.

When she picked up her overnight bag and stepped out of the phone booth, the snow was coming down more than before. Although her bag was small, it was surprisingly heavy, weighed down by a well-used dictionary and another large book.

Chiyo Wada was a senior in the English Department at Japan Women's University. At the age of twenty-five, Jane Prescott was three years older than Chiyo and an American exchange student studying in the graduate school at the same university. Jane was specializing in modern Japanese literature and had come to Japan after completing a master's degree in Japanese at the University of Oregon. She had been in Japan for a year and a half on a grant, but finding that her subsidy did not cover all her expenses, had taken a part-time job tutoring Chiyo in conversational English.

4

The makeup of Chiyo's family was rather complicated. Her great uncle, Yohei Wada, was the patriarch of the family and the president of Wada Pharmaceuticals, one of the largest pharmaceutical companies in Japan. His name and that of his company were household words all over the country. It was a tradition in the Wada family to get together every year for the New Year's holiday at one of Yohei's several villas. After dismissing their retainers, the entire clan would spend two or three days in seclusion enjoying the holiday. This year they had selected the summer home on the shores of Lake Yamanaka for their reunion. Properly speaking, Jane should not have been invited to the private family gathering, but Chiyo had asked that Jane be allowed to join them because her graduation thesis would have to be submitted soon, and she needed Jane's help in revising it.

The theme of Chiyo's thesis was Virginia Woolf; more precisely, a critical study of *Mrs. Dalloway*. Chiyo had enough innate sensibility to understand and appreciate Virginia Woolf, but her ability to write in English was shaky at best, perhaps because she had been educated in private girls' schools and had never had to study for college entrance examinations. Nevertheless, as a student majoring in English, she was required to write her graduation thesis in that language. In addition to submitting her thesis, she also had to sit for an oral examination. The thesis was due on January 10 and in order to meet the deadline Chiyo had asked Jane to read the entire thesis and check the places where her use of English was awkward, as well as to rehearse her for the oral examination.

Chiyo had waited until after Christmas before suddenly asking Jane to join the family for the holiday, apparently because she had lost confidence in her ability to complete the job herself. Seeing Chiyo's desperate face and realizing that she was on the verge of tears, Jane had felt she could hardly refuse to help. Chiyo had always lived a sheltered life and was such a delicate person both physically and emotionally that most people's natural response was to be protective of her. It was a certain kind of natural charm the girl had. Even among the complex personal relationships that existed within the Wada family, Chiyo was the one person everyone loved.

Shizuko Natsuki

This fact was the source of the tragedy that was to follow.

There were perhaps ten people waiting at the bus stop by the time the bus was ready to leave. It left promptly at 2:30 and threaded its way through the shop-lined streets of the city and out onto Highway 138, Mt. Fuji soaring majestically in front of them. Although capped with snow, the mountain was not completely white; dark blue streaks running down from the peak accentuated the steepness of its slope.

The clean, paved road wound its way through the foothills in gentle curves. As they drove along, Fuji remained fixed in its position, filling the very center of the windshield. This view of the mountain was much different from the impression one got seeing it at a distance from the window of a bullet train. At this close range one was made aware of its powerful, imposing presence.

As the landscape unfolded around her, Jane was caught up in the natural beauty of the Fuji Five Lakes region. It was snowing off and on, sometimes falling heavily only to let up moments later. The road they followed was alternately lined with fields of vegetables and groves of cedar. Occasionally there would be a beautiful stand of bare, winter trees. Larch forests towered over them with sharp, angular branches that reached up into the sky. The branches were heavily laden with snow, and the red light of the late afternoon sun shone dimly through the treetops. Mt. Fuji was always in front of them, but the gently sloping ridges of the hills continued to act like a screen, cutting off the view as the bus ran through the broad fields on the lower slopes of the mountain.

At each stop the driver would announce their location on his microphone and two or three people would get off. Only a few new passengers boarded the bus. Within an hour they passed the Tsuzura grade and approached their destination. Rounding a sharp curve they saw a sign announcing, LAKE YAMANAKA TOWN-SHIP—YAMANASHI PREFECTURE. A short distance further on was another sign, KAGOSAKA PASS. A tape-recorded message came on the bus's loudspeaker: "This is Kagosaka Pass; we are one thousand fifteen meters above sea level. In ancient times this road was called the Kamakura Highway. It was along this route that fresh fish and salt as well as the culture of Kamakura and Edo were taken into the mountainous provinces of the interior. This pass is famous for the snow drifts that gather here. In a few moments we will be arriving at our destination of Asahi Hills." As the recorded message ended, the bus began a steep descent.

The snow was falling harder than ever and the houses along the road were powdered with it. They had obviously arrived at the shores of Lake Yamanaka, a region dotted by summer houses. The construction of the houses was different from that of the farmhouses they had passed earlier; many of these were elaborately designed villas.

The lake spread out before them at the bottom of the slope, where the road turned at a sharp right angle and followed along the shore. The Asahi Hills bus stop was at the point where the road curved.

As Jane got up from her seat, she could see Chiyo waiting at the covered bus stop. Chiyo was wearing a short, cherry pink coat and a dark brown scarf over her head. Her skirt was the same color as the scarf, and beneath it Jane could see the short, high-heeled boots that encased her slim, straight legs. Chiyo always presented a slender, delicate silhouette. The moment she saw Jane, a smile bloomed on her pale face and she waved.

As Jane stepped off the bus, Chiyo's first words were the traditional New Year's greeting. Jane returned the greeting in Japanese. Since Jane spoke Japanese comfortably, the two women made a practice of conversing in that language except when they were working on Chiyo's English lessons. Their breath hung in white clouds as they chatted in the cold air.

"I hope it's not too cold for you here," said Chiyo with concern. She had classic Japanese features: a long, oval face with narrow eyes and a thin nose. The clean line of her chin was delicate and attractive.

"It's certainly every bit as cold as I expected it would be. But that's all right, I'm fine," replied Jane with a shiver.

"I guess I should have met you with the car."

"How long does it take to walk from here?"

"If we hurry, it will take about fifteen minutes."

"That's not so bad."

Gas stations, drive-in restaurants, and real estate offices lined the highway. Behind them was another street that served as the main business street of Asahi Hills.

Chiyo turned toward the lake and pointed to the mountains off to the left. "Our house is this way. It is in a very quiet neighborhood on the west side of town."

The two women crossed a pedestrian bridge over the highway and walked along the road following the shore of the lake. Snow continued to fall. There was a continuous stream of cars on the road, but virtually no other pedestrians in sight.

"It looks like the lake is already frozen over."

"Only in some places. Underground springs bubble up in other places and keep the water from freezing."

The surface of the lake was white with an icy blue cast. Here and there it appeared to be frozen in ripples or waves, but occasional patches of open water were smooth and peaceful. Two boats floated in one of the open patches, fishing for fresh-water smelt. Apart from this, there was nothing, not even the usual groups of people skating. The dry reeds along the shore shivered in the wind. The surroundings were desolate, but the soaring peak of Mt. Fuji in the background gave a majestic quality to the scene.

Along the shore of the lake were a number of resort hotels with New Year's pine decorations adorning their gates, white birches in their front gardens, and stereo music coming from within. As they passed the hotels, Chiyo explained, "The only time they have guests here in the winter is at New Year's time."

The main commercial district in Asahi Hills was surrounded on three sides by summer homes that looked out over the north end of the lake. The main road ran along the edge of the lake and branched into many smaller streets only a few meters wide. These in turn branched out into small lanes leading to individual homes. Chiyo turned left where the street sloped up away from the lake at the third street from the Asahi Hills intersection. The frozen surface of the street was lightly dusted with snow, and more was beginning to collect atop the wooden fences on both sides. Away from the streets the snow was deeper, as though left over from an earlier snowfall.

"The street is slippery, so be careful," cautioned Chiyo.

The first summer homes they passed were built close together, nearly touching at the eaves, but the further they climbed, the more spacious the lots became and the larger the houses. Many of them were elegant, Western-style homes, but occasionally mixed among them was a traditional Japanese-style home, or one built with the steep roof of the traditional Japanese farmhouse. Between the houses were groves of pine, larch, maple, and birch.

Nightfall came early in the mountains, and this, combined with the lowering snow clouds, made the women feel chilled. Here and there were streetlights designed like the old-fashioned gas lamps of London. On every side the summer homes were quiet and deserted, their gates closed, but there were indications of life in a couple of the larger buildings that displayed signs announcing them to be businesses, hostels, or resorts.

The hill grew steeper and the two women began to breathe heavily as they walked on in silence. Suddenly they heard the sound of a motor and a small, white, compact car came slowly down the hill toward them. The lane was so narrow it was difficult for even a single car to get through. To get out of the car's way, Chiyo and Jane had to press close to the wooden fence that ran along the street. Just as it came abreast of the two women, however, the car stopped. A young man stuck his head out the window and smiled at Chiyo. He had short, trimmed hair and wore gold-rimmed glasses.

"When I heard you'd gone out on foot in all this snow, I thought I had better come out and give you a lift."

"It wasn't snowing like this when I left the house," said Chiyo cheerfully.

"Well come on, hurry up and get in." The man unlocked the back door and the two women got in.

"Let me introduce you. This is Takuo Wada, he is my granduncle's nephew. Takuo's father was my granduncle's younger brother. Takuo works in the accounting department of Wada Pharmaceuticals." Chiyo then went on to introduce Jane. "This is Jane Prescott, who has been teaching me conversational English since last spring. I call her my teacher, but of course she is not much

9

older than I. She is studying modern Japanese literature as a graduate student at the university."

Jane felt Takuo's quick, birdlike eyes appraising her. The next question came from him. "Which writers are you particularly interested in?" Takuo addressed her in Japanese, and there was a certain disagreeable tone to his voice, as though he was testing Jane.

"Right now I am reading Yasunari Kawabata and Yukio Mishima."

"Oh well, no wonder your Japanese is so good."

"I completed a master's degree in Japanese at the University of Oregon before coming to Japan, but I'm afraid I still have a long way to go."

"On the contrary, you're really doing very well." Takuo suddenly switched to English as he said this. Apparently he wanted to show Jane that his English was just as good as her Japanese. "Actually, my granduncle, Yohei, sent me to the University of Pennsylvania for a year as an exchange student."

Takuo laughed cheerfully and turned his attention to Chiyo. "Well, shall we go on back to the house? Dinner will be early tonight, and afterwards Grandpa wants to talk to you about something." Though Yohei Wada was Takuo's granduncle, all the members of the family simply called him Grandpa.

As Takuo turned back to his driving, Chiyo pursed her lips and looked down.

Takuo shifted into reverse and began backing up with great speed and confidence. At the same time, Jane noticed a melancholy expression on Chiyo's face that contrasted oddly with the cheerful tone in Takuo's voice.

Jane had been meeting with Chiyo twice a week for almost a year, but only rarely did they discuss their personal lives. Jane did know that Chiyo's granduncle had been urging her to get married, and had made it clear he would prefer she marry someone in the family. Jane suddenly wondered if Takuo was a prospective husband for Chiyo. Her friend's forlorn expression silently but eloquently expressed her true feelings about Takuo.

Everyone loves Chiyo, thought Jane, and yet, I wonder if she isn't the loneliest one of all.

Takuo continued to drive in reverse over the slippery, snow-covered street without slackening speed. He did not stop until they were in front of a villa where the heavy iron gate stood open. At the top of the stone gatepost was a brass plate inscribed with the name Wada. The large, stylish capital *W* was reflected in the glow of the car's taillights.

Once they entered the gate, Takuo drove with great care and parked in the front yard. There were already two other cars parked there, their roofs turning white under the snow.

Jane had assumed that the villa of the president of Wada Pharmaceuticals would be luxurious, but the sheer beauty of this place left her breathless. Naturally, the grounds were extensive. Like the other villas in this exclusive neighborhood, the house was surrounded by lawns and groves. The two-storied house had white walls with small windows and a dark, slate roof in the style of northern Europe. From where they stood, the roof appeared to be a flat trapezoid crowning the sturdy, timbered walls. There were balconies on both floors, and the bay windows of the second floor repeated the trapezoidal outline of the roof. The iron handrails on the balconies gave the house a vaguely medieval appearance. At the very center of the roof, between a pair of lightning rods, shone a blue, star-shaped light. The blue glow of this light enhanced the imposing elegance of the house. Night was rapidly closing in and large snowflakes danced under the lowering, overcast sky. The whole scene had a lonely, mysterious quality that suggested an isolated house in the mountains.

"Oh, it's magnificent," murmured Jane.

"We can take a leisurely walk in the morning and I will show you everything. Why don't we go inside now," said Chiyo, taking Jane by the hand.

Takuo picked up her overnight bag saying, "Let me carry that for you."

Passing in front of the first floor balcony, they climbed a flight of stone steps to the front door of the L-shaped building. Though the door was a massive one of carved wood, it was surprisingly simple and understated. Perhaps this was in keeping with the style of a country house, thought Jane.

In the entry hall Jane was greeted by Chiyo's mother, Kazue

11

Wada. Jane had met her on countless previous occasions when she
made her twice weekly visits to Chiyo's home in Tokyo, but this
time she was dressed even more stylishly than usual. She always
wore her hair in a formal, swept-up style. Its elegance reminded
Jane of Marie Antoinette. Kazue was a proud, aristocratic woman,
but not at all arrogant.

Kazue was the niece of Yohei Wada and was probably in her
mid-forties by now. Her features were striking. She felt a great
deal of love and affection for her only daughter, Chiyo, and also
lavished much attention on her husband. It was Jane's impression
that she was a self-sacrificing woman who treasured her family
above all else.

"Well Miss Prescott, you made it. Do come in, you must be
frozen. Chiyo only told us at the last moment that you were coming, but now that you're here, I hope you plan to stay a while."
Sweeping back the skirts of her long dress with one hand, she set
out a pair of slippers for Jane.

As they entered the living room on the left, Kazue introduced
her to Sawahiko. He was Kazue's husband, but not Chiyo's father.
Chiyo was the child of Kazue's second marriage, but that husband
had died in a plane crash overseas. After his death, Kazue and
Chiyo had returned to the Wada family, and later she had married
her third husband, Sawahiko.

They found Sawahiko in the spacious living room seated beside
the fireplace. He reluctantly got to his feet as they entered. He was
a slightly overweight man of medium build wearing a bulky car-
digan. Jane had only met him two or three times before.

"Good to see you," was Sawahiko's curt greeting. He was in his
early forties, a few years younger than Kazue. He customarily
spoke very deliberately.

Kazue explained, "Chiyo says she just can't possibly get her
graduation thesis done on time without some help, so she asked
Jane to come all the way down from Tokyo."

"Well, good to see you," said Sawahiko repeating his earlier
words.

His eyes were set close and he had a large, beaklike nose on his
long face. A professor of biology at a private university near

12

Tokyo, Sawahiko tended to be rather conservative in his views, and gave the impression of being a serious and honest person. His hair was always neatly combed and there were only the first signs of graying at the temples. His features were those of a moderate and gentle man, but his smile failed to conceal a trace of annoyance. No doubt he was irritated that an outsider had been brought into a private family gathering.

Chiyo had once told Jane, "At home Father never talks very much and sometimes he is irritable, but he is very generous whenever I ask for something. Every time he goes out of town to make a speech or something, he always brings back presents for Mother and me."

Jane had taken the opportunity to observe, "I guess that's what they call a scholarly disposition; a lot of professors are like that. Sometimes those people who don't talk very much turn out to be quite warmhearted inside."

Chiyo had merely murmured, "Yes, I suppose you are right, but it's a lot nicer when people are more sociable. It seems as if all Father cares about is his research."

"We've prepared a room for you upstairs," said Chiyo, leading the way up the carpeted stairs. Jane was embarrassed to have Takuo carry her luggage for her, so she picked up the overnight bag herself and followed Chiyo. Jane halted when they reached the landing halfway up the stairs. There, perfectly framed in an oblong window, stood Mt. Fuji. The white peak of the mountain appeared dramatically imprinted against the black ink wash of the winter sky. The lower slopes of the mountain were hidden by forests of desolate, bare trees powdered with snow. The whole scene was like a traditional Japanese painting and the window had clearly been designed to show it off.

"Nearly all the homes in Asahi Hills are built facing the southwest, since that is where Mt. Fuji is," explained Chiyo.

"The setting sun over San Diego Bay is a famous view, so they've built all the hotels there facing west. This is the same thing, isn't it?"

Turning away from the window, Jane was about to resume her climb up the stairs when she let out an involuntary cry of astonishment. A large man wearing a black turtle-neck sweater and gray flannel slacks was coming down the stairs toward them. He had heavy eyebrows and dark, coarse-textured skin. The moment Jane's gaze met his, the man stopped in surprise.

"This is Dr. Shohei Mazaki. He's a professor of surgery at the university hospital and is also my great-uncle's personal physician." This time as she made the introduction, Chiyo's voice was lighter and more animated than when she had introduced Takuo.

"So we meet again," said Shohei with a faint smile.

"I'm afraid I was rather rude to you."

Surprised to hear this exchange, Chiyo asked, "Do you two know each other?"

"We happened to meet in front of Gotemba Station this afternoon when I stopped to ask directions," said Shohei. This time there was no smile on his face.

"What a coincidence," said Chiyo. She stood for a moment, gazing after Shohei as he went down the stairs.

When they reached the second floor, Chiyo opened the first door on the left and turned on the lights in the room. Near the window stood a bed and a writing desk, while closer to the door were a dresser and a bathroom. Jane walked to the window and drew open the curtains. She had a view of the front lawn where they had parked the car. In the opposite direction she could see the other wing of the house where the living room was located. The living room curtains were open and the soft light streamed out over the snow.

"Over there is the dining room. We will be eating early this evening, a little before five, so why don't you rest for a bit, and then come down and join us?"

Consulting her watch, Jane saw that it was already ten past four.

"We have to eat early because the head of the accounting department and the two maids are returning to Tokyo tonight, and with all the snow, we thought it would be better if they left early."

"I understand. Then we can get to work right after dinner."

Although Chiyo and the rest of the family would be staying for some time, Jane felt it would be best to get the graduation thesis finished and leave as quickly as possible.

14

"Yes, and thanks again for coming," said Chiyo with a sweet smile.

As Chiyo went out, closing the door behind her, Jane had a sudden impulse to ask her something. She wanted to find out what sort of relationship there was between Chiyo and this Dr. Mazaki she had met earlier. She restrained herself, however, and left the question unasked. Jane could not tell if the look that Chiyo had given the doctor on the stairs earlier was one of hope or frustration, but it was clearly some complex and deeply felt emotion. This heightened her curiosity about the strange Dr. Mazaki.

Jane sat on the bed for a time and pondered these things.

The lonely isolation of the lakeshore seemed to engulf the house. Large, soft snowflakes continued to fall outside the window. The thought crossed Jane's mind that they might become snowed in, and this left her feeling a bit uneasy.

But it was not the snow that would keep her there.

Jane was wearing a sweater and a pair of jeans, so it was a simple matter to change for dinner. She pulled on a green wool dress and matching earrings and necklace. Jane had open, boyish features and short, naturally curly hair, so when she wore earrings it gave her a rather dressy look.

Downstairs she found the dining room with its crystal chandelier ablaze and the table being set while three or four men stood in a group watching. The living room was to the left of the front door and the dining room was to the right. A pure white tablecloth had been spread on the long table and place settings for nine people were being laid. Large platters of various foods were elegantly set out. Looking at what was there, Jane saw cold, Japanese-style New Year's food as well as various kinds of hors d'oeuvres, such as escargot, salmon, and raw oysters. There was also some marinated freshwater smelt that had surely been caught in the lake. Two maids were placing a large, silver tureen on the long sideboard. Steam rose from the tureen, and there was a stack of bowls beside it for serving whatever it held. The two maids made several trips back and forth to the kitchen, and soon the sideboard was filled with other food as well.

"Excuse me, but . . ." An elderly man wearing a checked sports coat approached Jane as she stood by the folding door of the dining room. Speaking in Japanese he asked, "Are you Miss Prescott, the one who is here to help Chiyo?" The man had thinning, nearly white hair combed straight back, and a thin, white mustache to go with it. There was a smile in his eyes as well as on his lips.

"Yes," replied Jane with a nod and a smile of her own.

"I'm Shigeru Wada, Yohei's youngest brother and Chiyo's youngest granduncle."

"I'm Jane Prescott. I'm pleased to meet you."

"It is very nice of you to come out here to help Chiyo. I'm afraid you are probably very busy at New Year's time."

Shigeru stepped closer to Jane and she could smell the fragrance of expensive aftershave lotion. Jane was average height for an American woman, but Shigeru was easily half a head taller, nearly six feet even in bare feet. He must have been about sixty years old and had something of a sophisticated and urbane air about him that reminded Jane of David Niven. Nevertheless, she sensed a certain tenseness in his features, and there was something about him that suggested a venal nature.

"I hope I'm not intruding."

"Not at all. We're delighted to have an attractive young lady like you join us. Where exactly do you come from, Miss Prescott?"

"Please call me Jane."

"All right, Jane, where does your family live? I would guess that you come from a small university town surrounded by large farms."

Jane's hazel eyes shone with their natural brilliance as she recalled the landscape of her hometown in America. "I was born in San Diego, but my family moved to Eugene, Oregon, when I was in high school."

"Isn't it rather unusual for an attractive young American girl like you to have an interest in Japanese literature and to come to Japan to study?"

"Perhaps. I have heard that there are about seven thousand foreign students in Japan enrolled in degree programs, and I believe about ten percent of them are Americans. But most of the foreign

16

students come to Japan to study science or economics; only a very few are involved in the study of Japanese culture as I am."

"How did you become interested in Japan in the first place?"

"Ah, that was my father's influence. He was in the Navy just after the end of the Second World War and was stationed in Japan for quite a long time. After he returned to San Diego he became close friends with a Japanese woman who was a war bride. When he retired from the Navy he went to work for a wood products company in Eugene that exported many of its products to Japan. My father was deeply impressed by Japan, and it seemed I was always hearing about Japan from the time I was a small child.

"I see. In that case we all owe a debt of gratitude to your father. After all, it is thanks to him that we have you here as our guest tonight. So you just made up your mind to come to Japan and took off, leaving all your family and lovers behind?"

"What does that mean? Are you asking if I have a lover or a fiancé, or something like that?"

"Do you?"

Jane saw no reason to evade his question and answered, "Why no, as a matter of fact there isn't anyone at the moment."

The old gentleman cocked his head and looked at her for a while before saying, "There is something about you, maybe it's the way you talk, that makes me think you are a very passionate person. I can't believe you don't have any lovers."

Suddenly Jane remembered the blue sky of Eugene and the beautiful university campus. She had had many boyfriends during her years at the university, and several had proposed marriage, but she had not been ready to get married and settle down. Instead, she had felt she wanted to live on her own for a while longer. She was still looking for something in life, and even though she was not quite sure what it was, she was not ready to get married and stop her search just yet.

Jane turned to Shigeru Wada and gave him a quiet smile. "You speak of having many lovers, but I can assure you that isn't my style."

Shigeru nodded his head. At the same time there was a kind of desperation in the look he fixed on Jane. No doubt he had had intimate relations with a great many people over the years and was shrewd at gaining some insight into another person's feelings. This thought flitted through Jane's mind.

Suddenly Shigeru's face lit up with an odd smile and he spoke to her confidentially. "Perhaps you would be wise not to let it be known around here that you have neither a husband nor a lover."

"Why in the world do you say that?"

"Well, the fact is that the men of the Wada family, all of them, have a reputation for womanizing. To put the matter bluntly, we're lechers. It seems to be some sort of unfortunate inherited trait that has been handed down in the family. The really peculiar thing about it is that it's infectious; even the men who marry into the family develop this trait. So be careful—around here you're pretty much like a lamb that's been thrown to the wolves. Oh look, here's another poor lamb." Shigeru pointed toward Chiyo, who was just at that moment entering the dining room, but Jane's attention was drawn to the couple who accompanied her. She realized, without prompting, that this must be Yohei Wada and his wife, Mine.

Chiyo was on one side of Yohei, and Mine stood close to him on the other side.

Yohei closely resembled Shigeru with his slim, graceful build and pure white hair; the only difference was that he did not have a mustache. Mine was a slight woman wrapped in a pale violet dress. She had a small, oval face and wavy, silver hair. Her face had an odd sort of symmetry, and her gray skin, creased with countless tiny wrinkles, seemed to emphasize this. Her features, Jane decided, resembled those of a Kewpie doll.

Chiyo beckoned to Jane. As Jane approached them, Chiyo spoke in her gentle voice, "This is my granduncle and my grandaunt." She completed the introduction by saying, "This is my teacher, Jane Prescott."

Jane noticed that Yohei Wada had the same crescent-shaped eyes that Shigeru had. She also noted that he used those eyes to carefully scrutinize her. At the same time, Jane was looking at Yohei. She remembered hearing from Chiyo that he was sixty-six years old. His complexion and the texture of his skin suggested a man still in the prime of his life. The pure white hair and the general air of distinction he had about him were appropriate to his age. The curve of his nose and the shape of his lips held a particular charm, and Jane decided that he was a refined, elderly gentleman. While there was a remarkable resemblance between him and his brother, Shigeru, there was an air of alertness about Yohei that suggested he was still an active businessman.

"So you're the one Chiyo has been telling us about," said Yohei in a dry voice, and once again he looked Jane in the eye. A thrill ran through her as he held her gaze. One thing, she felt, that distinguished Yohei from his brother was a certain intensity and a lustful glint in his eyes.

"How lovely to meet you, my dear," said Mrs. Wada in a high-pitched voice. "Please have a seat."

Everyone, including the men who had been in the room earlier, took their seats at the table. Yohei sat on one side of the table, flanked by Mine and Chiyo, with Shigeru next to Chiyo. On the other side of the table were Sawahiko, Kazue, Shohei, Jane, and Takuo.

The mood at dinner was far less formal than Jane had anticipated. Chiyo was wearing a billowy, cream-colored dress, and the men were dressed in a variety of styles, some wearing suits and others more casual in sweaters and slacks.

Yohei began by serving himself and the others followed suit, helping themselves to whatever suited their fancy. One of the maids began dishing up the soup while Chiyo and Kazue stood up to help with the steamed dishes. After everyone had been served, Mine turned to the maid and said, "We can manage now. You can get ready to leave."

As the maids left the dining room, they passed the chief accountant, who was coming in to say good-bye. Apparently he had already eaten.

Mingled with the sound of cutlery were the occasional murmurs of conversation and muffled chuckles. Everyone seemed to be relaxed. There was a convivial atmosphere of intimacy as they ate.

Presently they heard the sound of a car engine starting, indicating that the chief accountant and the two maids were leaving. After that, no sounds at all reached them from the outside. Darkness shrouded the house while large, feathery snowflakes continued to fall and accumulate on the ground.

Thus nine people were gathered at the villa on the shores of the lake. One of them would soon be dead.

2

The Curtain Rises
on a Blizzard

The early dinner continued until after six o'clock. As the diners consumed wine, sherry, and other drinks, they became more talkative and the mood at the table grew more festive.

Yohei was in good humor as he talked about golf and discussed plans for a trip abroad. The others discussed similar topics. Sawahiko and Shohei were rather quiet, but not unsociable. From time to time Kazue would dish more food onto Sawahiko's plate and, leaning toward him, would talk in a low voice. At these moments especially, the love and affection she felt for her husband became obvious.

When the meal was finished, the men moved into the living room with their drinks, and a short time later Yohei retired to his room. The other men dispersed to bathe, make phone calls, and do other small chores. The job of clearing away the dinner things was left to the women, but since the kitchen was equipped with a dishwasher, it wasn't much of a job. Mine, Kazue, and Chiyo were all loading the dishwasher and Jane offered to help, but Kazue said, "It would be better if you and Chiyo got to work on her graduation thesis as soon as possible."

Mine also chimed in, saying, "We can take care of this with no difficulty." With that the two younger women were virtually driven out of the kitchen.

Chiyo guided Jane to her own room on the second floor. It was the second on the left at the top of the stairs and was adjacent to Jane's room. The room itself was identical to Jane's, but the desk beside the window was piled high with reference books and littered with notes.

Chiyo had already completed the first draft of her thesis on eighty sheets of notebook paper. She was now going through it on her own and had revised about half of the manuscript.

"Why don't you start reading the section I have already revised? Just make a check mark in the margin beside those places where there is an error or something. I'll go back and make the revisions later."

"That sounds like a good idea. Let's have a look at it."

Originally Jane had only been asked to tutor Chiyo in conversational English, and she had some doubts about her ability to revise a graduation thesis, but she decided there was no point in worrying about that now.

"Uh, I would appreciate it if you would work on it in your own room though," said Chiyo apologetically. "I find it hard to concentrate if there is someone else in the room."

Jane found the request reasonable, and taking the forty or so pages that had been revised, withdrew to her own room.

The curtains were still open and as Jane drew near the window she could see that it had stopped snowing, but the trees in the front garden were blanketed in white.

She set to work reading the manuscript. Chiyo's handwriting was neat and precise, though the style was a bit stilted. Her sentences tended to be long, and it required a fair amount of concentration just to get the gist of what she had written.

The villa was wrapped in a profound silence. The only sounds that disturbed the quiet were the occasional murmur of a voice from downstairs or a knock at someone's door. The sturdy construction of the house along with the fact that all the floors were thickly carpeted seemed to muffle all else.

After two and a half hours of complete absorption in reading the thesis, Jane's eyes were becoming fatigued. Just then there was a knock at the door. Thinking it must be Chiyo, Jane opened the door only to find Kazue standing in the corridor.

"We've just made tea downstairs. Why don't you take a break and come join us?"

"Good idea. What about Chiyo?"

"I'm just on my way to invite her too."

"I'll be down in a minute, then." Jane went back to finish the page she had been reading.

22

When she got downstairs, she found that most of the folding door dividing the living room from the foyer was closed. On the other side, the door to the dining room was completely closed. Although the villa had central heating, it was more efficient to close off the rooms that were not being used at night.

Looking a bit uncertain, Jane stepped into the living room and hesitated. The spacious room was carpeted with a very chic, pale vermouth carpet, and there were six or seven members of the family seated in the sofas and chairs clustered around the fireplace at the far end of the room.

"Please come join us," called Kazue, with a cup of tea in her hand.

The living room was much warmer than the foyer had been. No doubt this was due to the fire glowing brightly in the fireplace, but when she got a closer look at it, she saw that it was not a real fireplace for burning wood, but a large, electric heater. On the mantel stood a clock with small ceramic figures that moved with the hour; according to the clock, it was just ten past nine.

"Please sit down," said Kazue, getting up from her chair. She placed Jane's cup of tea on a nearby end table. Mine was serving cheesecake on small plates. Sawahiko, Shigeru, Shohei, and Takuo sat around a low, oval-shaped coffee table. Chiyo, however, had not yet joined the group.

"How's the graduation thesis shaping up?" asked Sawahiko from a nearby armchair.

"I've only seen part of it, but I think it will turn out pretty well."

"Great. That's wonderful." There was a kindly look in Sawahiko's gentle eyes.

"I wonder what's happened to Chiyo?" said Takuo, using his forefinger to push his glasses up on his nose.

"She wasn't in her room when I went up to call her a few minutes ago," said Kazue.

"She had something to discuss with Grandpa this evening, so she's probably in his room. I heard voices in there," said Kazue, filling her own cup with tea and glancing toward the foyer.

"Grandpa's not here either, is he?" said Takuo.

Kazue set down her teacup saying, "I think I'll go find her. And

23

maybe Grandpa will join us too." She stood up and hurriedly left the room.

Yohei's room was in the wing opposite the living room, and was located at the very end of the corridor beyond the dining room. Kazue crossed the dimly lit foyer and could be seen disappearing down the corridor. Two or three minutes elapsed. Suddenly, they heard a door slam followed by Kazue's distraught cry. "My God, Chiyo! Why did you do it? Why?"

As the people in the living room looked at one another in bewilderment, the two women came running into the foyer together.

Chiyo staggered and collapsed to the floor weeping hysterically. Kazue beat her fists on her daughter's back saying, "Why did you do it, Chiyo?"

The six people in the living room quickly ran to the foyer and someone turned up the lights. What they saw was blood. The sleeves of Chiyo's cream-colored dress were soaked with blood. Shohei shoved Kazue aside and clutched Chiyo's wrists. "My God! She's slashed her wrist. Quick! Someone bring my bag, it's in my room."

"There's a first-aid kit . . ."

Kazue dashed to the kitchen. At the same time Shohei pulled out his handkerchief and pressed it tightly to Chiyo's left wrist. "The cut isn't very deep, it should be all right." It was not clear whether he was speaking to Chiyo or to the others. When Kazue got back from the kitchen with the emergency first-aid kit, he quickly, and with the easy competence of an experienced doctor, put disinfectant on the wound and bound it. It did not seem that all that much blood had come from the wound on her left wrist, yet there was blood all over the sleeves and breast of her blouse.

All the time she was being treated, Chiyo sat rigid and shaking, just like a child about to go into convulsions. She wept hysterically.

"Chiyo." Sawahiko knelt beside her opposite Shohei. His voice was calm and sympathetic. "What happened? Try to get hold of yourself and tell us what happened."

After a time she began to whisper, but all they could make out were the words "Grandpa . . . Grandpa . . ." All the rest was muffled sobbing. After repeating these words several times, she paused long enough to draw a deep breath. When she spoke, her voice was hoarse with despair. "I've just stabbed Grandpa to death."

Once again she dissolved into tears and began to writhe in agony. For a moment everyone was stunned into silence. They were no longer even conscious of Chiyo's crying; it was as though they had heard her statement, but had to wait before they could fully grasp its meaning.

Chiyo's words were indelibly printed on Jane's mind; she was sure she would never forget the sound of that voice. It had been hoarse and almost inhuman; certainly it had not sounded like Chiyo's voice. Terrible as it was, Jane intuitively knew that this was only the opening act of a much greater tragedy which was about to unfold.

"You idiot! What do you mean? Why would you kill Grandpa?" screamed Takuo with an incredulous laugh, as though the whole thing might be some sort of elaborate charade. But the laughter quickly died away on his lips.

The one who continued to respond with immediate action was Shohei. As a way of reassuring Chiyo, he transferred her to her mother's arms and Kazue accepted her daughter in a tearful embrace.

Following Shohei, the men all rushed down the corridor of the east wing. The door to the foyer through which Chiyo and Kazue had recently entered remained open. The corridor passed beside the dining room and led to the end of the east wing of the house. Mine followed after the men; she had not uttered a single word from the very beginning. Finally, Jane, too, followed the older woman along the corridor. They all automatically avoided stepping on the bloodstains along the corridor.

There were two doors on the left side of the corridor, both of them closed. The farthest one was the door to Yohei's room. Shohei barely paused long enough to knock before throwing the door open. A floor lamp brilliantly illuminated the entire square room. At the far side of the room was a bed and in front of it lay Yohei's crumpled body, clad in a light bathrobe, facing the door. The front of the robe was open and they could see that he was wearing the same silk shirt he had worn at dinner. Blood had flowed from a wound on his chest and made a dark stain on the

25

light gray carpet. Also on the floor, halfway between the body and the door, was a small fruit knife. A low moan of horror and disbelief arose simultaneously from everyone's lips.

Shohei knelt at once beside the fallen figure. He lifted the upper part of the old man's body and said, "Hold on, we're here to help you." But Yohei made no response.

Shohei searched for a pulse, then examined the pupils of the eyes. Finally he pressed his ear against the man's bloody chest to listen for the sounds of a heartbeat. Quickly he snatched a small lamp from the night stand and took off the shade. As he did so, his foot hit a silver fruit plate, knocking it over and spilling pears and oranges across the carpet.

He brought the lamp close to Yohei's face. Apparently he wanted a better look at the eyes, but the pallor of death had already stolen across the old man's face as he lay on the floor, his lips parted slightly.

"Nothing we can do," murmured Shohei. "There is no pulse and the eyes are fixed open. It's too late to help him now."

It was too late to help Yohei. If there had been even the faintest sign of life, everyone's subsequent actions might have been much different, but the blood had already stopped leaking from Yohei's chest and was beginning to congeal. There was really not all that much blood. The wound was about an inch long and slightly above the left nipple. It was evident that the wound had been made by the fruit knife. There were also cuts on the fingers of both hands. The knife on the floor was stained with blood, and there was a bloody fingerprint on its wooden handle. Together Shohei and Takuo lifted Yohei's body onto the bed. They closed the front of the bathrobe and covered him with a blanket.

Having done that, they all returned to the living room. Under the circumstances there was no urgency about calling an ambulance or the police. Clearly the victim was dead and the assailant was safely in her mother's arms. Just as in some cheap thriller, the circumstances surrounding these events seemed obvious to everyone. All that remained to be explained was why.

The clock on the mantel struck ten as Chiyo lay in front of the fireplace and began to relate the details of what had happened. "As Grandpa left the dining room after dinner, he asked me to come to his room later. Apparently there was something he wanted to tell me." Thus Chiyo, lying on the sofa, still half in her mother's embrace, began to tell her story, through her tears and in a wavering voice. Her face, swollen from weeping, was completely changed. "I worked for a while revising my thesis, but I had trouble concentrating. It must have been about quarter past eight when I went to Grandpa's room. He seemed a little drunk, but I was in pretty good spirits when I first got there." Here Chiyo bit her lip and fell silent for a time. Sawahiko prompted her quietly, "What did Grandpa want to talk to you about?"

Sawahiko was normally rather somber and moody; this was the first time Jane had seen him respond tenderly to his daughter, and the tenderness was clearly evident in the look he gave her.

"First of all he told me that since I would be graduating from the university this year, we ought to start thinking about who I would marry."

According to the girl's account, Yohei had invited her to sit down and had seated himself nearby. He then began to question her quite frankly about whom she might marry. He had asked if there wasn't someone she had already set her heart on, and when she said no, he had wondered if she was being completely honest with him. He insisted that she be honest with him and had said he was certain she would not try to deceive him. Then he had asked again if there wasn't someone she had in mind. He had also asked if she had ever been in love, and even asked if she was still a virgin.

This was about all they could make of Chiyo's fragmentary account of what had happened. Chiyo said she had noticed an unnatural gleam in his eyes and Yohei had seemed excessively interested in the fact that Chiyo was sexually inexperienced. He had asked what sort of man Chiyo liked best and assured her he would find her a suitable husband. Then he had asked her to sit beside him as he told her that in order to find the right husband for her he would have to know everything there was to know about her.

He had repeated these words over and over and finally insisted

27

that she lie down on the bed. Then he had locked the door, but she had still not realized what his intentions were.

"But then Grandpa came back to the bed and put his hands on my shoulders and said, 'You're fond of your old Grandpa, aren't you?' And then he . . . he . . ." Chiyo's body began to shake uncontrollably. She let out a wail and buried her face in her mother's bosom.

Chiyo was not the only one whose face was swollen with weeping. Large tears were also streaming from Kazue's eyes as she stroked Chiyo's back.

"It's all right now. It's all right. You don't have to tell us about it. I will explain it to the others if you like." Apparently Kazue had heard the whole story from her daughter when the others had all been in Yohei's room examining the body.

The mother clenched her jaw, and with an occasional sob, continued the story. "He tried to take possession of Chiyo's body. When she realized what he was up to, she attempted to escape, and at that moment she picked up the fruit knife that was on the nightstand. Grandpa was in the habit of eating a piece of fruit before retiring at night, so it was normal for the knife to be there. Chiyo was dazed as she picked up the knife, but she certainly never meant to hurt him with it. It was an accident. Why did he try to do that to her in the first place. . . ? How could he do it?" Kazue stifled back a sob and her words momentarily broke off at this point.

Regaining her composure, she resumed. "Chiyo wasn't even trying to threaten him. She intended to kill herself if he became violent. The truth is that she had the blade of the knife against her own throat. Grandpa had taken leave of his senses by that time and attacked her. He managed to get both hands on the knife, they struggled, and the next thing Chiyo knew, he had been stabbed in the chest."

Kazue appeared exhausted by the time she reached the end of the story, and her cheek was resting on her daughter's shoulder.

"Chiyo, that's the way it happened, isn't it? The way your mother has just explained it?" Sawahiko pleaded for confirmation.

"Yes. . . . I knelt for a time beside Grandpa. I was dazed. I

28

truly felt that my own life had come to an end. Then I heard mother in the corridor calling to me. She was calling me to come drink tea with the rest of you. I made up my mind to end my life on the spot, so I pulled the knife from Grandpa's chest and tried to slash my wrist, but I guess I didn't do a very good job of it. I think I was in too much of a hurry, and anyway, by that time mother was knocking on the door. I felt I wanted to see her one more time before I died, so I opened the door and . . ."

Seeing her mother, Chiyo had suddenly lurched wildly from the room. Kazue caught only a glimpse of the room and was so shaken by the scene that she slammed the door and pursued Chiyo, catching up with her just as they stumbled into the foyer together.

Kazue went on. "Poor Chiyo. If you had been successful with your suicide, I don't know what I would have done. I couldn't have gone on living myself. I still wonder why that man tried it?" For a moment there was a terrible look in Kazue's eyes and her lip trembled.

Kazue was Yohei's niece and she had reminded him of his deceased sister. Since Yohei had produced no children of his own, he had always treated Kazue as his own daughter. And she, too, had always felt very proud of Yohei; this mutual affection had been apparent to Jane earlier in the evening. Kazue, like the others, had always referred to Yohei as "Grandpa." Now it seemed she could only refer to him as "that man."

The quiet weeping of the two women died away and the group lapsed into mournful silence.

Mine was the first to break the silence, her high-pitched voice muffled by heavy sighs. "It was my fault. I was negligent."

Everyone's startled gaze turned to Mine, whose complexion seemed grayer than ever. "For some time now, ever since Chiyo had matured physically, I knew that the way he was looking at her was not natural. It was wrong of me to assume that nothing would happen. I should have known that he was capable of something like this." Mine sighed deeply and shook her head two or three times. As she spoke her voice was filled with resignation laced with shock and sorrow, but it remained quiet and controlled. As Jane looked at the round, cherubic face with all its tiny wrinkles, she felt she

29

could see engraved there a heart that had seen the truth and understood it.

"He always had a weakness for women," murmured Shigeru. "In a sense I suppose Mine is the chief victim of his weakness, but all of that is finished now." When Jane's gaze met his, she could see a glitter of sadness in his crescent eyes that reminded her so much of Yohei's. Shigeru's look seemed to be telling her, You see, what I told you earlier was true. All the men of the Wada family have an uncontrollable lust for young ladies. It is an unfortunate trait that seems to have been passed down in our family. Jane also recalled the lustful look she had recognized in Yohei's eyes, and she shuddered at the memory.

Once again the group relapsed into a strained silence. As the initial shock began to wear off and each of them came to grips with the dizzying turn of events, they began to realize the enormity of what had happened, and that too weighed on them.

Presently Sawahiko frowned gloomily, bringing his eyebrows together and pursing his lips. "It doesn't matter any longer what the cause of the tragedy was, it's clear that Chiyo overreacted. There is no way she can undo what she has done. That's just the way it is." Having said this, he nodded his head several times. Even though he was not related to the Wada family by blood, the fact that he would have to bear much of the responsibility for what had happened seemed to strengthen his resolve. "We can't just sit here forever in a state of shock. We have to start thinking about what we are going to do now."

The men nodded their agreement.

"I suppose the proper thing would be to inform the police right away. No matter what happens, Chiyo is going to have to pay a price for what she has done."

Kazue clutched Chiyo closer to her and looked wildly about. "What a terrible thing to say. I can't bear to have the police come and take away my daughter."

"I suppose she can always argue that it was a legitimate case of self-defense," said Shohei in a somber voice.

"I don't know about that," murmured Takuo thoughtfully. "After all, it wasn't Grandpa who picked up the knife and started waving it around."

30

"Still, the fact is that Chiyo did not have any murderous intent."

"What are you talking about?" asked Mine with a certain amount of dignity in her voice. "You have all failed to see the problem we are facing. I will not approve of taking this matter to the police. For one thing, that would be too harmful to Chiyo, and for another, it would bring to light too many things Yohei did long ago that are better left forgotten. The only thing we would accomplish by going to the police is to expose the family's dirty linen. For the time being . . ." She struggled to maintain the restraint in her voice as she looked around at the others. "The best we can hope for now is to try to protect his reputation and the name of the Wada family. Isn't that right?"

Sawahiko raised a question. "Are you suggesting that we should cover this up and keep it from the police and from the world at large?"

"Well I'm not saying we can keep something like this completely covered up, but I do think we need to take steps to protect Chiyo. That will also prevent anything unpleasant from being said about my husband."

Sawahiko did not reply to this but merely nodded his head in silence.

Suddenly Takuo broke in, his words uttered with such violent emotion he could hardly get them out. "Are you proposing that we make it look as though he died of natural causes? Are you saying we should simply hide the wound on his chest under his clothes and ask Dr. Mazaki to make out an appropriate death certificate?"

"I rather think that's a bit out of the question. He was wounded by a knife thrust into his chest, a wound that was opened even wider when Chiyo pulled the knife out. If anyone caught sight of the wound, of course, the game would be up," said Shigeru, inclining his head to one side.

"There is another problem here as well," murmured Shohei in his sepulchral voice. Earlier, during all the excitement, he had acted alertly as a doctor should, but since then he had merely watched the proceedings quietly without uttering a word. "Five years ago Yohei came to the university hospital for a gallstone operation. At that time he promised the surgeon who performed the operation that he would stipulate in his will that after he died his

31

body would be given to the university for dissection purposes. It would be a normal procedure in such a case to have the pathologist make out a consent agreement, and I assume that was done in this case."

"Yes, that's right. I heard him say something about that," said Mine. Apparently Sawahiko and Kazue also knew of this arrangement, for they too were nodding their heads.

"In that case, then, I guess we have no choice but to inform the police, but we do not have to tell them that Chiyo was the one who did it, though they'll become suspicious right away if she continues this hysterical crying," declared Takuo, looking at the prostrate Chiyo.

"I think there may be a way we can handle this," announced Shohei firmly.

"What do you mean?" asked Takuo sharply.

"All we have to do is get Chiyo out of here, get her to some place far away. We could send her back to Tokyo, then arrange things so that the body is discovered later. Since it would look like she hadn't been here at the time of the killing, there would be no reason for the police to want to question her."

"Do you think we could pull off something like that?" asked Sawahiko.

"There are several ways we could handle it," said Shohei.

"Yes, but isn't it going to seem odd if she goes home ahead of the rest of us?" asked Takuo. There was a subtle hint of provocation in his rejoinder to Shohei.

"Oh, I'm sure we could come up with some sort of reason to explain that. We might say, for example, that there was some important reference book she needed for her thesis that she had left behind in Tokyo, and she had to rush back to get it."

Up to this point everyone's gaze had been focused on Shohei, but now they shifted to Jane, who sat beside him. The members of the Wada family had forgotten all about her. When the thesis was mentioned, however, they suddenly remembered her. As one by one they turned their gaze on her, Jane felt they were like a pack of wolves; their eyes cold, suspicious, and vigilant. She felt a bewildering rush of feelings, but most of all, she was acutely conscious of being an outsider and a foreigner in the eyes of the Wada family.

"All right, then," said Sawahiko, taking charge of the situation. "We'll get Chiyo as far away from here as possible, and we'll make every effort to conceal her crime from the police and from everyone else for that matter. Do you think we can manage that?" He spoke as calmly as possible, but his voice quavered slightly as he asked the group for their help.

Mine was the first to nod in agreement. "Remember, we're not just doing this for Chiyo's sake, we're doing what's best for all of us."

Choking back her tears, Kazue made a little bow of thanks toward Mine.

Sawahiko turned to Shigeru for his confirmation.

"Yes, I believe this will be the best course of action." He stroked his mustache with his fingers in a gesture that belied his uneasiness.

"You can count on me, one hundred percent," said Takuo stoutly. "Nevertheless, after Chiyo has returned to Tokyo, there still remains the problem of what we are going to tell the police."

"The only thing we can say is that it was a burglar who broke in," murmured Shohei.

"Right. We will say a burglar broke in and Grandpa confronted him."

"Good idea. If we say anything else, it would simply mean that one of us did it."

The two men held each other's gaze for a time.

"You're right, of course. That's the only story we can tell." Takuo once more nodded his head vigorously. There seemed to be a note of regret in his voice, but since he could not think up a better plan on the spur of the moment, he quickly agreed to cooperate with this one. "If we all tell the same story, and tell it convincingly, then when the police get here, they will have to believe us."

But Shohei shook his head and frowned. "No. We can't make it look too neat and tidy for them. I'm pretty sure the Fuji Five Lakes

33

precinct has jurisdiction in this area. Last year there were two murders here that appeared to be a lovers' suicide, but they solved that one beautifully. They have some very outstanding detectives here."

Takuo shrugged his shoulders lightly.

Finally Sawahiko turned to Jane and asked, "You've heard our plan, Miss Prescott, I wonder how you feel about it? Now is the time to say exactly what you think."

Jane was bewildered and sat in silence.

"What I am asking is this; are you willing to cooperate with us in covering up what Chiyo did, and to make it appear that a burglar broke in? If not . . ."

"If you are not willing to cooperate with us," broke in Takuo, "I trust you will agree to remain absolutely silent about the matter." There was a hint of a threat in Takuo's voice.

"That's right," said Sawahiko firmly. "You have two choices. You can go back to Tokyo with Chiyo and pretend you don't know anything, or you can stay here and help us with our plan. You may choose either course."

"I guess I would like to ask all of you, which choice would you prefer I make?" Jane finally responded, the question giving her a little time to think.

"Well, actually—"

Sawahiko was about to tell her either choice would be all right, but Takuo broke in. "Since you ask, we really would prefer that you stay here with us. From the point of view of the police, the story we give them will be much more believable if it is confirmed by a number of outsiders, rather than just having the statements of family members." This time Shohei was nodding in agreement with Takuo's suggestion. In a sense, even Shohei could almost be considered one of the family.

"I know it's a lot to ask of you, but it would be best if you stay here," said Mine, speaking very precisely. But Jane had caught the glance that had passed between Mine and Shigeru a moment earlier. If she were allowed to return to Tokyo, there would always be the possibility she might tell someone what had happened, or even go to the police with the story. On the other hand, if she were kept

34

here, everyone would be able to keep an eye on her, and to the extent that she cooperated in the cover-up, she would be implicating herself as one of the conspirators.

Jane took a long look at Chiyo, who, feeling her gaze, looked up. Her eyes were slightly swollen, her cheeks pale, and whisps of disordered hair clung to her cheeks. It was an exhausted face. Surprisingly, Chiyo did not question the family's decision to cover up her crime. Her large, marvelous eyes that had always seemed so cool were now shaded with grief and she seemed completely willing to accept whatever happened to her. "Please let Jane do as she wishes," whispered Chiyo, though Jane gave no sign of having heard this.

The other members of the family, meanwhile, were still waiting for Jane's response. In order to relieve some of the strain of the moment, Jane gave them a wry smile. "I appreciate your kind words. I'm afraid my presence here has been something of a nuisance for you. I only want to do what is best." Certainly Jane loved Chiyo as much as the other members of the Wada family did.

Sawahiko looked at the clock on the mantel; it was just a bit past 10:40. "If we are going to make up our minds about this, we had better hurry."

"How is she going to return to Tokyo anyway? The snow has gotten pretty deep out there." As she raised this new problem, Kazue looked across at her husband.

"That's no problem. It stopped snowing around seven o'clock, but we do have to decide which car she will take."

"Naturally she will have to use a rented car with a driver," said Takuo with authority. "We will need an outside party who can affirm that Chiyo left here at a certain time and returned to Tokyo."

"Yes, of course, that's right." Sawahiko had taken it upon himself to be the leader of the group, but all heads were turned toward Takuo and Shohei.

"I will telephone for a car," said Kazue, getting to her feet.

"Well, at least there is one thing in our favor. New Year's is the only time during the winter when businesses are open this late at night in Asahi Hills."

"Is that hotel still open this late?" asked Shohei as though he had just thought of something.

"Do you mean the one with the restaurant and bar?"

"Yes."

"During the summer tourist season and at New Year's they're usually open until eleven o'clock. I remember we went there once for a late dinner."

"I see. I suppose they deliver meals as well?"

"Deliver meals?" asked Takuo in disbelief. The others were also staring at him.

"Let's see, they have a Western restaurant and a sushi bar at the hotel. We've ordered food from both of them in the past."

"Would they deliver at this hour?"

"They probably would today," said Kazue, consulting her watch and giving an affirmative nod.

"So you think this would be a good time to order up some dinner, do you?" asked Takuo sarcastically.

Shohei ignored this and continued with a note of urgency in his voice. "All right, I want you to give them a call right now and find out."

"Do you really want me to ask them to send some food over?"

"What sort of menu do they have in the Western restaurant?"

"They have things like stew, croquettes, gratin, and pizza."

"Okay, the gratin is fine. Order enough for eight people."

"Not for me, thanks, I'm not hungry."

"I don't need anything either. Under the circumstances, I don't think I could eat anyway," said Takuo.

"No, no. You don't understand. It is very important that we have dinner," said Shohei. "It is essential that we make it look as though Grandpa stayed up late tonight and decided to have a late dinner. After Chiyo left for Tokyo, the rest of us sat around playing cards. In the middle of the card game, we decided to call in some food. That's why it is absolutely crucial to make it appear that Grandpa had a late dinner with us."

Kazue went to the kitchen to get the local telephone directory and then went to the telephone in the corner of the living room. As everyone watched, she called the rental car place located on the main street of Asahi Hills and then called the restaurant. Since the car rental place had done business with the Wada family before, they promised to have a car and driver at the villa within fifteen minutes. The restaurant said that it would be thirty or forty minutes before they delivered the gratin.

Chiyo had to hurry. With Kazue urging her on, they had gone to her room on the second floor where she had removed her bloody clothing, changed into fresh ones, and repaired her makeup. Chiyo now stood before the front door, her coat draped over her shoulders and wearing gloves, the bandage on her wrist hidden from view. In the red, leather overnight bag beside her were packed her discarded clothing along with the fruit knife that had killed Yohei as well as his document case and some jewelry—a diamond tie tack and a pair of emerald cuff links. In the leather document case was nearly a million yen in cash, some important company documents, and some stocks. These were the items the burglar would "steal" later on when he showed up to "murder" Yohei.

The doorbell rang at 10:55. Luckily, the middle-aged driver was a man who knew both Kazue and Chiyo by sight. They had hired his car in the past during other stays at the villa.

Sawahiko asked about the snowy conditions right away, and the reply he received was, "There is about five inches of snow where the roads aren't plowed, but of course I have snow tires on the car; that will help. Traffic has been running all evening on the main roads, so they won't be a problem. We can get on the Tomei Expressway at Gotemba, and at this time of night ought to be able to make it to your house in Tokyo in about two hours." The cheerful driver seemed unconcerned about the snow. "Nevertheless, it's a terrible night for the young lady to be traveling."

"Yes. That's certain, but the deadline for her graduation thesis is almost here and she just can't go on without that reference book, so there's no choice," said Kazue by way of explanation.

"I'll try to be back as soon as I can. I hate to keep Jane waiting like this," said Chiyo with a nod. She seemed to be taking in the complex meaning of what her mother had just said. In any case, Chiyo would surely have to return here the following day. After all, Yohei had been especially fond of her, and after his death was

37

discovered, it would seem strange if she did not come home right away.

"Be careful."

"Thanks for everything."

With these brief words of departure, which belied the true depth of their feelings, Chiyo got into the waiting car at the front gate. She hardly spoke, fearing perhaps that if she opened her mouth, her nerve would give way and everything would come rushing out. Just before she walked out through the garden, Chiyo caught Jane's gaze; she frowned and turned away with a slight nod.

The snow tires of the car squeaked as they ran over the snow, and the group that remained behind stood listening until the sound had died away in the distance.

"All right. We'd better get the table set up right away," said Shohei in a tense voice. "When the delivery person arrives from the restaurant we have to make it look as though we're playing cards."

"Good idea. If we make it look like we're playing poker, we can continue the game until morning," said Sawahiko, turning away from the window.

"What do you mean, until morning?" asked Shigeru, suddenly looking exhausted.

The two looked at each other intently and Sawahiko explained, "I mean just what I said. In the morning someone will discover that Grandpa has been killed by a burglar, and we will report it to the police right away. Until then, though, we have our work cut out for us. If we make even a single slip at any point, we'll all be putting our necks in the noose."

Takuo walked over to the stereo and selected a record. Soon soft Latin music was flooding the room. The sound of the music was kept low enough so that it would not disturb their further discussions, but was intended to serve as a cover to explain why they did not hear the sounds of a struggle from Yohei's room.

Kazue found a deck of cards while Sawahiko and the others set up the table.

Jane, who had been gazing intently at the winter wonderland outside the window, was invited by Shigeru to return her attention to what was happening in the room. She had the feeling that one act in this drama had just come to an end, and the second act was about to begin.

38

3

Desperate Measures

The living room of the Wada family villa was awash with popular Latin music while the card players sat around an oval table. All together there were seven people: Mine, Shigeru, Sawahiko, Kazue, Takuo, Shohei Mazaki, and Jane Prescott. The green felt table was cluttered with cards and chips. Sawahiko looked at the clock on the mantel and raised an eyebrow. The metal hands on the ceramic face indicated ten past eleven. "I guess it's time to get the poker chips distributed."

"Do we really have to do this?" asked Shigeru. It seemed as though he had suffered particularly from the tense atmosphere in the room. His hand automatically went to his mustache and he pursed his lips.

Although they were not really playing a game, they felt it would look better if they had the chips and cards out when the delivery boy arrived.

Shohei and Takuo exchanged glances, and Shohei gave Sawahiko a nod, inviting him to distribute the chips. "The restaurant said the food will be delivered around eleven thirty. We have to be busy playing cards when the delivery boy arrives."

"We have to be sure we create the proper mood," added Takuo. His mouth was set and he had an intent look on his face.

Kazue quickly stacked the chips in piles and placed one pile in front of each player. Jane knew the basic rules for playing poker, but Takuo explained briefly various rules used by the Wada family. It turned out that the family members often played cards when they got together for the New Year's holiday or some other family get-together. They all enjoyed gambling and the bidding was usually high.

They played two hands. As the game progressed, Shohei fixed his gaze on Sawahiko, but he spoke in such a way as to urge the whole group to continue their plan, saying, "We have to be sure we carry out our plan in every detail until morning. Remember, it was just eleven o'clock when Chiyo left for Tokyo. That means the murder had to happen after eleven."

Gradually Sawahiko had taken charge of things and brought the conversation around to the real topic by saying, "Our story is this: After dinner we began playing cards. We had some records on and became very engrossed in the game, and in any case did not hear any suspicious sounds from Grandpa's room, where he was alone all evening. The most important question is establishing the time of the murder." Sawahiko looked at Shohei. After all, Shohei was a doctor and it had been his idea in the first place to try to make it appear that the killing had happened later than it really had.

For a time Shohei remained silent, sunk in thought. Beneath his heavy eyebrows, his eyes were staring intently at the foyer. It was almost as though he was reliving the scene when Chiyo, with an unnatural sob, had come running into the foyer and collapsed.

"Let's see now, it actually happened around nine-fifteen or nine-twenty, so we can suppose that Grandpa was stabbed at around nine o'clock." Shohei turned to look at Sawahiko as he said this. "Now the snack we ordered should be delivered around eleven-thirty, so we'll have to make it look as though the murder happened at around midnight. We will say that Grandpa ate dinner with us and was murdered at around midnight on the evening of January third when he was assaulted by a burglar."

"From the beginning I have opposed this idea of sending out for food and having your so-called dinner—" Just as Takuo was about to raise an objection to the plan, the doorbell rang.

They heard a voice on the door step calling, "Hello. It's the delivery boy from the Kohan Restaurant." Suddenly strain and tension clamped its grip on everyone's features. The curtain was about to rise on the main act.

"Coming," called Kazue, going into the foyer and heading for the door.

In his excitement Shigeru got up from his chair and started to follow her, but tripped over his own feet and stumbled. He put one hand to the carpet to steady himself while Takuo and Jane, one on either side of him, helped him up.

Meanwhile, Kazue was in the entry hall opening the door for the delivery boy. She took a tray containing plates of food and returned to the living room. The delivery boy was a young man who stood by the folding door and looked into the room.

"Do you need some help?" asked Sawahiko, keeping his eyes on the cards, "There must be a lot of plates."

"Yes, you're right," said Kazue, turning to the delivery boy. "Would you bring the rest of it in here and put it on the table?" The boy kicked off his snowy boots and lugged his heavy delivery box into the living room. He showed no sign of having any idea that he was being set up as a witness.

The plates of food were set out on the table where the poker game had been suspended, and on the tea cart nearby.

"Is it still snowing?" asked Shigeru, still trying to cover his confusion at having stumbled over his own feet.

"No. It has completely stopped," replied the young man, with a plate of food in his hands. "Where shall I put this?"

A cunning look gleamed in Kazue's eyes and she turned to Shohei saying, "Where is Grandpa going to eat?" Her question sounded innocent and natural enough. When Shohei was slow in answering, Mine quickly broke in. "He should be about done with his bath by now. I'll go ask him; he may want to join us here."

She stood up and crossed the living room, passing close beside the delivery boy. The others watched her go, stunned by her display of calmness and the audacity of her performance. Both her words and her actions seemed completely natural.

"All right, then, just put it down here for the time being."

Doing as he was told, the young man from the restaurant set the plate on the tea table and returned to the entry hall where he put on his boots and left after Kazue paid him for the gratin.

"Why don't we eat as we play? That way we can have the food before it gets cold," said Sawahiko in such a way that he surely would be overheard, but even so his lines were not nearly as convincing as Mine's had been.

Mine returned to the room after the sound of the van had died away in the distance. Looking toward the front door where Kazue was just locking up, Mine murmured, "You wonder what the world is coming to these days when the delivery boys and the hired help all come to the front door instead of using the servant's entrance."

As the seven players once again resumed their places around the table, their collective gaze was drawn to the extra plate of food that had been ordered for Yohei. It was a gratin with plenty of white sauce over it and the steam still rising from it.

"How are we going to handle this?" asked Jane in a whisper. From the moment Shohei had suggested doing this, it had simply been for the sake of appearance to put in an order for food and to order a portion for Yohei as well. But Jane was the one who now realized that this implied that Yohei would also have eaten the food that had been ordered for him.

Shohei glanced quickly at Jane and then turned to Kazue. "Is there any of the consommé left over from dinner?"

"Why yes, there is."

"Then bring it here. Don't bother to heat it. I'm going upstairs for a moment."

As Kazue and Shohei hurried from the room, Shigeru heaved an exhausted sigh.

"Well, we might as well eat something, even if it's just a little bit. It's going to be a long night," said Sawahiko in a loud voice as he picked up one of the forks wrapped in a napkin and began to unwrap it. "Besides, if everyone doesn't eat at least a little bit, they might find that out later and become suspicious."

"That's true," said Mine in agreement.

A moment later Shohei reappeared. In his left hand he carried a plastic bag and a huge hypodermic syringe. The bag contained a coil of slender, brownish-orange rubber tubing.

Right behind him came Kazue, returning from the kitchen. She was using both hands to carry a deep soup bowl filled with consommé.

"What are you going to do with all that?" asked Shigeru.

Shohei laid the hypodermic syringe on the table and opened the

42

plastic bag. The tube he drew from it was about five millimeters in diameter and over a yard long. Measurements were marked on it every five centimeters.

"This is called a stomach tube; it's something we physicians always carry in our bag. Ordinarily we use it to pump a person's stomach when they have taken poison or something like that. We also use it to lave a person's stomach. It's used any time we have to clean out a stomach in a hurry." Shohei explained all this with the deadpan professionalism of a physician.

"You mean you put that thing right down into a person's stomach?"

"That's right. If you insert it through the nasal passage, it generally takes about a foot and a half of tubing to reach the stomach. It can also be used the opposite way: as a way of putting nutrition or fluids into the stomach. When a patient is unconscious for a long period or in a coma, we can use this to feed him."

"You can feed a person who is unconscious?" muttered Shigeru in an astonished voice as he nervously fingered the hypodermic syringe. It was already clear to Jane how Shohei intended to use that instrument.

"After we discover the body and call the police, they'll certainly perform an autopsy. Not only will they examine the external appearance of the body, they will open it up as well," continued Shohei in his usual gloomy fashion. "So in order to make them think that Grandpa really died after Chiyo had left, we have to be very careful about taking care of this point."

"How do they usually determine the time of death when they examine a body?" asked Sawahiko. Although he was a biologist, these things were outside his area of expertise.

"That's a question of forensic medicine and it's not my specialty either, but there are several ways of doing it. One is to check the condition of the body for rigor mortis, discoloration of the skin, the state of decay, and so on. Another way is to examine the contents of the stomach and calculate how long death occurred after the victim had eaten." As he explained this, Shohei looked at his watch. "We finished eating dinner around six. All he ate was a good cut of meat and other foods that are easily digested, so they ought to have passed through the stomach in two hours' time. In any case, the sooner we get this done, the better."

His tone had suddenly grown very abrupt and professional as he picked up the syringe and tube with one hand, and the plate of gratin with the other. Turning to Kazue he said, "Please bring the soup and come with me."

She shook her head and handed the bowl to Takuo, saying, "You'd better do it. I don't think I could bear to watch."

"I think I'll wait here as well," said Mine.

Shohei and Sawahiko set out for Yohei's room. Shigeru hesitated for a moment, then followed. Takuo carried the bowl of soup, but kept his eyes on Jane. Behind his steel-rimmed glasses his eyes somehow resembled those of a bird, but there was also some commanding authority in them that seemed to be telling Jane, "You come with us."

The implication was that as long as she was here in the villa with them, she should be directly involved in the cover-up. She would have to be a party to their conspiracy.

The party of five proceeded across the foyer and along the corridor toward the kitchen and Yohei's room beyond.

The room itself was just as cold as the corridor had been. Apparently someone had turned off the heat earlier when they had laid Yohei's body out on the bed and returned to the living room. Shohei noticed this for his eyes went immediately to the switch on the heater and he nodded with evident satisfaction.

Yohei was lying face up on the bed with a blanket pulled up to his chin. At first glance he appeared to be merely sleeping. Suddenly it seemed to Jane that the events of the evening must have been only a dream. But when she noticed the dark spots of blood staining the gray carpet, it was no longer possible to delude herself.

Shohei placed the things he was carrying on the table and bent over the bed. The first thing he did was hold a hand to Yohei's temple, but there could be no doubt that the skin was stone cold. There were age spots on Yohei's skin, and his complexion had turned a grayish color; his face appeared small and his cheeks sunken.

Shohei got out the stomach tube. Turning to Takuo, who was still holding the bowl of soup, he said, "Mix that with some of the gratin. I want the mixture to be thin, like fluid. I have to be able to get it through the syringe and through the tube into his stomach."

This was the first time Shohei had explained concretely what he meant to do. As Takuo approached the table, his gaze once again came to rest on Jane. "You seem to be pretty clever with your hands. Why don't you give me a hand with this?"

Without a word Jane carried the bowl of soup to where the plate of gratin had been placed. Takuo poured some of the soup on the side of the plate. Using the spoon, Jane mixed the shrimp, meat, macaroni, and white sauce with the soup and mashed it into a thin, pasty mixture.

Meanwhile Shohei had already inserted the tip of the stomach tube into Yohei's left nostril. He passed the tube through the trachea, feeling the course of its progress with his fingers.

"There is no chance, I hope, of the tube ending up anywhere but in his stomach," said Sawahiko.

"The throat is divided into two passages. In the front is the wind pipe; in back is the alimentary canal. As long as I make sure the tube follows the back wall of the throat, it can't go anywhere but into the stomach. Even a nurse could carry out a procedure like this." As he answered, his hands never ceased moving. After he had inserted nearly a foot and a half of the tube, Shohei drew a small pair of surgical scissors from his breast pocket and cut the tube. Then he turned to Jane and Takuo, saying, "Put the gratin in the syringe."

The syringe was a huge affair about a foot long and more than an inch and a half in diameter. Jane filled the syringe with the gratin mixture and handed it to Shohei, who applied it to the mouth of the tube. There was no needle attached to the syringe, so its opening fit perfectly with that of the tube. When the plunger on the syringe was pressed, the gratin flowed through the tube and disappeared into Yohei's nasal cavity.

Each time the syringe was emptied, they would fill it again from the plate. The food passed through the tube and into Yohei's stomach. Shohei supervised the operation, making sure everything was

45

done properly. He did not tell them to stop until there was virtually no white sauce left on the plate.

"We've probably fed him enough to make it safe," said Sawahiko, hardly able to conceal the amazement in his voice.

Shohei withdrew the tube and replaced it in its plastic bag.

"Once I wash this up, there will be no evidence. No doubt the conclusion will be that Grandpa was murdered shortly after eating his gratin. Of course it is still going to be somewhat unnatural in the sense that there will be very little in the way of saliva or digestive juices mixed with the food, but as long as they don't become suspicious of this right away, there is little reason to suppose that the doctor who does the autopsy will notice it.

"It was eleven-thirty when the gratin was delivered," said Sawahiko, "so the murder must be discovered some time after that."

"Wait. I'm afraid we're not finished with this yet. Just as we said earlier, the deterioration of the body begins at the moment of death. I don't know much about these things, but the colder the body is kept, the slower the process of decomposition will be. So, if we want to make it appear that he died later than he really did . . ."

"How would it be if we put the body outside?" said Takuo, pursing his lips. "It's stopped snowing, but the temperature must be below freezing out there. It would be just like putting the body into a refrigerator."

"Ah, that sounds like a good idea," said Sawahiko, looking at Shohei for confirmation. Instead, Shohei was staring at his watch thoughtfully. "He actually died around nine o'clock, and if we want to make it look as though he died around midnight, or half an hour after the gratin was delivered, we have to cover up an interval of some three hours. We will have to bring the body back inside before we call the police. Also, if we warm the room up before the police arrive, we ought to be able to move back the estimated time of death."

Shigeru crossed to the window looking out into the balcony and drew aside the heavy curtain. Outside the glass doors the world was wrapped in lonely silence and the dark of night. In the faint light reflecting from the snow they could barely make out the dark trunks of the trees and shrubs in the garden.

Sawahiko went to the door and pressed his face against the glass. "It looks as though the floor of the balcony is wet. We had better lay out a sheet of plastic," he said, marching out of the room with long strides.

"Where shall we say Mr. Wada ate the gratin?" asked Jane to no one in particular. She had stopped asking herself if all this was right or wrong, or whether or not she was afraid. All she felt was a curious sort of emotional emptiness.

"It would be most natural if he had eaten it in the living room with the rest of us, wouldn't it?" said Takuo.

"Okay. I'll collect all the plates and wash them."

Shohei nodded his assent and Jane began to stack the plates, being careful not to spill any of the food that was left on them.

Sawahiko returned to the room with a vinyl tablecloth from the kitchen table.

Sawahiko and Takuo released the catches on the French doors and opened them out onto the balcony. The harsh metallic shriek of the rusty door hinges made everyone cringe. The clear, cold air rolled in through the open doors.

The balcony itself was not all that wide. The iron handrails were in keeping with the rest of the house and were designed in a sort of medieval pattern. Since the balcony was protected by the eaves of the house, it was damp but no snow had accumulated there. They spread Sawahiko's tablecloth on the floor.

Shohei grasped the body's shoulders while Takuo got the legs, and they laid Yohei out on the balcony. Apparently rigor mortis had already begun to set in because the frail body in its bathrobe was already stiff as a board, and the neck was so rigid that his head did not move.

As a precaution, Sawahiko looked out over the dark garden, and once he was sure there was no sign of anyone about, returned to the room. This time they tried to close the doors without making a sound, but of course there was no way to avoid the harsh, metallic shriek. As the doors were closed, a swirl of cold air rushed through the room.

"Well," said Shigeru, collapsing into a nearby chair, "that's taken care of."

"Yes. Now all we have to do is wait for three hours and bring the body back into the room. That should make it look like the murder occurred around midnight."

Jane looked at her watch; it was twenty past twelve. She wondered if Chiyo was still in the hired car. They had left about eleven and the driver had said it would take about two hours to reach the house in Tokyo. At least Chiyo was safe for the time being. At the very least, Yohei's death would not be calculated any earlier than eleven-thirty. Jane felt a warm sense of satisfaction at this thought.

Meanwhile, however, Sawahiko had begun to frown and was looking nervously and with some exasperation at Shigeru. "We're not even half done with this job yet. The seven of us who are left here at the villa have to arrange things so that there is no doubt that the killer came in from the outside. We will have to make some footprints coming into the house."

"Oh yes," said Shigeru weakly, "I had forgotten about that."

"But before we do that, I think it would be a good idea if we take a break for a while and go to the living room and have tea."

"I think we can take care of things," said Takuo curtly. "If you want to go to bed Uncle Shigeru, that will be all right."

"No. Don't. You can't go to bed yet," said Sawahiko with a note of urgency in his voice.

After Shigeru had departed for the living room, the remaining four found themselves seated on nearby chairs or on the bed. The aging Shigeru was not the only one who was tired.

"What exactly needs to be done to make it look like an assailant came in from the outside?" asked Jane. She had come to realize that they had no choice now but to work at this job until it was finished.

"I guess it will all depend on where we decide to have the burglar enter the house," said Sawahiko.

"Why don't we just let it be that door right there?" suggested Takuo, pointing to the door at the end of the corridor, which opened onto the back garden.

"No one ever uses that door. We could say that somehow the key for it disappeared and no one noticed it missing."

48

"Um, that's probably the best one to use," agreed Sawahiko thoughtfully. "That would explain the bloodstains in the corridor. The story will be that the burglar had the key and came in through that door, entered the bedroom looking for valuables, and that's when Grandpa woke up. He was startled by the intruder, jumped out of bed, and the burglar, thinking he was about to call for help, pulled a knife and stabbed him in the chest. After that he gathered the briefcase and the valuables from the cabinet and departed through the corridor."

"One more point, before he fled, the killer put Grandpa's body back on the bed," amended Shohei in his quiet, melancholy voice. "Rigor mortis set in while the body was lying flat on its back. It wouldn't look right to have him collapsed on the floor that way," he said, pointing to the bloodstained carpet.

"Right. As he left, the killer took the bloody knife with him, and that will explain the bloodstains in the corridor. We'll have him flee by the same route he entered, and make his escape through the back garden."

"In that case we'll have to make some footprints out there. There should be a clear trail in the snow, both coming up to the house and leaving it," said Takuo enthusiastically.

"We may want to have him cut the telephone lines too, as a way of giving himself time to get away," said Shohei.

"He could also break the outdoor yard light."

"Don't you think that will be enough?" said Sawahiko with some strain in his voice. "If we try to do too much we are more liable to make a mistake."

"Whatever we do, we might as well do it now," said Shohei, getting to his feet. He was used to spending long hours in the operating theater and appeared to have more endurance than the rest.

The first thing they needed was a pair of shoes with which to make the killer's footprints. Sawahiko enlisted the help of Kazue, who was waiting in the living room. He had her rummage around in the storeroom adjacent to the kitchen. A while back a number of Sawahiko's students had come to the villa for a visit, and one of them had left behind a pair of gym shoes.

Meanwhile, Takuo was examining the door they would have the

49

intruder use. It was solid oak with metal fittings on the inside that were quite rusty. It did not look like it would be too hard to dislodge the door.

Jane took the gratin and soup dishes from Yohei's room and washed them while Shohei crawled around on the floor of the foyer examining the carpet. He was checking the place where Chiyo had collapsed after slashing her wrist. If there was any sign of blood here they would have to revise the killer's route and have him pass through the foyer on his way to Yohei's room. Fortunately, however, there was no trace of blood on the moss green carpet in the foyer. Chiyo had not wounded herself very badly, and apparently all the blood had been absorbed by the sleeves and front of her blouse.

"We found them," said Sawahiko, emerging from the storeroom with an ordinary pair of rubber-soled gym shoes with white laces. They were dusty and the canvas upper part had yellowed, but they were definitely a pair of men's gym shoes.

Now that the problem of the intruder's shoes had been decided, the next question was who would put them on and make the necessary tracks.

"I remember reading somewhere," said Sawahiko, "that a skilled investigator can examine the pressure made by footprints and estimate the weight of the intruder. If that's true, it would be best to have someone of average build."

Since it was a question of average build and average height, Takuo was the obvious choice. Sawahiko was a bit on the plump side, and Shohei was far too large. Shigeru was too unreliable.

"Okay, can do," said Takuo, thrusting out his chin and assuming a belligerent pose. "I'm prepared to do whatever has to be done to protect Chiyo."

If it was true that Yohei had actually been thinking to make Takuo Chiyo's husband, what would happen now that Yohei was dead? This thought crossed Jane's mind, as she watched the young man prepare for the next bit of deception.

Takuo went into the corridor and put on the gym shoes. Everyone including Shigeru and Mine came out of the living room to watch. When Takuo was ready, Shohei opened the door. Through the open spaces between the white birch and silver fir trees they could see the wood and iron fence that separated the garden from the public road beyond. In a corner of the garden stood the yard light that was an imitation of a traditional London gaslight. It was hooded with snow and cast a melancholy light over the garden. There wasn't a single footprint or blemish on the pale, flourescent snow.

"I don't think the houses on either side are occupied, so you won't have to worry about anyone seeing you," said Sawahiko softly. All the villas in the neighborhood were large with extensive grounds surrounding them. Across the road to the east and to the north they could dimly make out the shapes of trees, but there was no sign of a building or of any lights.

Showing great determination, Takuo stepped down from the doorstep and set out across the garden. He walked with normal strides to the yard light. After leaving the protective eaves of the house, he found himself sinking into the snow up to his knees. The back garden was quite a contrast from the front garden in that the snow had not been cleared away. Tonight's snow, or rather last night's snow, had fallen on what was already there, resulting in an accumulation of more than two feet.

Takuo trudged step by step through the deep snow. After a few minutes he had reached the far side of the garden, and climbing over the low fence, left the premises. The street sloped away down the hill, but since it was routinely plowed, and an occasional car drove by, it made sense that the footprints would be lost there. In order to make sure he had gone far enough, Takuo raised his arm and waved. Then with his head down and his eyes on his feet, he started back toward the house. He began the return trip making a trail parallel to the set of tracks representing the assailant fleeing the house, and had just crossed the fence when Sawahiko held up his flashlight and said, "There's the telephone line. It's the lower line, the thick one."

Takuo signaled with his hand that he understood. The cement telephone poles lined the road. They had metal spikes protruding from them that served as footholds, and using these, Takuo energetically climbed up the pole. When he reached a point nearly twenty feet above the ground, close enough to reach the lower wire, he pulled the knife he had remembered to bring from his jacket pocket. Before cutting the wire, he turned once again in the direction of the house, but the watchers merely looked back in anxious silence.

Moments later, the line dangled to the snowy ground. Takuo then climbed halfway down the pole, reached out and swung his arm in an attempt to smash the yard light, but he could not get to it. Leaping from the telephone pole, he walked to the base of the yard light, where he searched for a suitable stone, but the deep covering of snow made the task difficult. He finally managed to find two small rocks, which he threw at the square, glass panes of the light, with no success. In frustration he hurled his knife, but that, too, only grazed the light.

"Don't bother with that, just leave it. The yard light doesn't really matter," called Shigeru. The others could hear the tension in his voice. Giving up, Takuo retrieved his knife and returned to the house across the pale, phantom snow, sinking in up to his knees. Step by step he marked out the path of the intruder.

"Be careful now, don't cross your earlier trail," said Shohei in a low voice. Takuo had stumbled and come perilously close to treading on his earlier path.

"Don't worry. I know better than to do that," came Takuo's instant rejoinder.

When Takuo reached the door, the whole group let out a collective sigh of relief. Still wearing the shoes, he entered the hallway and headed toward Yohei's bedroom. But before he had reached the bedroom door he saw that his wet footprints were soaking into the carpet and although they were disappearing without a trace, he stopped and removed the shoes.

"Okay! Nice job," said Shigeru enthusiastically. "Now we can all relax and get some rest."

But Sawahiko only sighed and said, "I'm afraid we can't rest yet. If we don't add some finishing touches, everything we have done so far will have been in vain."

There were a few finishing touches they could not afford to

overlook. For example, there was the matter of replacing the fruit knife. The knife that had originally been on the bedside table with the fruit had been carried away to Tokyo by Chiyo. It had to be replaced by another one from the kitchen.

And there was the matter of fingerprints. Naturally Mine had been in and out of Yohei's room several times and her prints were on the door knob. Takuo, acting as the assailant and wearing a pair of cotton gloves, opened and closed the door. They also wiped the knob of the door leading to the back garden and had Takuo open it when they went in or out.

They arranged Yohei's room so that the only light burning was a small night-light beneath the bedstand. This provided a dim glow rather than leaving the room completely dark. It could be assumed, of course, that a serious burglar would carry a flashlight with him.

Finally, the seven conspirators gathered once again in the living room. It was 1:30 in the morning.

"I hope Chiyo made it home all right," murmured Kazue in a worried voice. If everything had gone as planned with the hired car, she should have been at home in Tokyo by now. Jane was just about to say that they could easily telephone and see, but restrained herself at the last minute, remembering that the telephone line was cut, and the seven occupants of the villa isolated.

Shigeru topped off the glass of brandy he had been working on for some time.

"Why don't you make coffee for us?" Sawahiko suggested to Kazue.

"Maybe it would be better to have mild tea so it won't keep everyone awake."

"No! We need coffee, and make it strong."

This time everyone looked at Sawahiko in astonishment. "How can you suggest strong coffee at this hour of the night?" exclaimed Shigeru.

Sawahiko looked around at them with a troubled expression on his face and said, "Our whole story is that we were here playing poker from nine in the evening until one o'clock in the morning. There were some exceptions, of course. Chiyo and Jane were upstairs working on the graduation thesis until just before eleven. At that point they suddenly realized they were lacking a certain, essential reference book, so Chiyo decided to return to Tokyo on the spur of the moment. Our story is that Yohei played poker up to that point, then took a bath, had a little of the gratin with us, and retired to his bedroom around eleven forty-five."

"We resumed the game," added Shohei, "and were all preoccupied with playing poker at midnight when the murder occurred. That's why no one heard any sounds from the bedroom." It was clear that Shohei already understood the point Sawahiko was making.

Sawahiko continued by pointing out, "Our main alibi will be that we were all together playing cards."

"Naturally the police will try to verify that point by questioning each of us individually about the details of the game. That's their usual method to see if they can turn up any discrepancies in the evidence given."

"Right." Takuo was snapping his fingers and clucking his tongue in excitement. "If we get a sharp detective who's persistent, he'll figure it out right away if we don't really play a game."

"But of course," muttered Shigeru, turning up his hands with a dramatic shrug as he sat down heavily in his chair. Obviously, he also recognized the need for actually sitting down and playing a game of poker.

"I don't think we'll have to play it out for the entire four hours, but we should play for at least two hours to account for the time from eleven, when Chiyo left, until one. To actually play a game will be much better than rehearsing a story about a fictitious one."

"If we start now and go for two hours, we can be done by four. That should be just about the right time to bring Grandpa's body in from the balcony." Shohei's words brought tension back to everyone's face by reminding them that Yohei's body was lying rigid out on the cold balcony.

Kazue and Jane prepared hot coffee and cookies and cheese for snacks. They resumed the seats they had occupied before the delivery boy had arrived with the gratin, and began playing poker. Naturally, they were betting real money.

All seven players got caught up in the game, but it seemed as

54

though they were also trying very hard to fix the details of the game in their minds. Nevertheless, whenever someone mentioned the killing, everyone's thoughts were drawn in that direction. They all wondered if they had left anything undone. Would the police really be convinced that the murder had been committed by an outside intruder? By actually playing cards as a part of their cover-up scheme, they also gave themselves time to think about what might follow.

Holding the deck in her hands, Kazue suddenly sobbed out, "Listen, everyone, you have all joined in tonight to help protect Chiyo. I will be indebted to you for this for the rest of my life."

"Exactly so. Our daughter's misconduct has caused trouble for all of you. We can't apologize enough." Sawahiko's voice was strained, but a tighter note of tension crept into it as he looked hard at each of the people sitting around the table and continued, "Nevertheless, now that we have embarked on this conspiracy, there can be no turning back. We must all work to ensure that the true facts never come to light. That means we will all have to work together. If any one of us weakens in his resolve, or becomes careless, all the others will be in jeopardy. If the truth does come to light, we will all be in a lot more trouble than if we had done nothing. This started out as Chiyo's problem, but from now on, it is all our problem. We must never forget that."

"Since we're on the subject, there's something I would like to say as well," said Mine in her high-pitched voice. Everyone's attention turned to her. The poker chips were piled high in front of her, evidence that she had been winning steadily. Jane recalled Chiyo telling her once that whenever the family got together and played cards or roulette, Mine usually won.

"Once the police begin their investigation, they will surely probe the relationships among the various members of the Wada family. We must stand together in this and be careful not to say anything that will hurt one of the others. For example, we must not say anything about someone having a grudge against Grandpa, nor should we let on that some of us don't get along very well together. And if the subject of Grandpa's moral behavior comes up, please act as though you knew nothing about it. While we have a responsibility to protect Chiyo, we also have to protect the Wada family from any embarrassment. We have to be sure we protect all members of the Wada family." At last, Mine turned her attention to Jane and said, "You, too, must join us in doing this." With this final remark she dropped her eyes and looked at the floor.

Jane nodded and tried to control her feelings.

By this time it was 3:40. They had been playing poker for exactly two hours when they brought the game to a conclusion. Takuo had come out on top, and Mine, too, had won substantially. Sawahiko and Kazue were the big losers. Takuo had won seventy thousand yen from Sawahiko, who wrote out a check for the amount. Takuo gathered up the score sheets and threw them in the wastebasket. The check and the score sheets would all become important pieces of evidence.

"Will it be all right if I go to bed now?" asked Shigeru, who was clearly at the limit of his physical endurance. He had been steadily drinking brandy while they played cards, and now his eyes were unfocused and his mouth slack. His elegant, David Niven appearance was now slovenly and derelict.

"That's fine. Go ahead and go to bed," said Sawahiko gravely. "You really look like you've had it."

"Then we will see you at nine o'clock tomorrow morning," said Kazue, reminding him of what they had planned earlier.

"The more time that elapses, the harder it will be to predict accurately the time of death," said Shohei with a bitter smile directed toward Shigeru. "So we should delay the discovery of the body as long as possible, but we can't put it off too long; it would arouse suspicions if we slept too late in the morning."

"Well, I'll go up to bed now and pray for the prosperity of the Wada family." Shigeru gulped down the last of the brandy that remained in his glass and started precariously up the stairs.

The six who remained said good-night to Mine, who set off down the hall. Her bedroom was next to Yohei's. Jane once remembered hearing Chiyo say that even in their Tokyo home Mine and Yohei used separate bedrooms and had done so for years, perhaps even decades.

"Will you be all right by yourself . . . after what's happened tonight?" Kazue inquired solicitously, but Mine merely took a deep breath, nodded her head, and said, "Yes."

"Well, I hope you have a good rest."

"Good-night." Mine paused at the doorway and looked back as though she had something on her mind, but then switched on the light and closed the door softly. Watching that wrinkled, gray face, Jane suddenly wondered how Mine really felt about her husband's murder.

The ones who remained now trooped to Yohei's room. By this time the body lying on the balcony was completely rigid. When Shohei and Takuo picked him up as they had earlier, one taking the shoulders, the other the feet, it looked as though they were carrying a stone statue. Behind the ears, on the nape of the neck, and all the lower parts of the body, the purple, mottled spots of postmortem lividity had formed.

After they had laid the body out on the bed, Shohei looked at his watch. "It is almost four. It was shortly after midnight when we put him out on the balcony, so it's been just about four hours. I think that ought to be long enough."

"It's pretty chilly in here now, too," said Takuo, trembling. The French doors that opened onto the balcony were closed but the curtains remained open and the freezing cold could be felt in the room.

Takuo folded the plastic tablecloth they had spread under the body and closed the curtains. Meanwhile Kazue straightened Yohei's robe and put a blanket over him. Once again the night-light was turned on and the room was plunged into gloomy half-darkness. The five people paused briefly to face the bed in a moment of silent prayer. The only sound that broke the silence was a sob from Kazue.

Throughout all of this, the door was always opened and closed by Takuo. When all of this was done, Takuo, wearing his cotton glove, opened the door and the remaining conspirators exited into the corridor as he closed the door behind them.

Back in the living room, everyone pitched in and carried the plates and coffee cups into the kitchen in one trip. The uneaten gratin was put in a plastic bag and dumped into the rubber bucket that was used for wet garbage. By now everything anyone could think of had been taken care of. It was 4:15 on the morning of January 4.

Sawahiko and Kazue were using a small room behind the living room for their bedroom, while Shohei, Takuo, and Jane were staying in rooms on the second floor. Briefly, all five paused in the foyer.

"Thank you again for all you have done," said Sawahiko, but his thanks had an empty ring and left the others feeling that he had only said it because he felt he should.

"I'm going to take a shower," said Takuo, talking to himself.

"Well, good-night," murmured Shohei as the group went their separate ways. Whatever each of them may have felt in his heart, they were too tired to try to put it into words, and went to their rooms in leaden silence.

Since she had left the radiator on, Jane's room was warm and cozy when she entered it. The manuscript for Chiyo's graduation thesis was still on the writing table by the window. She had been in the middle of reading it when she was called away by Kazue to come downstairs to have tea. The events that had occurred since then had happened in such dizzying sequence that she could not remember them all clearly. It did occur to her, however, that after the events of the evening, Chiyo's graduation thesis would probably not be completed on time.

Jane's mind was numb and she felt as if she had been drugged. Moving somewhat shakily, she went into the bathroom and washed her face with warm water. Taking off her earrings and necklace, and discarding her dress, she collapsed on the bed. Heavy silence and deep fatigue embraced her.

She was not sure how deeply asleep she was, but at some time during the night, in the very deepest part of her mind, she heard a sound. It did not seem to be very near, but it did seem to come from somewhere within the house. It was a faint sound, but remarkably clear; a harsh sound, like the scraping of a rusty tool. What could it be? Jane knew what made that kind of sound, but she could not quite remember what it was before she sank back into a deep, deep sleep and her mind went blank.

4

The Hidden
Clue

The sky was still leaden and overcast, but it looked as though it would burn off. More snow appeared unlikely.

The Fuji Five Lakes police station was located on the national highway between Lake Yamanaka and Lake Kawaguchi. The windows on the southwest side of the building looked directly out on Mt. Fuji, whose lower slopes were covered with larch forests. The massive, snow-covered higher slopes soared up into the sky, and on this day, the peak was hidden in the clouds. The hard chill of the previous night was gone and an air of quiet tranquility enveloped the scene.

What a lovely day, thought police detective Ukyo Nakazato as he lingered by the window of his second-floor office. This year, January 4 had fallen on a Sunday, so only about a fourth of the usual number of officers were on duty. The first three days of the New Year holiday had seen a few traffic accidents, but not enough to make overtime necessary, so Nakazato felt adequately rested. Knowing that he would be on duty today he had not had much saké to drink the previous evening and, as a reward, even his huge stomach felt refreshed. In addition, it was customary for the superintendent to make his annual New Year's speech to the assembled officers on the fourth, but this year he had postponed it for a day. Not having to hear the superintendent's harangue made it that much easier for the detective to retain a bit of the holiday's festive spirit even though he was back at work.

As was his habit, Nakazato sat stroking his belly with one hand, while the other reached for the pack of cigarettes on his desk. He remembered that his wife had urged him to quit smoking for New Year's, or failing that, to at least use a little plastic filter that was

59

supposed to reduce the amount of tar he inhaled. He rummaged through his various pockets in search of the elusive filter, but failed to find it.

As he searched, Nakazato heard the sound of tire chains on the street below his window. The vehicle in question stopped in front of the precinct station. Glancing out the window, he saw a cream-colored van pull to a stop and two men quickly get out, one from the passenger's seat, and one from the rear seat. On the side of the van was the lettering of logo of the Kohan Restaurant.

Nakazato had time for two or three drags on his cigarette before he heard a uniformed officer ascending the stairs and approaching his office. He had given up trying to find his plastic filter.

"We have just received a report from a villa in Asahi Hills. They say that during the night a burglar apparently broke in and murdered the elderly gentleman who owned the house."

Nakazato was aware of a certain self-consciousness in the young policeman's voice at being in the presence of a detective.

"Did they come directly here from Asahi Hills?" asked Nakazato.

"They say they first tried to telephone, but the telephone lines had been cut, so were unable to do that. Just as they were putting chains on their car, the delivery truck from the Kohan arrived to pick up some dishes, so they caught a ride in the van and came straight here."

"Did they notify the local police box?"

"Apparently not."

Nakazato got up from his desk with startling agility and rapidly propelled his vast bulk toward the stairs. At forty years old he was barely five feet tall and weighed one hundred and seventy pounds, giving him a bulky figure. His legs were short, but he moved shrewdly and with surprising speed.

It's like I was supposed to have a holiday today and find that I have to climb a mountain instead, he thought as he went down the stairs and approached the two men near the door who were talking to a police officer.

The officer introduced Nakazato as the chief detective on duty.

"Oh yes, of course," said one of the men, pausing for a moment before continuing with his agitated account. "We belong to the Wada family, and have a villa at Asahi Hills. The whole family has been staying there for the holidays, but this morning Grandpa, I mean Yohei Wada, who is president of Wada Pharmaceuticals . . . Well, we found his bedroom a mess, and he had been murdered. Oh, I forgot, my name is Sawahiko Wada and I'm married to the niece of the victim. I teach at a university near Tokyo."

With flurried movements he produced a business card from the pocket of his heavy tweed overcoat. Sawahiko, with his high, patrician nose, long face, and swatch of gray hair at the temples gave the impression that he was a serious, reserved sort of person, but at the moment he was clearly upset.

"You say someone was murdered; are you sure the man is dead?"

"Unfortunately there is no question about that," came the reply from the other man, who had a large build and was in his thirties. "He was stabbed in the chest, and by the time we found him this morning, a good deal of time had already elapsed. You see, I'm a physician, and I know something about these things."

Nakazato interrupted to ask if they had come directly to the precinct station without notifying the Lake Yamanaka police on the way. Learning that this was indeed the case, he sent a nearby officer to call the local police and tell them to investigate the scene of the crime. He also dispatched two officers from the precinct station to the villa. Since it would only take a few minutes for the local police to get to the Wada villa, they would soon have confirmation by radio that the crime had been committed.

While this was going on, Nakazato seated the two men in an office and called in a stenographer to take notes while he asked them about the circumstances surrounding the murder.

"Last night after dinner all nine of us started playing poker, and it went on until late. No, actually there were only seven of us because my daughter, Chiyo, and her American friend, Jane, were upstairs working on Chiyo's graduation thesis until about eleven o'clock."

Most of the time it was Sawahiko who answered Nakazato's questions, though he thought the questions themselves seemed to skirt the main issue and not really get to the heart of things. But this was Nakazato's technique of amassing the fine details, so that later he could sift through them for discrepancies that might provide clues.

"It turned out that there was one essential reference book Chiyo had left behind in Tokyo. Apparently she could not get along without it, so suddenly at eleven o'clock she called a taxi and returned to Tokyo. At that point Jane joined us at the card table and we continued to play cards until one o'clock this morning."

"You left out something," interjected the physician, Shohei Mazaki. "Grandpa joined us for a light meal, but retired to his bedroom at about eleven-forty."

"Oh, that's right. Looking back on it now, all of this would never have happened if he had stayed and played cards with the rest of us." Sawahiko closed his eyes for a moment, his lips quivering, before continuing. "After Grandpa went to bed, the rest of us played a ruthless card game until one o'clock. We were all in bed by one-thirty, but because it was so late, we slept in this morning. Shortly before nine, Grandpa's wife, Mine, and my wife, Kazue, got up."

"Who discovered the body?"

"Mine did. Grandpa was always up by eight at the latest. Since there was no sound coming from his room, she thought it strange and went to investigate. You see, Mine slept in a separate bedroom adjoining Grandpa's."

Hearing Mine scream, the other six had rushed to Yohei's room, where they found his body lying on the bed. According to Sawahiko's story, that had happened around nine o'clock this morning.

"Naturally we tried to contact the police right away, but the telephone was dead. We figured the burglar had cut the lines. Just then the boy from the Kohan Restaurant showed up and we got a ride with him to get here as quickly as possible."

As a matter of routine thoroughness, the delivery boy from the Kohan was asked about this, and he said all had happened just as the Wadas had described.

It was approximately 9:50 when they received a report from the local police. They confirmed that the body had been positively identified as that of Yohei Wada.

At that point all the officers at the precinct station met in conference. They also sent a message to the Kofu Prefectural Police Headquarters requesting that they dispatch a team of special investigators. It was decided that eight detectives and two supervisors would report immediately to the scene of the crime.

The precinct superintendent, Katsubei Aiura, lived in the official residence directly behind the precinct station. He arrived at the station within five minutes of being called. He was almost fifty-four years old and only one year away from retirement, but he was still energetic and scrupulously neat in his personal appearance. His slim figure invariably attired in a dark suit gave one the immediate impression that he was a business executive or a high-level government official. It was widely acknowledged that he was an eloquent public speaker, and there was a rumor that he would run in the mayoral elections after retirement from the police force.

"All right, follow up matters at the scene of the crime and make a report," rapped Aiura as Nakazato hurried out of the building. "This is the first major investigation we've had since that phony suicide last year."

Early the previous spring there had been an incident in which the bodies of a middle-aged man and woman were dredged up from Lake Kawaguchi. At first it was thought to have been a lovers' suicide, but a few minor details in the case seemed suspicious. By investigating these, the Five Lakes police were able to prove that it had definitely been murder disguised to look like suicide. In the end, they caught the culprit and, quite naturally, had received the attention of the national media. Superintendent Aiura, with his glib tongue, had been the darling of the press.

"Here's a chance for you boys to wrap this thing up quickly and show the whole country what you can do." It was clear from the tone of Aiura's voice that he was looking forward to having this develop into a major incident. He relished the prospect of finding himself once again in the national spotlight.

Nakazato merely shrugged his shoulders, slipped into a pair of blue overalls, and headed for his car in the parking lot behind the building.

The Wada family villa was located on the high ground to the west of Asahi Hills, and the first police officers to arrive on the scene had roped off the entire area in preparation for the investigation that would follow.

After Detective Nakazato and the other officers entered the front door, they proceeded directly to Yohei's room. Sawahiko had returned in the police car to act as guide. He opened the door on the right side of the foyer leading to the corridor along the eastern wing, and as he did so, pointed out a spot of blood on the carpet. Slight stains could be discerned, but they were unable to make out any footprints. As a precaution, Nakazato instructed one of his subordinates to put down boards to keep the carpet from being trampled, and to insure that the bloodstains were not obliterated. Then, walking along the edge of the corridor, they proceeded to Yohei's room.

The door had been left standing open and as they entered Sawahiko explained, "We were careful not to touch anything after we discovered the body."

The room was square, the curtains were drawn, and a dim light emanated from under the bedside table. There was light coming into the room from the corridor as well, and some light reflected from the snow was able to penetrate the curtains, so it was possible to see in the room.

On the far side of the room was the bed with the old man lying on it, face up. He was covered to his chin by a blanket. On the floor scattered beside the night table was a silver fruit plate, pears and oranges, a fruit knife and fork, and some pharmaceutical magazines. In the middle of the carpet were spots that appeared to be bloodstains. At the foot of the bed stood a cabinet with its drawers and doors flung open. It was clear that someone had ransacked its contents.

The room was warm. It felt like it was in the low eighties and Nakazato looked at the heater, noticing that even now it was giving off heat.

Sawahiko explained, "It was Grandpa's custom to sleep with the heater on all night and to use only a light blanket." As they entered the villa Nakazato had noticed two men and three women clustered in the living room, but it had been left to Sawahiko and Shohei to accompany the police and provide explanations.

After looking carefully at everything in the room and getting an initial impression of it, Nakazato told his assistant Narumi to open the curtains. Only after the curtains facing onto the balcony were opened did Nakazato approach the bed.

He gazed for a time at the finely chisled features of the old man, and then, after closing his eyes for a moment, drew back the blanket. Beneath his light robe, Yohei was wearing a silk shirt. There were what appeared to be stab wounds in the middle of the chest and also on the left side. There was not much blood around the wounds, and what there was had already dried. There were also cuts on the fingers of both hands.

"Apparently he was awake when he was attacked by the intruder," murmured Nakazato in mild surprise.

Sawahiko gave him a startled look and said, "Of course he wasn't asleep, you can see he is not wearing pajamas; he had on a shirt and bathrobe." A momentary look of confusion crossed Sawahiko's face.

"Yes, I expect Mr. Wada's wife may be able to explain that," added Shohei quickly, though his voice remained calm.

Nakazato noted, however, that the doctor, with his rough-hewn, masculine face, had remained calm from the very beginning.

"It was his custom to lie in bed with his robe on and read a book or magazine until he fell asleep. I would imagine that was the situation when the burglar entered. I expect he was awakened by some sound, leaped out of bed, and the burglar, fearing he would call for help, just stabbed him," continued Shohei evenly.

"In that case it means the assailant laid him back on the bed after stabbing him," whispered Assistant Detective Narumi. Narumi was a handsome young man in his thirties who seemed somewhat lacking in character. He had not had much experience with homicide, so he spoke in a whisper out of deference to the dead man.

"Not only did he lay him out on the bed, he covered him with a blanket and dimmed the lights. But of course he probably did that so it would be a while before anyone discovered something was wrong," said Nakazato. He spoke as though he wanted to persuade himself of this. There seemed to be no flaw in this reasoning, but there was one thing missing from the scene—the murder weapon. Nowhere in the room could he find a knife that might have made the wounds in Yohei Wada's chest. There was a knife that had fallen to the floor, but it had no bloodstains on it, and besides, it was very small and had a rounded tip. Nakazato thought it would be hard even to peel an apple with such a knife.

Nakazato left the bedroom, leaving the medical examiner to look at the body. He decided that the first thing he should do was to get a clear picture of the sequence of events that had taken place.

"The key to this door is missing and there are footprints outside, so we think this is probably where the intruder entered," said Sawahiko, indicating the door that led from the corridor to the back garden. It was a solid oak door with metal fittings beneath the knob to prevent it from being jimmied. And yet the door had been unlocked.

"No one remembers having used this door for a long time, and who knows how long it has been unlocked?"

Nakazato put on a pair of gloves, and being careful not to disturb the fingerprints, opened the door.

As the door swung open, revealing the full sweep of the garden, an involuntary cry escaped the lips of the detectives. The garden was a pure white expanse of snow with thick growths of silver fir and white birch; and there in the snow were two lines of clearly visible footprints.

Obviously the footprints represented one line coming into the house, and one line going away. In a corner of the garden, near a tall yard light, the trail entered the public road.

"Now how do you like that," murmured Nakazato in astonishment. His first impulse was to hurry down into the garden and examine the footprints carefully. But the snow was nearly two feet deep, and at the thought of trundling his own one hundred and seventy pounds out into it, he suddenly hesitated. He was not reluctant to get his feet snowy, it was just that he realized that if a lighter man examined the footprints the site would not get as badly torn up.

Without hesitation he waved Narumi out into the snow to examine the footprints. He also ordered one of his technicians to accompany Narumi to measure and photograph the footprints.

Both of them brought their boots around from the front door and went down into the garden. Narumi probably weighed no more than one hundred and thirty-four or one hundred and thirty-five pounds, yet with each step he sank into the snow up to his knees. He trudged across the garden and back, following the line of the footprints. He paused for a time near the road at some distance from the yard light, looking at the thick, black wire dangling from the telephone pole.

"It looks like the intruder climbed this pole and cut the telephone line with a knife or some other sharp instrument." Narumi's voice seemed still with cold and stress.

"Is there any sign of blood at the point where it was cut?"

"No."

"How about on the snow?"

"I don't see any signs of blood. It doesn't look like he dropped anything."

That meant there was a strong possibility that the intruder had cut the telephone line before committing the crime. After all, it seemed natural that he would have used the same knife he used to stab Yohei. So, the intruder had already cut the telephone line before he broke into the house. Perhaps he had done that to give himself more confidence. Surely this meant the intruder had known the door was unlocked, and that the owner of the villa was likely to have valuables with him in his bedroom while he slept.

Nakazato mulled over these thoughts in his mind.

Judging from the traces, the intruder had gone directly to Yohei's bedroom, so it seemed likely that it was someone who was familiar with the layout of the house.

And yet, one had to wonder why there were bloodstains on the carpet right next to the door, but none on the snow.

"Is there anything unusual about the footprints?" he asked again.

The technician was photographing the prints in the garden and measuring them for both length and width.

"It looks like he was wearing rubber-soled gym shoes, about a size ten, I'd say."

"The length of the stride is just about the same as mine," said Narumi. "That means he was probably slightly over five and a half feet tall."

Nakazato turned to Sawahiko and Shohei, who were watching over his shoulder, and said, "Tell me, who has been to this house?"

"Not that many people, really. During the summer season we probably use it two or three times. It's a family tradition for us to gather here at New Year's time. But we have other villas we use, and generally this one is closed up for most of the winter," replied Sawahiko.

"When was the last time anyone was here?"

"Well, you'll probably have to check with Mine or my wife to be sure, but as far as I know, no one has been here since last summer."

That meant the house had been uninhabited for four or five months. There was no way of telling when the intruder had learned that the door was unlocked, but if he (and there was a strong possibility that it was a man) had observed the house over a long period of time, it probably meant he was waiting to make a big strike. But in that case, why would he choose a snowy night and try to break in through the back garden, which was piled deep with snow that would record a clear set of footprints?

Nakazato turned his thoughts in another direction and cast about for a different image of the intruder. "Is there any indication that someone has been watching this house?"

Sawahiko was just about to say something, but paused and finally hung his head in confusion. Shohei interjected, "I think we can be pretty sure that if there had been any suspicious people lurking about since we arrived on January second, we would have noticed them."

About an hour later another team of investigators and technicians arrived on the scene from the prefectural headquarters. They joined forces with the officers from the Fuji Five Lakes precinct and went through the basic procedures once more, meticulously, from the beginning.

The investigation of technical matters was handled by a prefectural authority who issued instructions to various technicians. These investigations took about an hour to complete. Afterward, they assembled the major players in the drama and presented them with the objective results.

"The weapon was a small, sharp blade, like that of a fruit knife. It penetrated the left side of the chest between the third and fourth ribs. It appears that one thrust pierced the heart." All this was explained by the medical examiner. "Either the heart, or one of the major arteries of the heart ruptured, causing blood to gather between the heart and the pericardial membrane. This put pressure on the heart, causing it to collapse. It is what we call a cardial tamponade. Ordinarily death results within one minute. Now we have to calculate the time of death."

Both Nakazato's investigation team and the prefectural one were listening closely to this.

"Since rigor mortis sets in pretty uniformly throughout the body, there is a strong possibility that at least twelve hours have elapsed. Also, there are no longer any signs of hemorrhaging."

The medical examiner pointed to Yohei's body, which had been returned to its original position, lying face up on the bed. Behind the ears and at the nape of the neck was a dark purple mottling that looked like bruises on the ashen skin.

"As you know, these dark spots are purpura or postmortem lividity and are caused by ecchymosis as the blood settles to the lower parts of the body. If the position of the body is altered within four to five hours after the time of death, these spots will also shift accordingly. In other words, the old spots will disappear and new ones will form. But if the position of the body is changed between eight and nine hours after the time of death, the spots will only partially change, and traces of the old spots will remain even though new ones are formed. After more than ten hours, there is no change in the spots no matter how much the body is moved.

"There is also another method for estimating the time of death, and that is to apply finger pressure to these purpura spots. At first when you press it, the color blanches, but as time passes, the spot stabilizes and there is no blanching even when pressure is applied. Generally speaking, between six and twelve hours after the time of death you can cause one of these spots to partially blanch by pressing it. After more than twelve hours, there may be some fading of the color, but it will not entirely blanch. Using these three principal methods we can estimate the time of death, but don't forget that the age of the victim, his physical condition, the cause of death, and the environment in which the body is found are all variables that can have a great effect on determining the time of death."

"How about in a closed room like this?" interjected Inspector Tsurumi, a member of the prefectural investigation team. The examiner ignored this question and continued his explanation.

"Ordinarily we expect that in summer all the changes take place faster than in winter. This is due to the higher temperature and humidity of summer compared to the cold, dryness of winter. Once putrefaction sets in, the differential becomes even more marked. In cases where death has resulted from a loss of blood, the presence of these purpura spots is much less pronounced. We should also note that the purpura are relatively unaffected by temperature, but in a warm environment, the spots will lose their ability to blanch under pressure somewhat earlier. In this case, for example, the purpura spots show no response to my finger pressure. Judging from the temperature of the room I would say that the victim has been dead about ten to twelve hours. But we must keep in mind that after a body has been dead for more than half a day, we have to allow for an increasingly wide margin of error."

"Following this line of reasoning, then, at what time would you estimate the death occurred?" Inspector Tsurumi seemed quite excited and could hardly contain himself.

"The condition of the body is rather advanced, and the rectal temperature is extremely low. So low I can't account for it by the method I have just outlined, but calculating back from the time I began my examination of the body at eleven o'clock, I would say that he had been dead for between eleven and fourteen hours."

"That means you estimate the time of death to be between nine o'clock and midnight last night."

"Umm. We may be able to tell a little more precisely after we've performed an autopsy."

Nakazato recalled Sawahiko saying that Yohei had eaten a meal at 11:30.

After their preliminary investigation at the scene of the crime, Nakazato and the other officers put out an alert throughout the region around Lake Yamanaka, and also along the national highway from Fuji Yoshida to Gotemba. Policemen were stationed at intersections, bus stops, and other key locations, and all suspicious cars and travelers were checked.

For the investigation around Asahi Hills, Superintendent Aiura called out all his men and directed matters himself. Fortunately, the weather had cleared, so there was no difficulty in getting the investigation underway. They also put in a request to the telephone company to repair the severed phone line.

Detective Nakazato and Inspector Tsurumi, in the meantime, were seated in the dining room at the villa where they were individually questioning each member of the Wada household.

The first person they called in was Mine. Mine Wada, sixty-two years old, was from one of the old, aristocratic families, and had been married to the victim for forty-one years. She had also been the first person at the scene of the crime.

"Last night my husband joined us in the living room while we ate gratin. We ordered it from the Kohan Restaurant. Since it was just before bedtime, my husband mixed a bit of soup with the white sauce and macaroni to soften it and make it easier to digest. He only ate a little. After that he went straight to his room. I suppose it must have been about eleven-forty or eleven-forty-five." Mine spoke in her usual high-pitched, singsong voice. Her round face was very gray, her eyes bloodshot, and she seemed exhausted, but she retained an air of dauntless resolution as she answered the questions that were put to her. Nakazato was astonished at her determination.

"It was probably shortly after one o'clock when I went to bed.

We played poker until just about one. I left the younger people to do the cleaning up and went to bed."

"Your bedroom is the one that adjoins your husband's, is that right?" Inspector Tsurumi spoke rapidly, spitting out the words in a manner that reflected his own intensity.

Mine pursed her lips and replied, "We thought that while we were here at the villa, it would be just as well to have separate rooms."

"I understand. When you went to bed, did you look in on your husband?"

"Yes, I did. I peeked into his room, but only the night light was on, so it was quite dim. I just assumed he was asleep and quietly closed the door. I'm getting old and my eyes aren't so good anymore, but it was so dark in there I am sure anyone would have had difficulty in seeing what had happened. I suppose he was already dead by then, and no doubt if I had gone right up to the bed, I would have seen it." Mine took a deep breath.

"And you didn't notice any of the bloodstains on the carpet in the hall between your room and the foyer?"

The woman sat with her eyes downcast, taking a few breaths before replying, "The hallway was also quite dark."

Since Tsurumi made no comment on this, Nakazato followed with the next question. "Just now when we were looking for evidence of what happened, we saw that your husband's dresser had been broken into. We were told that a diamond tie pin and a set of emerald cuff links were taken along with a briefcase containing some papers." Nakazato had learned this by asking some questions of his own before the other officers arrived from the prefectural headquarters.

"That's right."

"Can you tell me once more just for the record what was in the briefcase?"

"I can't say for sure, but I believe there was about a million yen in cash and fifty stock certificates worth a thousand shares each, so that would be fifty thousand shares. He told me he was bringing them with him because the company had issued new certificates at the end of the year and he was waiting for the banks to open after the holiday so he could put them in a safe-deposit box."

The news of Wada's murder had been relayed by the Fuji Five Lakes precinct to the Tokyo head office of Wada Pharmaceuticals, and information concerning the stolen stocks had been passed along to the head of the accounting division. He took steps to publicly announce the theft.

"I don't think the thief could very easily convert the stocks into cash, but I wonder what sort of price he can get for the jewelry?"

"Well, the diamond in the tie pin weighed more than one carat, and the emeralds were of very high quality. Altogether I would say they would bring about ten million yen."

Counting the cash, that would mean that the thief had made off with something in the neighborhood of eleven million yen.

"This may seem an odd question to ask at this point, but I wonder if you have any paintings, prints, vases, or other objects of art in the house that are valuable?"

"Well yes, in fact we do. My husband always liked to surround himself with things of the best quality."

"Pardon me for being so inquisitive, but what would you estimate is the value of all the artwork you have in the house?"

"I'm afraid that's a rather difficult question to answer." Mine looked down at the hands folded in her lap, and twisting her fingers for a time, appeared to be making an estimate. "Altogether I would say it is probably worth twenty million, maybe as much as thirty million yen."

"Yes. I see. Pardon me for being so inquisitive." Nakazato looked amiably off into space. If the intruder knew that the door in the hallway was not locked, one would have expected him to have slipped into the house when it was unoccupied and made off with at least twenty million yen worth of art objects. Instead, he had chosen to break in at a time when the house was occupied and face the danger of being discovered in order to steal an unpredictable amount of valuables.

"Do you know of anyone who might have had a grudge against Mr. Wada?" Tsurumi asked bluntly.

Mine's head jerked up and her gaze met and held that of the two detectives. This time she answered formally and clearly. "It is entirely out of the question that anyone would have had a grudge against my husband. Wada Pharmaceuticals was founded in the last century as a drugstore. It is an old, established business looking forward to its one hundredth anniversary. My husband represented the fourth generation to serve as president of the company. The family has always been very strict about who ran the business. In the second and third generations they adopted sons to head it. The family had heirs, of course, but they were not judged to be up to running the company adequately; the family was that strict. But my husband took over from his father as president of the company before he was forty years old. He was a devoted and serious man who worked very hard. He developed new pharmaceuticals, and he was successful in expanding into foreign markets. No one will deny that Wada Pharmaceuticals achieved the success it enjoys today as a result of my husband's efforts. All the people who worked for him held him in great esteem; I can assure you that not one of them had a grudge against him."

"How about the person who was to succeed him; how did he feel about that?"

"We never had any children of our own. Long ago we adopted a child to be heir to the family, but he later died of illness. I am sure that all my husband thought about was how to select the very finest person possible to take over as president. He always maintained that he was still young, and I am sure he must feel chagrined at suddenly losing his life in this way." Suddenly Mine's voice broke and she looked away. For a moment Nakazato glimpsed Mine in the grip of emotion. And yet even while her face was turned away, he noticed her stifle a small yawn.

Next they talked to Kazue, who, even more so than Mine, was grief-stricken over what had happened. Kazue was forty-five years old and Yohei's niece. She was a large woman with prominent features and an ample bosom, but this body housed a very feminine nature. This, at any rate, was Nakazato's assessment.

"My mother was Yohei's younger sister. My father was adopted into the family, so that's why I also have the name Wada. Both my parents died years ago. Sawahiko is my third husband. After my second husband died in an airplane crash overseas, I resumed using the Wada name, so that is why I still go by the name Kazue Wada."

74

Kazue was constantly dabbing at her large eyes, which were swollen and bloodshot. She responded to the detectives' questions rather erratically.

Tsurumi led by asking, "What about your husband, Sawahiko, in whose family register is he listed?"

"My husband married into the Wada family, so he is officially listed on the Wada family register. For the sake of the university where he teaches, he did not change his name, but legally we thought it would be better for Chiyo and me if we were officially members of the Wada family." Kazue added that she was grateful to her husband for his understanding in this matter.

"Yes. I understand now. I believe your daughter, Chiyo, was also here last night. Is that correct?"

"Yes." Suddenly Kazue was alert and on guard. As soon as the detective mentioned her daughter's name, Kazue was ready to stand fast and defend her. "But of course she had already returned to Tokyo before all this happened."

"Does she know yet what has happened?"

"She was probably notified by the company. I am sure she is very surprised and grief-stricken, as we all are. Grandpa always treated her as a favorite, and Chiyo respected no one more than she did him. She was very fond of him." At this point Kazue broke down in a fit of weeping.

"Did Chiyo plan to return here from Tokyo?" asked Nakazato.

"Yes. Jane Prescott is waiting here for her, and she was supposed to have come back today, but now I don't know what will happen. I imagine that once she hears the news, she will come with the people the company sends."

"In that case, we will probably want to talk to her later." Nakazato said this routinely. After all, it was his job to question anyone who had been in close contact with Yohei, but Kazue burst into tears once again when she heard this, and turned to Nakazato with a look of desperate entreaty.

"No! Please, you musn't let Chiyo get involved in this. She is very easily hurt. It would be a terrible ordeal for her to be questioned by the police right after a horrible event like this. I am quite certain her nerves would never stand the strain."

* * *

Shigeru Wada and Takuo Wada were each called in turn as the police continued questioning members of the household.

Shigeru Wada was sixty years old and Yohei's youngest brother. As a young man he had married a French woman and fathered a child, but he had divorced her shortly afterward and the woman had returned to her homeland. For years now he had lived alone and held a managerial position at Wada Pharmaceuticals. He had apparently been something of a dandy and a playboy since his younger days, and it would probably be accurate to say that he had spent most of his life as a parasite on Yohei. It was no more than a hunch, but when Nakazato looked at Shigeru's face with its neat mustache and fine features, he got the strong impression that the man was self-indulgent.

"Last night I was in the living room from nine o'clock until one, playing poker with the others. If you want to know how the game turned out, I pretty well broke even, but young Takuo was the big winner. Mine also did quite well. The score sheets may still be in the wastebasket if you care to look at them." Shigeru appeared haggard from lack of sleep and responded to the questions in a toneless voice. "My brother was with us until about eleven. At that point he went to take a bath, and afterward, though he joined us to eat gratin, he soon retired to his bedroom."

"You say Mr. Wada took a bath?"

Perhaps it was because Nakazato asked the question so abruptly that Shigeru was startled and his hand automatically went up to stroke his mustache.

"Uh, yes, that's right."

"If he took a bath before going to bed, I would have thought he would have changed into pajamas, but he was still wearing his shirt when we found him."

"I suppose Mine had just forgotten to lay out his pajamas in the bath. She was never very attentive to that sort of detail." Shigeru chuckled at his own statement, but somehow the laughter seemed hollow.

"At this point it seems likely that Mr. Wada was assaulted shortly after he retired to his room. Did you hear any suspicious sounds at all?" asked Tsurumi.

76

"No. I'm afraid I heard nothing. After all, we were in the living room and we had the stereo on and were very much involved in our game, so I'm afraid I can't help you with that one." Shigeru shook his head several times. Suddenly he slumped back heavily in his chair and rubbed his face with the palms of his hands. The action eloquently bespoke his desire to get the questioning over with as quickly as possible so he could get back to bed.

Though still very young, Takuo Wada responded to the policemen's questions with great authority. He was twenty-eight years old and the son of Yohei's younger brother, who had been dead for some time. Takuo worked in the accounting department of Wada Pharmaceuticals.

When Tsurumi asked, "Excuse me, but are you still single?" Takuo pushed his glasses up on the bridge of his nose and thrust his chin out belligerently before answering, "Grandpa Yohei was planning to announce in the near future that Chiyo and I are to be married. That was his wish and it was also something that she and I felt we wanted to do. But now this has happened. It's really a shame. I hope you'll make every effort to catch the killer as soon as possible."

Takuo's eyes darted quickly back and forth and he looked at the two detectives as though trying to size them up. He stated that he had been playing cards the previous evening from nine until one, and Tsurumi asked him about the outcome of the game. It was clear that he intended to systematically ask each member of the household about the progress of the game.

"My impression is that the turning point really came about halfway through the game when I drew a straight flush and Uncle Shigeru and I fought it out by raising each other a number of times. It turned out that he was betting on a full house."

Nakazato silently noted that, so far, everyone's testimony about the poker game had been consistent.

Tsurumi remained undaunted. "I understand that Mr. Wada had shown you a great deal of favor, both as a member of the family, and also as an employee of the company, but I wonder if you might know of anyone who might have had a grudge against him?"

Takuo, as was his habit, pushed his glasses up on his nose and replied firmly, "I can't think of anyone or any reason why anyone would hate Grandpa."

As he pushed his glasses up, Nakazato noticed that there was some white, powdery substance under Takuo's fingernails—something that seemed out of place.

Since Sawahiko Wada and Shohei Mazaki were busy making arrangements to announce to the press what had happened, the detectives decided to ignore them for the moment, and called Jane Prescott. Of all the people who were in the house at the time of the murder, only Jane and Shohei were not members of the family. Nakazato had been somewhat uncertain at first when he learned that there was an American woman staying at the villa, but after he found out that she had been living in Japan for a year and a half and spoke fluent Japanese, he heaved a sigh of relief. Nevertheless, taking testimony from a young American woman would be a new experience for him, and he felt rather tense.

Jane appeared wearing a dark blue sweater and a pair of black, designer jeans. She was slightly over five feet tall and had short, brown hair with a natural wave. She seemed an artless, uncomplicated sort of person.

"I am twenty-five years old, and I came to Japan after graduating from the University of Oregon. At present I am living in a dormitory at the Japan Women's University where I am studying modern Japanese literature. I make a little money on the side by tutoring English."

Jane answered their question in a low, feminine voice. Her green-gold eyes showed a lively intelligence, and her pert nose and friendly smile, revealing dazzling, white teeth, suggested a good-natured, outgoing personality. Nakazato decided she possessed a mature, confident air somewhat beyond her years.

"Chiyo asked me to come here to help her with her graduation thesis, and I arrived yesterday afternoon. It was only later that we realized that Chiyo had left one essential reference book back in Tokyo."

After that, her story corresponded with what the others had al-

78

ready said; at eleven o'clock they had sent Chiyo off in a hired car, and Jane was invited to join the poker game, which she did until it broke up at one o'clock.

"How long have you been tutoring Chiyo in English?" asked Tsurumi.

"Just a little over a year. I meet with her twice a week."

"At Chiyo's home?"

"Yes."

"I see. In that case, then, you are in a position to know something about the relationships among the various members of the Wada family."

"No, not really. I'm not that intimately involved with the family."

"Tell me quite frankly, what sort of impression did you have of Yohei Wada? What I mean is, did he have any unusual habits; was there anything about him that might have made people hate him?"

Inspector Tsurumi was watching Jane very closely as he asked this question, but she returned his gaze steadily and said quietly, "I met Mr. Wada for the first time last night. From all that I have heard about him, however, I would guess he was the sort of person everyone respected."

"Observing the Wada family as an American, I wonder if you noticed any problems or difficulties?"

"Until last night the only members of the family I knew were Chiyo and her parents, but her parents seem perfectly content, and she seems to enjoy the love and affection of both. I've been told that Chiyo's real father was killed in a plane crash, her parents weren't divorced or anything like that. Certainly in America these days, and increasingly in Japan too, it is not uncommon for parents to be divorced and for children to be living with a stepparent. As far as I can tell, Chiyo and her stepfather seem to get along quite well. But then Chiyo is the sort of person everyone loves . . ." Jane had a faraway look in her eyes as she murmured these last words, and then suddenly broke off without finishing what she was saying. She darted a swift glance at Nakazato and their eyes locked for an instant. In that moment, however, the detective thought he saw a look of sadness and pity.

*　　*　　*

It was past three o'clock in the afternoon when Superintendent Aiura arrived at the villa. He had spent the day sending out all available men to make inquiries throughout the region around Asahi Hills, and although he had personally taken charge of the matter, the results had been disappointing. The police check had turned up no suspicious vehicles or people, and they could find no eyewitness who had seen any sign of an intruder anywhere near the villa. The New Year's holiday was the off season for Lake Yamanaka, so most of the villas in the area were vacant, and because of the heavy snow the previous night, those few people who were in residence in the villas or at the hotel had been indoors. Nevertheless, since the crime had been committed in the middle of the night, it would have been a real breakthrough if they had been able to come up with an eyewitness.

After having gathered all the evidence they could at the scene of the crime, and after questioning everyone related to the incident, Superintendent Aiura, Detective Nakazato, Inspector Tsurumi, and a few other officers huddled together to review their progress. Shortly after four o'clock they held a press conference in the dining room. The news that the president of Wada Pharmaceuticals had been murdered at his villa had been discovered that morning by reporters routinely checking the police blotter, and all day long journalists had been trickling in and asking the police questions concerning the progress of the investigation; but this was to be the first official press conference.

Not surprisingly, taking a central role in the news conference was Superintendent Katsubei Aiura, who sat in front facing perhaps twenty local and regional reporters and cameramen. Aiura was wearing the same black suit he had worn that morning, but now he had added what appeared to be his New Year's necktie, which had a red and silver design on a black background. He sat with his back straight, leisurely looking over the roomful of reporters with what he hoped was an intellectual air.

The dining room crackled with tension and anticipation. When he judged the time to be right, Aiura stood up to face the crowd and began to speak. "I expect you all know in rough outline what has happened, but just to make sure, I will review today's events from the very beginning."

Aiura's clear, resonant voice reached every ear as he described in detail all that had happened from the time the first report of the murder had reached the precinct station. As he spoke, his delivery became more inspired, and even his features changed; he was the type who reveled in his own bombast. Meanwhile the reporters were busily taking notes and the police investigators who had examined the scene of the crime also gathered around and listened. Even Sawahiko, Takuo, and Shohei were there on the edges of the crowd. Kazue and Jane waited in the living room, while Mine and Shigeru were upstairs resting.

"So that's where things stand right now. Next we come to Special Prefectural Inspector Tsurumi and local Chief Detective Nakazato. They have been gathering evidence and testimony here at the scene of the crime, and I will now tell you the results of their work. They have verified that the victim, Yohei Wada, was stabbed to death in his bedroom in this house. They discovered bloodstains on the carpet in the hallway leading to his room. They also found an unlocked door leading from that hallway into the rear garden. They verified that there are two sets of footprints; one set leading up to the house, and one set leading away. They also found that the telephone line had been cut. At this time we are assuming that the murder was committed by a lone burglar who broke into the house at some time between nine o'clock and midnight, though we believe it was probably closer to midnight. Our theory is that he broke into Mr. Wada's bedroom, was discovered there, and that he stabbed Wada to death. Before fleeing he also broke into a cabinet and stole a briefcase containing stocks and cash as well as some items of jewelry. We believe that the motive was burglary and that the killing was incidental."

Here Aiura shrugged his shoulders, but an exultant light glowed in his eyes. "Nevertheless, we are not yet certain whether the motive was simply burglary, or whether it was someone who had a score to settle with Mr. Wada and knew that he would be in the bedroom, someone who killed him and took the valuables only to make it look like a burglary. One of the problems we have with the burglary theory is the fact that the intruder apparently knew that the door was unlocked. If money is what he was after, he could have entered the house before the Wadas came or after they had left, and made off with something in the neighborhood of twenty million yen worth of art objects. If the intruder noticed that the door was unlocked after the Wadas arrived here on January second that would be a different story, but there is a strong possibility that he knew about it earlier. Since they arrived here on the second, there were plenty of family members and maids on hand, so it would have been very difficult for someone snooping around the neighborhood looking for unlocked doors to go undetected. So, even though our intruder could have entered the house when it was unoccupied, he chose a time when the Wada family was in residence, and moreover, he entered Mr. Wada's room at a time when there was a light on in it. It is these facts that lead us to believe that perhaps the intruder's real objective was to take Mr. Wada's life. Although it is possible, of course, that Mr. Wada's room was only dimly lit at the time of the killing, the evidence suggests otherwise. Apparently Mr. Wada was lying on his bed wearing a silk shirt and robe and reading a magazine, which we found on the floor. From the testimony of family members we have learned that it was his custom to read in bed before going to sleep at night, so this indicates that the room was light enough to read in. Judging from the evidence, there can be little doubt of that."

The superintendent was the first one to have contact with the media regarding this incident and he presented his theories and ideas eloquently in his rich, resonant voice, but the fact was that from the very beginning these were the ideas and theories put forward by Detective Nakazato and Inspector Tsurumi.

Halfway through Aiura's presentation, Nakazato slipped from the room and made his way to the hallway in the eastern wing of the house where everything was quiet. He passed through the door on the right side of the foyer and once he had closed it, the voices in the dining room could only be faintly heard. He opened the door leading to the back garden. Ever since the special investigators had arrived from the prefectural police headquarters, they had had men examining the footprints, and now the back garden was disfigured by a great mass of muddy footprints, in addition to those left by the intruder. The pale light of the afternoon sun broke through the clouds momentarily, but the footprints remained frozen; there was no chance they would melt soon in this weather. The early winter twilight was already approaching and the sky was overcast again with heavy, snowladen clouds. The whole landscape appeared to be frozen.

Nakazato slipped on a pair of overshoes that were lying nearby, and stepped down into the snow. He followed the intruder's footprints around the garden. The snow had crusted, so he did not sink in too deeply. The telephone line had been repaired, and there had been no one in the garden since the repairman left. He was thankful at least for the fact that for once the scene of the crime was remote and he was not troubled by crowds of spectators, as he often was in the city.

A hunch was forming in Nakazato's mind, and though he kept playing with it, it did not seem to jell into anything substantive. He had verified the time at which Yohei had eaten his last meal by sending one of his men to the Kohan Restaurant at the Asahi Hills intersection. The people at the restaurant testified that they had sent eight servings of gratin to the house at 11:30, and this corresponded with what the members of the Wada household had told him. At that time they were halfway through their poker game, and according to the delivery boy, Yohei was in the bath. He had testified, "The old woman said it was about time to get him out of the bath, and she left the room." This corresponded nicely with what Shigeru had said about Yohei going to the bath at that time. And yet the body had been discovered wearing a silk shirt and trousers.

The people in the house that night had been the members of the Wada family, plus Yohei's personal doctor, Shohei Mazaki, and the foreign guest, Jane Prescott: why did they all look so sleepy this morning? Even if they had stayed up until 1:30 in the morning, they had slept in until nine, so they must have gotten at least seven hours of sleep. Even taking into account the fact that this sort of emotional shock can have an exhausting effect on people, how was he to account for the fact that all of them had bloodshot eyes and that many of them had been yawning during the questioning? The recollection of this latter fact was especially troubling, but his ruminations were cut short when he realized that he had returned to the house. Suddenly Nakazato stopped and sucked in his breath. Slowly he bent down and looked carefully at his feet.

Just beside the large stone step that led to the door he could see the intruder's footprints, and it was only at this point that the two trails, the outgoing and the incoming, crossed each other. There was the outgoing footprint, and clearly visible over the heel of it he could see the toe of the incoming footprint. He knelt in the snow and examined the prints more carefully, but there could be no doubt about it—the outgoing prints had been made first, and the incoming ones later.

What did this mean? If an intruder came in from the outside and then left again, there was no way he could have left footprints such as these. But that was not all. As he stared at the footprints, Nakazato noticed something on the snow beside one of them. Scooping up a handful of the snow, he found it covered with a gray-white powder.

Still staring at the powder in the palm of his hand, Nakazato kicked off the boots and entered the house. Judging from the sounds in the dining room, the reporters had begun asking questions. Nakazato pushed his way through the door leading to the kitchen on the opposite side of the corridor. In the middle of the spacious kitchen was a table on which lay a rumpled, plastic tablecloth. Removing the snow, he placed the bit of powder in a fresh plastic bag, and put it in his breast pocket.

Switching on the light, he looked around thoughtfully, and crossed the rectangular kitchen. In the back of the kitchen was a storeroom with bare wooden floors. The room had a number of shelves cluttered with all sorts of items. In a corner of the storeroom were stairs leading to the basement. On the floor near the top of the steps was a bit of the white powder that looked like wheat flour.

After carefully searching the storeroom, Nakazato descended the stairs and turned on the basement light. Apparently the basement room was used for food storage, for it was quite chilly and smelled of food stuffs.

Nakazato stood still and let his eyes wander, examining every corner of the room. The walls were lined with shelves loaded with

cans and jars, tea boxes, and bags of rice. There were old-fashioned, square, glass jars, and tubs with wooden lids, and there on
the floor. . . Suddenly his roving gaze halted. On the floor, diago-
nally across the room in plain sight, was a small pile of spilled
flour. Beside the pile was a large tin canister.

Nakazato put on his gloves and opened the can. Inside he found
it partly full of wheat flour. Removing one glove and pulling back
his sleeve, he thrust a hand into the flour. The first thing his fingers touched were shoe laces, and a moment later he pulled out a
white gym shoe. Soon he had retrieved the other shoe as well.
They were a pair of men's shoes, about size ten from the looks of
them. He would have to take them out to the garden to make sure
they matched the intruder's tracks, but he was willing to bet they
would.

Nakazato closed the can, and with the gym shoes tucked under
his arm, ascended to the kitchen. The first thing he did was find a
large plastic bag and put the shoes in it. Next, he went to the sink
and washed his hands, but found that he had difficulty removing
the flour that had lodged under his fingernails.

As Nakazato was crossing the foyer with his bag of shoes, he
could hear Aiura's mellifluous voice answering a reporter's question. "That's right, there is no doubt that the murder was committed by an intruder who broke into the house. We are presently
conducting a thorough investigation, and as soon as we can turn up
an eyewitness, it will only be a matter of time before we arrest the
culprit."

Detective Nakazato silently shook his head and took a deep
breath. The fact that he had found the so-called intruder's shoes
concealed inside the house made it quite evident that the culprit
was someone in the villa.

At that moment there came the sound of a car pulling up in front
of the house. Kazue came rushing out of the living room, and at
the same moment the front door burst open and a delicate young
lady entered. She was followed by two men wearing identical
black ties who appeared to be company employees. The two
women stood for a moment gazing at each other, dumbstruck.

"Chiyo!"

85

"Mother . . ."

As they embraced, each buried her face in the other's shoulder and sobbed.

"Chiyo, Chiyo, oh Chiyo." Kazue was unable to say more than this as she held her daughter in her arms, stroking her on the back and arms.

So, it really was true, everyone loved Chiyo. As he observed the scene, Jane Prescott's words came back to Nakazato.

5

Details of
an Inside Job

For a time the two women embraced and wept.

Chiyo buried her face in Kazue's shoulder and Nakazato was unable to see her features, only the hands twined around her mother's neck. Chiyo was wearing a black dress beneath her fur coat. Nakazato also caught a quick glimpse of something white around her wrist where her left hand protruded from the sleeve. Instinctively his eyes fastened on that flash of white, but just at that moment, Kazue turned toward him, pulling away from her daughter.

"You must be exhausted, why don't you rest for a while?" Whispering these words, she held her daughter's shoulders while the girl removed her shoes. Kazue beckoned to the two company employees who were hovering in the background, and they all went into the living room. Kazue closed the accordion doors behind them, flashing a large opal ring on her finger as she did so. Nakazato had the feeling that Kazue was being overly protective of her frail daughter, by not allowing her to be exposed for a moment to the harsh scrutiny of the detectives or the press.

Nakazato headed down the corridor of the eastern wing and once again opened the door onto the back garden. Putting on the overshoes, he went down into the garden. He took the gym shoes from the plastic bag and fitted them to the footprints in the snow. Both the left and the right one fitted perfectly. Even the tread pattern on the bottom of the shoe matched perfectly. With a look of satisfaction on his face, he replaced the shoes in the bag and returned to the house.

The news conference, which had lasted some forty or fifty minutes, at last came to an end and the reporters and cameramen filed

87

out of the dining room. Nakazato loitered in the hallway for a time, as though avoiding them. He did not enter the dining room until he saw that all the reporters, as well as Sawahiko, Shohei, and Takuo, had left the room.

In the dining room he found Superintendent Aiura, Inspector Tsurumi, and two other investigators seated at the table. The rest of the investigative staff had returned to the precinct station along with Yohei's body. The body would be kept at the precinct station overnight, and first thing in the morning it would be taken to the nearest hospital for an autopsy.

As Nakazato approached the group the superintendent gave him a look that clearly said, "Well where the hell have you been?" He looked trim and jaunty in his dark suit, but his narrow, questioning eyes asked, "Why weren't you present to hear my masterful handling of all those reporters?"

Without a word Nakazato tossed the plastic bag on the table in front of the superintendent. With a puzzled look on his face Aiura took the white, flour-dusted gym shoes from the bag and set them on the table.

"These were concealed in a large canister of flour in the basement storage room. They exactly match the footprints that were left in the back garden; these are the intruder's shoes. Or rather, I should say, these shoes were used to make it appear that there was an intruder. There is no question about it."

Nakazato went on to briefly explain how he had discovered that the incoming footprints overlapped the outgoing footprints, how he had found some flour beside the footprints, and how this had led him to the storage room. From there he went on and described how he had discovered the shoes. From his breast pocket he removed the plastic bag containing the flour sample and displayed it.

"Uh . . . what . . . but . . ." For once the superintendent was at a loss for words.

"It's really quite simple. Those footprints were deliberately made by someone in this house to make us think a burglar broke in. First he made the outgoing tracks, then returned to the house making the incoming tracks, but he was careless in one place and stepped on his own tracks. It was only in that first step, everywhere else he was careful to keep the two lines of footprints separate."

"Why didn't you notice this when you did your preliminary investigation?" muttered the crestfallen Tsurumi.

"The important thing is now that we have found these shoes hidden in the basement, we have to make a fundamental change in the way we are viewing the case."

"So you're saying this was an inside job made to look as though someone had broken in from the outside?" was Tsurumi's immediate response. He was a quick-witted fellow compared to Superintendent Aiura, who still had his jaw thrust out in uncertainty and confusion. Clearly this new development showed that progress had been made in the investigation, but that was not as important to him as the fact that he had just explained to the assembled reporters that the crime had been committed by an intruder. How was he going to change the story without making a fool of himself?

Tsurumi broke Aiura's reverie. "If it was an inside job, then the murder weapon and the items that were stolen should still be on the premises."

"That's right. It means we will have to do another, more thorough search."

The investigative team had already searched the villa once, but they had done so on the assumption that there had been an intruder, which meant they were looking for things that had been taken rather than for things that had been concealed.

"Under the circumstances, I think it would be a good idea if we don't let on right away that we've discovered the shoes. Sooner or later the culprit will realize that we've found them, but until then he'll feel complacent knowing that we're still looking for an outside intruder. If he knows that we know, he may change his strategy."

Nakazato's discovery made the matter far more complex and difficult than it had initially appeared to be. For one thing, it was not clear whether the murder had been committed by one person, or by several. Also, they did not know the motive for the killing. But there was no question about it, the killer was one of the members of the household, and even though he couldn't prove it yet, Nakazato was convinced of this.

"I agree," said Tsurumi grimly.

"All right, then, what we have to do is send investigators to Tokyo to check out the personal relationships among the members of the Wada family. It seems inconceivable to me at this point that a member of the family would have killed the old man just to get some jewelry and stock certificates."

Again Tsurumi nodded his agreement. "We should probably send several teams of investigators."

Superintendent Aiura stood between Tsurumi and Nakazato, and it appeared that his mood had changed once again. He said, "If it was an inside job, that means it was done by one of the seven people who spent the night here: Mine, Shigeru, Sawahiko, Kazue, Takuo, or one of the guests, Shohei Mazaki or Jane Prescott. So the rat is in the trap; we've narrowed it down to these seven." Once again his expression radiated the simple self-confidence that was so characteristic of his demeanor.

In any case, he thought, it's nice to have another major incident in my jurisdiction, and the way things are going, it could be quite dramatic to announce a great reversal in the case. Aiura was so excited by the thought of this prospect that one would hardly guess he was only a year away from retirement.

Using the newly repaired telephone, Nakazato called the Fuji Five Lakes precinct and instructed them to send four investigators back to the house. Meanwhile, the superintendent returned to the precinct station, where he selected a team of six detectives and told them to get ready to head out for Tokyo in three unmarked cars.

When the four officers remaining at the house were joined by the four sent from the precinct station, they divided themselves into teams of two and set about systematically searching the house. It probably would have been a good idea to search the grounds as well, but by this time it was already dark, and besides, at the time of their earlier investigation, they had focused their attention more outside the house than inside it. There were no signs that anyone had tried to hide the briefcase or the knife in the snow. On the other hand, there was no telling how many hiding places could be found in the spacious house.

It was shortly after six o'clock and they were just getting this second search underway when Sawahiko approached Nakazato. He had an unhappy look on his face and asked, "Is it really necessary to search the house again?" As a prominent university professor, he was used to commanding authority, but at the same time he was a man whose expression usually revealed his feelings.

"I'm sorry, but we have to make sure the intruder confined his activities to Mr. Wada's bedroom. It is unlikely that he was in any other part of the house, but there is a remote possibility, so we have to check it out," said Nakazato reassuringly.

"But I am sure that if he had ransacked any of the other rooms, we ourselves would have noticed it."

"But don't you see," interjected Kazue, "He might have gone into one of the bedrooms that is not being used."

They decided that for the time being the search would be limited to the unoccupied rooms. As night fell, the members of the Wada family looked exhausted and perhaps it was for that reason that they were unable to conceal their exasperation about the search. Since he did not have a search warrant, Nakazato knew he would have to show some restraint.

"Why don't you have dinner first? You detectives have had a long day, you must be tired. We are going to have some food sent in, you may as well have some too." Kazue continued to try and calm her husband with soothing looks.

When the food was delivered from the Japanese restaurant in Asahi Hills, Shohei and Takuo helped Kazue and Jane bring the dining table into the living room, and there they set out the boxed lunches. Both the Wada family and the police officers had missed lunch that day.

The Wada family members and the company employees who had arrived from Tokyo with Chiyo ate their dinner in the living room. But Mine and Chiyo had retired to their rooms and did not appear for dinner.

The police officers were invited to continue using the dining room, and they ate their meal there. Later Nakazato and his men commenced their search. One group combed through the kitchen and the storeroom again. Another team was assigned to search

Yohei's room and the corridor in the east wing. A third group searched the closets and unoccupied bedrooms on the second floor.

Behind the living room was a small cubicle Sawahiko and Kazue were using as a bedroom, a billiards room, and a small conference room. The conference room was lined with shelves of old books and mementos that the Wadas had collected over the years.

The searchers had to keep in mind that they were looking for a place where the culprit could conceal a briefcase containing a million yen and fifty stock certificates, a diamond tie pin and a set of emerald cuff links, as well as the knife that was used to murder Yohei Wada. It was likely that the murderer would also have had to hide some blood-stained clothing. If they searched every room from wall to wall and did not turn up anything, the investigation would be brought to a standstill. Nakazato and his partner searched the billiards room and the surrounding area. They worked intently for more than an hour without success. Then a young detective who had been searching Yohei's room looked in on them, his face drawn with fatigue. "How's it going? Did you find something?" asked Nakazato from where he stood on top of a round table peering down behind a cabinet. There was an unconscious note of hopeful anticipation in his voice.

Before replying, the young detective's worried gaze fastened on the round table legs, wondering if they would support the heavy detective's weight. Finally he looked up at Nakazato and said, "No, not really, but in a corner of the balcony we found this." Holding the object in the fingers of his left hand, he thrust it in front of Nakazato. "Inspector Tsurumi says they didn't notice it earlier today when they searched the area the first time."

At first glance Nakazato thought he was holding up a small worm. Tsurumi was a notorious practical joker and Nakazato wondered if they were playing a joke on him. But then he remembered it was hardly the season for worms, and besides, this was too long.

Being careful not to lose his balance, Nakazato climbed down off the table. When he took the object in his hands, he saw that it was an orange-brown strip of rubber; no, it was actually a tube. It was about a foot and a half long with a diameter of about five millimeters. One end had been cut cleanly, as though by scissors. Looking closely, he saw that it was marked every five centimeters.

92

"What is it?"

The other man tilted his head as though to say, "How should I know?" What he in fact said was, "When you open the French doors onto the balcony, the space behind the door is hidden. That's where we found it."

At the time the body was discovered, the French doors had been closed, as well as the curtains. Earlier they had assumed that the robber had entered by way of the door in the hallway, and had not paid much attention to searching the balcony. They must have overlooked this.

It occurred to Nakazato that the metal balcony door had been badly rusted, and that it made a terrible noise whenever they opened it. Obviously the balcony wasn't used often, so he was doubtful whether or not this rubber tube had anything to do with the murder. He cocked his head and pondered the matter.

The next day was Monday, January 5. The sky was leaden and overcast with snow-bearing clouds. It was intensely cold, but there was no wind and the morning was calm.

At 9:15 that morning Detective Nakazato and seven other officers got into two cars at the Fuji Five Lakes precinct station and set out for the Wada villa. Nakazato had wanted to leave promptly at nine, but Superintendent Aiura had insisted on delivering his annual speech to the assembled police officers. Thankfully, this morning he had been briefer than usual, but his delivery had been unbearably pompous. Some of the reporters drifted in early that morning, and when Aiura realized they were there, his speech became even more grandiose. The previous evening he had officially established the Special Task Force Investigating the Murder of the President of Wada Pharmaceuticals. Inspector Tsurumi had been placed in charge.

Through the windshield of the car they could see the forests of bare trees dusted lightly with snow, and towering above them, the gloriously white peak of Mt. Fuji. Miraculously, the peak was not hidden by clouds and the entire mountain was visible. As the car approached Lake Yamanaka, they looked directly at the eastern slope of Mt. Fuji; viewed from here the peak appeared broader than from any other location, and the whole mountain seemed dignified and resolute. Nakazato puffed on a cigarette as he squinted and took in the view. The surface of the lake was a chilly blue, and out in the middle it was frozen in white, wavelike ripples. He realized that again today he had forgotten the plastic filter his wife had wanted him to use to cut down on tar consumption.

When the two cars arrived at the Wada home, two plainclothes detectives came out to greet them. They had spent the night at the villa.

The previous evening Nakazato and his men had searched the whole house with the exception of the living room and the occupied bedrooms. They had finally abandoned the search at 9:30. The eight searchers had left nothing unturned, but they found neither the stolen goods, nor the murder weapon. This only increased the possibility that they were concealed in one of the occupied bedrooms.

During the course of the evening Nakazato had questioned the members of the household again, and had told Sawahiko that he wanted to search each of the occupied bedrooms, but this time Sawahiko refused outright. Both Shohei and Takuo broke in to say that they were all very tired and wanted to get some rest. In fact, it appeared that Mine and Shigeru had already gone to bed.

One could suppose that the terrible physical and emotional shock of these events had exhausted the family, still, it could hardly be called late. This aroused Nakazato's suspicions. Since they were adamant in their refusal to permit him to continue the search, there was nothing he could do about it, but this only reinforced his conviction that it had been an inside job. In the end he decided he would have to keep them happy because he knew that he would need their cooperation as the investigation progressed.

Nakazato decided to put off any further searching until the following morning and returned to the precinct station. In exchange for this concession, the Wada family agreed to allow two detectives to spend the night at the house. They would keep an eye on things to make sure that the culprit did not try to remove evidence from the house.

"Nothing seems to have changed during the night. Everyone retired to bed around eleven o'clock, and they all seem to have slept through the night," reported one of the detectives who had stayed at the house. "We took turns staying awake, but no one tried to leave and there were no suspicious movements."

"Is everyone awake now?"

"Everyone got up about eight o'clock, and they just finished breakfast."

"How about the daughter, Chiyo?"

"She was at breakfast too."

Chiyo had gone straight to her room on the second floor after her arrival the previous evening, and stayed there. She did not even show up for dinner.

Nakazato assigned half his men to search outside the house, since it had been too dark the previous day to do so. All they had done was make sure there was no sign that anyone had buried something in the snow, or had built a fire to burn evidence.

Nakazato and his assistant, Narumi, divided the rest of the officers into two groups and set about searching the occupied bedrooms. Inspector Tsurumi had remained at headquarters since he was now in charge of the entire investigation.

As they entered the foyer, they could see a cluster of people in the living room including Mine, Shigeru, Takuo, and the two company employees. They appeared to be talking among themselves. Perhaps they were making plans for the funeral. An autopsy would be performed on Yohei's body that afternoon, and then it would be taken to the Wada home in Tokyo. Apparently they were going to hold a public funeral, and the company was making most of the arrangements, so Nakazato had asked Mine and the others to stay at the villa for another day.

Glancing into the dining room, he found Kazue and Jane clearing away the breakfast dishes; they both said good morning to him. Chiyo was nowhere in sight. She had probably retired to her room.

Nakazato whispered to one of the detectives who had spent the night in the house, "Which room is Chiyo's?"

"It's the second room on the left at the top of the stairs."

After assigning tasks to each of his subordinates, Nakazato started quickly up the stairs. Before he joined in the search of the bedrooms, he wanted to meet Chiyo, and he preferred doing it without Kazue knowing about it. The previous evening, when the subject of Chiyo had come up, he noticed that Kazue became very tense. She had pleaded desperately, "No! Please don't get Chiyo involved in this. She can be very easily hurt. . . . I am quite certain her nerves could never stand the strain."

He turned left along the second-floor corridor and knocked softly on the second door. A small voice responded, "Yes?" Nakazato said nothing but merely waited until he heard the latch being removed. So Chiyo had shut herself in her room and locked the door.

The door swung back just a crack, and Nakazato shoved his way in. Since the safety chain had not been attached, he pushed his large body straight into the room and closed the door behind him. Chiyo retreated two or three steps and gasped. She was a slim, almost fragile-looking figure dressed in a black wool blouse, and a long, dark skirt. She had narrow eyes, a slim nose, and all the classic features of an aristocratic Japanese beauty. Her cheeks flushed and she stared at Nakazato, almost in terror. He quickly flashed his police badge and introduced himself.

"Please relax. Why don't you sit down over there? I'd just like to talk to you for a few minutes."

Nakazato kept his hands calmly at his sides as he approached her, but with each step he took, she took a step backward until she reached the window and sat down in the desk chair. The desk was littered with paper, dictionaries, pencils, and erasers.

Nakazato drew up a nearby stool and sat on it.

"You are Chiyo Wada, isn't that right?"

The girl said nothing.

"I believe the man who was murdered was your great-uncle, isn't that right?"

Chiyo nodded faintly without uttering a word. She had her hands clasped in her lap and kept her eyes cast down. Holding her body up rigidly in the chair, she would not look at Nakazato. Kazue had been like this yesterday, but hers was a defensive tension, while Chiyo gave the impression of one fearful of her fate.

Nakazato expressed his condolences simply and went on to say, "I understand you weren't here at the time of the murder."

"Yes."

"I heard that you left here in a hired car at about eleven o'clock on the night of the third. What time was it when you arrived home in Tokyo?"

"Shortly before one thirty," she replied in a small voice.

"What happened to the car?"

"The driver stayed just long enough to drink a cup of tea, and then left."

"I see."

The previous evening they had asked a few questions at the taxi rental place in Asahi Hills. The driver was a man in his forties, and his story was substantially the same as what Chiyo was telling him now.

"Was there anyone at home when you got there?"

"There is an old woman who looks after things. She took a holiday on the first and second."

"But she was back on the third?"

"Yes. Her daughter was also staying there with her."

"I see. Now as I understand it, if all this had not happened, you would have picked up your reference book and returned here on the fourth."

"Yes."

"You would have returned by taxi?"

"No. I would have taken the train, the Odakyu Line."

"What time does the train leave; the one you intended to take?"

"I was supposed to leave home before noon, but I was too late, I missed it." She suddenly seemed to choke up and bit her lower lip.

"Did you run any errands or go anywhere while you were in Tokyo?" Nakazato asked this last question very gently in order to keep the conversation going.

"No. I was in the house the whole time." Chiyo's voice had a note of desperation in it. "I was just too tired, I overslept."

"It was so late by the time you arrived in Tokyo that you couldn't get up the next morning, is that it? And I suppose that before you left the house, someone called up from the company and told you what had happened."

"Yes. Around one o'clock we got a call from the accounting department; I asked them to send a car for me at one thirty." She

97

went on and explained that the traffic on the highway had been heavy and it had taken a full three hours to make the trip from Tokyo to Lake Yamanaka, where they had arrived at approximately 4:40 the previous afternoon.

There were no inconsistencies or suspicious points to be detected in Chiyo's story. What impressed Nakazato was the girl's frightened manner and vigilance, which had caused her to spend the whole time since her return to the villa locked inside her own room. There was also the extreme protectiveness that Kazue had shown. This combination of factors impressed the detective. Added to that was the glimpse he had had the previous evening of something white wrapped around her wrist. Somehow that flash of white had stuck in his mind.

He idly walked over to the window and looked out, bringing his face close to the glass. In order to get to the window he had to pass behind the chair where Chiyo was sitting and he could hear her suddenly suck in her breath as he approached. It was like approaching a wild animal.

"It looks like there are still a few flakes coming down," he murmured to himself as he turned and directed his gaze to the back of Chiyo's neck. "Do you have any particular thoughts about the unfortunate way in which Mr. Wada died?"

A few moments elapsed before she replied, "I was told that you suspect he was attacked by a burglar who had broken into the house."

"What would you think if it didn't turn out to be a burglar? You understand, of course, that I am just speaking hypothetically now, but what if someone deliberately planned to kill Mr. Wada and only made it appear as though an ordinary burglar had done it? Now I know that Mr. Wada was always very fond of you, so I wonder what you think about what I have just suggested?"

She had her head bent so far down that it seemed her neck would break, and it did twitch two or three times. She gave a start as she listened to Nakazato. Chiyo clutched her left wrist with her right hand as she replied in a teary voice, "No, I'm sorry, I wouldn't know anything about that."

At this point Nakazato paused, then suddenly sucked in his breath and exclaimed, "Oh my! What happened to you there?"

"What?" said Chiyo, looking away, but instinctively clasping the fingers of her left hand with those of her right.

Nakazato grasped her left arm and raised it up. Under the light wool sleeve of her blouse he had observed an unnatural thickness. With his other hand he gently slid back the sleeve of her blouse to reveal a white gauze bandage. "Just as I thought. Last night I thought I saw a bandage on your left wrist." He let her hand fall back into her lap. Again she quickly concealed her left wrist with her right hand.

"I burned it."

"Did it happen while you were here?"

"Uh, no. It happened yesterday morning at home while I was making coffee."

"I see. Burns can be tricky; you may not think much of them at the time, but sometimes they can be very serious. You should be more careful."

Nakazato's impulse was to seize her hand again and remove the bandage so he could see the wound, but of course he hesitated to do that. For one thing, it would be far too violent, and for another, he felt sorry for Chiyo. She simply sat there with her head bowed and her white hands clenched in her black-skirted lap.

Assistant Detective Narumi and his men had begun their part of the search in the bedroom used by Sawahiko and his wife. Meanwhile Nakazato, with Chiyo's permission, had searched her room, and finishing that he called for his subordinate who had been waiting at the foot of the stairs. They went to Shohei Mazaki's room and knocked on the door. It was two doors down from Chiyo's room.

A harsh, husky voice responded, and Shohei opened the door. He was a large man wearing a dark green sweater and gray slacks. He had heavy eyebrows and thick lips, and an unpleasant expression clouded his rugged, masculine face as he looked down at Nakazato and his assistant. All of the people staying at the villa had changed into black or nearly black clothing out of respect for Yohei's death. Shohei alone was wearing ordinary clothes.

"You recall that last night we decided to search people's rooms today. It is possible that on the night of the murder the intruder may have visited other rooms besides Mr. Wada's, so we want to have a look around."

"Please make yourselves at home," said Shohei nodding and opening the door for them. Nakazato and his assistant followed him into the room.

The layout of the bedroom was pretty much the same as Chiyo's. There was a bathroom and closet, a queen-size bed in the middle of the room with a night table posted on either side of it, and a writing desk beside the window. On the desk were several paperbacks in a foreign language and a number of medical journals. Beside the desk chair was a heavy, black bag. On the bed were a discarded jacket, cigarettes, and a lighter.

Nakazato's assistant excused himself and began searching the bathroom. Ignoring the intrusion, Shohei simply picked up his cigarettes and walked over to the window where he lit one up.

"You returned to your room that night after you finished playing poker. I wonder if you found anything out of place, or anything missing?" asked Nakazato, looking at Shohei's stubborn back.

"Don't be silly. If anything had been disturbed or missing, I would have reported it at once."

"Do you have any theories or hunches about the intruder?"

Shohei did not even bother to respond to this question. Meanwhile, Nakazato's assistant was systematically searching the bathroom. He also peered into the crawl space above the ceiling and looked under the bed.

Unperturbed, Nakazato continued asking questions. "Dr. Mazaki, I know you teach at a prominent medical school in Tokyo, but what exactly was your relationship to Mr. Wada?"

"It was an ordinary doctor-patient relationship."

"So you were staying here at the villa as his attending physician?"

"Yes, that's right. Whenever it was possible for me to get away, Mr. Wada always liked to have me accompany him on long trips."

"Was there something wrong with him?"

"No, not at all. He was sixty-six years old, but he really didn't show much sign of old age. He was really very healthy."

"What makes me curious is the fact that you are a surgeon. Now

I can understand that a man of Mr. Wada's stature and prominence would want to look after his health, and it is very reasonable for him to have an attending physician with him, but I would have thought he would have chosen an internist."

"Ah, yes, of course. There is a reason for that. You see, five years ago Mr. Wada had an operation for gallstones. Members of my staff at the hospital performed the operation, and in the course of making my rounds during his recovery, I got to know him personally. He asked me to become his attending physician at that time. Besides, since he was in such good physical condition, even a novice like myself could take care of him."

Throughout this exchange Shohei had remained standing, looking out the window. Nakazato had learned earlier that Shohei was thirty-four and single. That meant he had only been twenty-nine when he met Yohei; quite literally a novice. Since that time he had occasionally accompanied Mr. Wada on trips and the two men had grown close.

The room was not all that large, and they were able to complete the search in less than half an hour. Nakazato had predicted they would not find what they sought in Shohei's room, and he had proved himself correct. They had not yet searched his personal possessions, however.

"I hate to ask this of you, but we would also like to search your belongings."

Nakazato had tried to speak casually, but as he said this, Shohei suddenly whirled around to face him. His thick lips were tense and his crescent-shaped eyes glittered as he returned Nakazato's gaze. For a moment the look on his face reminded Nakazato of someone else.

"You want to search my belongings? Why would you want to do that?"

"Well, we think there is a remote chance the intruder may have made off with some of your personal effects."

"If the intruder had stolen anything of mine, I would have noticed."

"It's also possible that he might have left some slight clue that would give us a lead."

"You're really going to go all the way on this, aren't you?" said Shohei with a bitter laugh. "What you're really saying is that one of us may have the money and jewelry that were stolen from Mr. Wada concealed among our personal effects."

"If the intruder was startled, he might have done anything."

"Don't try to kid me. You suspect one of us, admit it."

Silently Nakazato drew a deep breath, and put on a poker face, though he was sure the perceptive Shohei would see through it. There was nothing else he could do. Sooner or later he would have to tip his hand. Quietly he said, "To tell you the truth, that thought had crossed my mind. Things were quite frantic for us yesterday, and despite the questioning and searching we did, we did not do an adequate job of evaluating the intruder's footprints. If there really had been an intruder, somewhere, somehow, we would have found some evidence confirming that. Of course, if it had been a real, professional thief, it is quite possible that he might have disappeared without a trace, but in that case why would he have left footprints in the garden? Following that line of reasoning, there is a possibility that the footprints might be false and only made to look as though an intruder came in from the outside. After all, the only real evidence we have that there was an intruder are the footprints and the cut telephone line."

Shohei's features softened in astonishment, and his dark complexion paled. He seemed to lose some of the contempt he had earlier had for the detective. "Yes, of course. You have to take every possibility into account when you conduct an investigation. It's just like a doctor giving a patient a variety of tests to find out what is wrong. But you realize, I'm sure, that if you don't find the stolen items and the murder weapon in the house, your theory will be proved false."

"I have said from the beginning that there is only one chance in a million that anything will turn up."

"I understand. Go ahead, search anywhere you like." Shohei turned away and took out a fresh cigarette.

He did not have much in the way of personal effects. In the closet were a coat and suit, and aside from that, there was only an overnight bag and his doctor's black bag. Since he had driven to the villa in his Mercedes sports car, Nakazato borrowed the keys so he could search the car as well. He went through the pockets of the suit and checked the overnight bag. Shohei had a single, silver tie pin, and no cuff links. He had a couple of credit cards and less than fifty thousand yen in cash. At the very end, Nakazato turned his attention to the doctor's black bag. "Surely you won't object to my looking in this."

Shohei's only response was a slight frown.

Nakazato set the heavy bag on the bed and opened it. It contained all the usual medical equipment: stethoscope, blood pressure gauge, syringes, scalpels, scissors, and so on. The two scalpels glittered sharply; there was no sign of blood on either of them.

"You may look through those things, but be careful about handling them," said Shohei softly. Nakazato nodded and looked everything over with close scrutiny. There was a plastic bag containing a thin coil of orange-brown tubing. It was perhaps a yard long and had graduated markings every five centimeters. One end looked as though it had been cut with scissors. A label on the plastic bag identified it as a stomach tube, for pumping stomachs. The bag had been opened.

"What's this for?"

"It's used to pump a person's stomach when they have swallowed poison or for washing the stomach, and sometimes it can be used to empty the stomach when we have to administer an emergency anesthesia. You see, if a person receives anesthesia when he has food in his stomach, there is always the danger that he will vomit and choke."

"Have you used this on Mr. Wada recently?"

"No, never." Shohei's denial was spoken with sudden vehemence. He sucked in his breath in apparent consternation, but then resumed calmly, "There was never any need to use that piece of equipment on Mr. Wada."

"I see. Have you used it on one of your other patients?"

Shohei made no reply.

"What I am getting at is that it looks as though there is some white residue here on the inside of the tube."

Even though the tube had been used, it had been well washed

103

afterwards, and Nakazato might not have noticed the residue if he had not been examining the tube with special attention.

"Oh, that. A couple of weeks ago an emergency came up while I was making a house call on one of my patients. I need to get a new tube, but just haven't gotten around to doing it. It's not something I use very often."

Shohei's response seemed unnaturally quick, and he rubbed his jaw vigorously with the palm of his hand. It did not escape Nakazato's observant eyes that from the very beginning of this affair the young surgeon, more than any of the others, had seemed unflappable, but now for the first time he seemed flustered and uncertain.

11:05 A.M.

Inspector Saburo Tsurumi of the Prefectural Police Headquarters was sitting at a desk in the Fuji Five Lakes precinct station looking expectantly at the black telephone in front of him. The search at the Wada family villa was being continued from the previous day, but a considerable time had passed since the murder and hope was fading that the search would turn up any major leads. Nakazato and the seven men under his supervision had been looking both inside and outside the house all morning. There had been one phone call prior to eleven o'clock, but only to say that they had found neither the stolen items nor the murder weapon.

Now Tsurumi was waiting to hear word from the detectives who had gone to Tokyo to find out about the personal relationships between Yohei and his family and the employees of his company. So far the gym shoes found in the basement were the only concrete evidence they had that the crime had been committed by one of the members of the household. Still, it was enough to focus the investigation on the seven people who had spent the night at the villa. The fact that a team of six investigators had been dispatched to Tokyo indicated the police's determination to find out if there had been an elaborate deception.

The investigators had divided themselves into teams of two and had been questioning people and following up leads since their arrival the previous evening. The superintendent's instructions had been to report back by eleven o'clock this morning.

A short distance from Tsurumi at the head of a U-shaped cluster of desks sat Superintendent Aiura with a thoughtful look on his face. Today he was wearing a very stylish, dark gray, pinstripe suit, and having just finished lunch, he was using a toothpick and glancing frequently at his watch. He was going over in his mind what he would tell the reporters at this afternoon's news conference. The reporters would have to have their stories filed between 1:00 and 1:30 in order to make the evening editions, so Aiura had promised to meet with them by 12:30 at the latest.

The telephone rang. Tsurumi snatched it off the hook and immediately heard the voice of the senior detective. He reported that his team had visited Yohei's home in the Tokyo suburb of Ogikubo in order to find out what his daily routine had been like. "By last night, a large number of friends and relatives had already gathered at the house, but thanks to the fact that Mine is still there in Asahi Hills, it was relatively easy to make some inquiries. There is a maid here who has been with the family for forty years, and also Mine's stepsister, a middle-aged woman. I had some interesting conversations with these women. At first, of course, they were reluctant to talk to the police, but once they started, one thing led to another."

The veteran detective was in his forties and had seen it all. His specialty was a gentle, but tenacious form of interrogation.

"Tell me about these interesting conversations."

"It turns out that ever since his younger days Mr. Wada had been quite the womanizer, and apparently he didn't slow down in old age. He would fall for a young lady from time to time, and once that happened, he would lose all control."

"Ahh, that must have caused all sorts of grief for Mine."

"When these things first began to happen, she would leave home or threaten to commit suicide, but after they passed the age of fifty or so, she seemed to reconcile herself to his behavior, and from that time on they always maintained separate bedrooms. What I am not yet sure of is whether she had truly reconciled herself to his behavior, or whether she had simply concealed her jealousy and anger for the sake of the family's prestige and wealth, and had just played the role of the faithful wife."

Tsurumi rubbed his chin thoughtfully and pictured Mine in his

105

mind's eye. "Even here at the villa on the night of the murder they were using separate bedrooms, so it is possible that while they were here she had the opportunity to do away with him at her leisure."

"In any case, in recent years, instead of getting angry at Yohei's little flings, she just turned a blind eye to them and tried to maintain a social facade."

"I see."

The previous day, under questioning, Mine had whipped up her head and said in her distinctive, high-pitched voice, "It is unthinkable that anyone would have had a grudge against my husband. He was always a serious man dedicated to his business. All the people around him held him in great respect and there is no reason to suppose that any of them would have had cause to kill him."

Mine had been protecting the family's reputation by concealing her husband's excesses and by idolizing him. Perhaps it was just a pose to maintain her own pride.

"I don't think we can take at face value everything the maid and the stepsister said, so I tried asking some of the other relatives and people who work in the company, and even though no one would come right out and say it, I had the impression they weren't denying Yohei's behavior either."

"So you think he was keeping a woman?"

"He was probably keeping several of them. I haven't got the names yet, but I expect to turn up something today."

"Yohei and Mine had no children of their own. Did he have any children by any of these other women?"

"I think there's a good possibility of that. There's one other thing that came up. It seems Yohei's younger brother, Shigeru, also has these proclivities, and he's even worse than Yohei was. Yohei at least was very good at his job, but from early on, his younger brother made a career of sponging off Yohei. The fact that Shigeru also has problems with women is something I picked up from people in the company and also from relatives."

"I heard that when he was young he married a French woman and fathered a child by her, but that's all."

"He divorced her soon after the child was born and has lived alone ever since. Or I should say he pretended to live alone, but it's pretty certain that he has a mistress hidden away somewhere. This sexual indulgence seems to be a Wada family trait. One of Yohei's old friends even told me jokingly that this was so."

The detective completed his report to Tsurumi by promising to come up with more concrete evidence of Yohei's amorous activities. Next to come on the line was a young detective who had been checking leads within Wada Pharmaceuticals.

"Last night I visited the home of the company's legal adviser. He had been in the same class with Yohei since middle school and in addition to being legal counsel for the company, he and Yohei were longtime personal friends. He's a member of the bar association, and a very pleasant man. I think we can trust what he said."

Apparently this interview had also turned up some interesting information, for the young detective's voice became tense with excitement. "It turns out that Yohei had not drawn up a will. He was sixty-six years old and in good health, and it seems he did not give much thought to dying. He also had not made any definite arrangements for someone to succeed him as president of the company."

"Um. Did the counselor have any idea of what Yohei was worth?"

"He had several villas, lots of artwork, and several business enterprises. Altogether the lawyer thought Yohei was worth about two billion yen. In addition to that, he also controlled most of the stock in Wada Pharmaceuticals."

"If there is no will, it means everything will be inherited by the next of kin."

In this case Yohei's principal legal heir would be his wife, Mine. Since he had neither parents nor children, the others who stood to inherit from his estate were his brothers and sisters. Tsurumi calculated that in a case such as this the court would probably award three-fourths of the total to Mine, and the remainder would be divided among the brothers and sisters. Under Japanese law, since some of the brothers and sisters were dead, their children would inherit their share.

107

"From what I've heard so far at Wada Pharmaceuticals, there is not much factional in-fighting of the sort you would expect in a company that size. Ever since Yohei became president, there has not been a chairman of the board. There were two managing directors, but they did not have any real authority. Mr. Wada ran a one-man operation."

"Shigeru is one of the managing directors, isn't he?"

"Yes, and I heard something about him as well. It seems that Shigeru used his position as managing director to get the company to advance him some money. He was not able to pay it back, and the head of the accounting section fixed the books and charged the money to some other name. In another incident, in which the company bought a number of antique paintings—they were for the Wada collection—Shigeru made up some phony receipts to say that the paintings cost twice as much as they actually did, and then gave the dealer a kickback. Apparently this sort of conduct was going on all the time, and Yohei was just waiting for Shigeru's term of office to expire before forcing him out of the company."

"Did Shigeru know what Yohei was planning to do?"

"The counselor told me he thought Shigeru had some inkling that it was about to happen."

"Umm. Did you hear anything about Takuo?"

"Yes. It seems Takuo is sharp enough, but he always brags about being Yohei's nephew, and that has caused some resentment among his fellow workers. As far as his marrying Chiyo is concerned, there had been some vague talk about it, but nothing more. It is well-known that Mr. Wada was especially fond of Chiyo, and Takuo may have thought that if he married Chiyo, he would have been picked to take over as president of Wada Pharmaceuticals."

"I wonder if Yohei really intended for Takuo to marry Chiyo?"

"I haven't found anyone who can confirm that Mr. Wada ever actually said such a thing. I also picked up some other information." Here the young detective stifled a chuckle and lowered his voice. "I heard this from one of the women who works in the accounting department. I don't know what her motive was for telling me; maybe she had her own sights set on Takuo and he rejected her, or maybe he had dallied with her and then left her. I would guess something of the sort happened. Anyway, she says that for years now Takuo has maintained a steady relationship with a bar hostess, an older woman. She says he intended to break off with the woman once his engagement with Chiyo was formally announced, but until that time, he was afraid that if Mr. Wada found out about it, it would ruin his chances of marrying Chiyo. There's a rumor that Mr. Wada already knew about Takuo's mistress, so the girl in the accounting department may have told Yohei on the sly."

The investigators had heard nothing unpleasant when the members of the household had been questioned the day before. Yohei was loved and respected by everyone; it was unthinkable that anyone would feel hatred or resentment toward him. But after a single night's investigation, the detectives had uncovered a web of jealousy, mistrust, and deception.

The third team had been sent to follow up leads at the home of Sawahiko, Kazue, and Chiyo, and their report struck a somewhat different chord.

"Sawahiko and Kazue have been married for four years; he's forty-two and she forty-five. His first wife died, and while this is his second marriage, it's Kazue's third." The plodding, unassuming, middle-aged detective who was making the report typically began by reporting what was already known.

"Kazue has never had much luck with men. Her first husband ran off with another woman and divorced her. Her second husband was killed in an airplane accident. This time, fortunately, she has been able to create a happy family life. Sawahiko is apparently very devoted to her. Last year when he was hospitalized with a light bout of hepatitis, Kazue worried about him a great deal. So much, in fact, that by the time he came out of the hospital, he had gained about five pounds and she had lost just as many. She is a very passionate woman by nature and seems to love Sawahiko a great deal."

This team had assembled their report by interviewing the maid who worked at Sawahiko's house and her daughter who sometimes stayed with her, as well as some of the neighboring housewives. Sawahiko and his family lived in a wealthy suburb of Tokyo where

109

Kazue was well liked by her neighbors. She would often spend the day with two or three close friends who were also housewives in the neighborhood.

"Chiyo is the daughter from Kazue's second marriage, and although she is only Sawahiko's stepdaughter, he is very fond of her, and by all reports they make a very happy family."

All of this fit with what they already knew, namely that Yohei had been especially fond of Kazue and her daughter, Chiyo, and that they, in turn, had been very proud of him.

"What no one seems to know is what sort of relationship existed between Sawahiko and Yohei, and there is also the question of how Sawahiko and Kazue met each other in the first place," murmured Tsurumi into the phone.

"We've found the answer to that one. The husband of one of Kazue's friends teaches at the same university as Sawahiko. It was through this mutual acquaintance that they got together."

"Let's see, he teaches biology, doesn't he?"

"Yes, at the Institute of Medical Biology."

"What sort of research does he do?"

"Kazue has bragged about him to her friends in the neighborhood, saying that he does genetic engineering. This is a field that is attracting worldwide attention and is the cutting edge of scientific research right now. It has the potential for radically increasing the production of foods and medicines in the future, and Sawahiko is utterly devoted to his work. According to what Kazue has been telling the neighbors, there is no more serious or ambitious scholar than Sawahiko. But it also turns out that there is some suspicion that Sawahiko has been keeping a woman."

"What?" Tsurumi called to mind an image of the moody features of Sawahiko.

"It is only a rumor that one of the neighborhood housewives heard, but according to her, someone unexpectedly spotted Sawahiko in the lobby of a hotel in the city with a woman who appeared to be a courtesan or entertainer of some sort. The housewife thought the matter over for a time and finally decided not to tell Kazue about it, and was trying to forget about it herself."

Just what we need, another woman, thought Tsurumi with a

grimace. He had forgotten who had made the remark, but it certainly seemed true that the men of the Wada family were notorious womanizers.

No investigation had yet been undertaken in Tokyo concerning Shohei Mazaki or Jane Prescott.

Tsurumi instructed them to investigate two new points. These had been requested by Detective Nakazato in his earlier phone call from the villa. "Find out how Shohei Mazaki came to be Yohei's attending physician. There may be something behind that, so I want it checked out. The other item has to do with Chiyo. She returned to Tokyo in a hired car, arriving home at one-thirty on the morning of January fourth. That same day she got a call from the company telling her about the murder, and at one-thirty that afternoon they sent a car to pick her up and bring her back here. She claims she never left the house during the entire twelve-hour period. Just to be sure, we want you to check on her movements during that time."

By the time Tsurumi had given two or three other instructions and hung up the phone, it was a quarter past noon.

With a look of impatience, Superintendent Aiura demanded Tsurumi's report. For some time now reporters had been milling about in front of the investigation headquarters. Looking at his hastily scribbled notes, Tsurumi summarized the telephone conversation for the superintendent. "Well, I can't say that we've made great progress, but on the other hand, every line of inquiry we have pursued thus far has brought to light important information. In any case, the fact that it was an inside·job is undeniable. We can suppose that the true motive for the murder is to be found in the complex pattern of relationships surrounding Yohei Wada."

Katsubei Aiura nodded and stroked his eloquent jaw. At last night's news conference he had stated quite categorically that the murder had been committed by an intruder, and now he would have to reverse himself. Nevertheless, he thought such a reversal could actually be made quite dramatic if he handled it properly. The superintendent straightened his necktie, threw back his shoulders, and strode into the press room where the reporters were waiting. He began speaking immediately in a voice so young and vibrant that one would hardly believe his age.

"At last night's news conference I said that the murderer was an intruder who broke into the house. That statement was part of a carefully calculated plan worked out by my investigative staff. It was deliberately designed to deceive the culprit. Our ultimate goal, of course, was to penetrate a very cunning deception set up by the killer. We are meeting again and I can tell you that we now have firm evidence that the murderer of Yohei Wada was one of the seven people staying at the villa that night."

The furor that erupted at this news was more than Aiura had anticipated. From the midst of the uproar someone shouted, "You say you have firm evidence. What is it?"

"The shoes! We found a pair of gym shoes hidden inside a canister of flour in the basement. Those shoes exactly match the tracks that were made in the back garden."

The superintendent did not go on to explain that the tracks overlapped at one point, proving that the outbound trail had been made first, because he didn't want to disclose that they had overlooked it when they made their initial examination of the scene.

"Yesterday six members of our investigative staff were dispatched to Tokyo to clarify points about the motives and relationships of the suspects, and even at this early stage we have received several reports from them. I expect it's just a matter of time until we find the items that were stolen from the villa and the murder weapon."

"You say the murderer was one of the people who spent the night at the villa. Does that mean that of the nine people who gathered there on the third, you are excluding the man who was murdered and the young lady who returned to Tokyo for the night?"

Aiura took a deep breath and answered clearly, "That's right. The killer has to be one of the remaining seven."

6

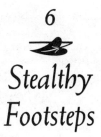

Stealthy Footsteps

After an interval of a day and a half, the snow began falling again and the trampled garden at the villa was once more covered with a smooth, soft, white layer that looked like sugar frosting.

Peace and tranquility had returned to the villa at last. Since morning the area around the house as well as the rooms of the occupants had been searched by Nakazato and his men, causing turmoil everywhere. But finding nothing, they had at last withdrawn. Shortly after noon Mine and the two employees from the company's accounting division had finished making the plans for the funeral, and the employees had returned to Tokyo. Yohei's body had already been taken to the Fuji Five Lakes Hospital, where an autopsy was scheduled, but since most of the doctors were away for the holiday, it could not be performed until 3:30 that afternoon. The body would be transported to Tokyo the following day, and the wake would be that evening in Tokyo. Mine and Shigeru were to escort the body back to Tokyo, but all the others were to remain at the villa.

Kazue and Jane prepared tea while the other members of the family gathered in the living room. All were present: Mine, Shigeru, Sawahiko, Kazue, Chiyo, Shohei, Takuo, and Jane Prescott. Of the nine who had gathered together on the third, only Yohei was absent.

It should have been a pleasant moment as the evening twilight settled silently over the large room, but this time there was no music, only the sound of the occasional clink of a teacup on a saucer. Judging from their expressions, all eight were sunk in gloom, or perhaps it was only deep thought. Only rarely since the murder had the whole group been together in the same room, and when they had been together, it seemed some emergency always came up that had to be discussed.

"As far as our cover-up goes, our first line of defense has been breached." These words came from Sawahiko as he placed his cup on the saucer and stretched. He seemed to reluctantly accept the role of being the leader of the group. "I have discussed the case with some of the newspaper reporters. The police held a news conference this afternoon and announced that they had concluded that the murder was an inside job. Our story about a burglar having broken in is gone."

The content of the news conference was not made known to them by the police; immediately after Superintendent Aiura completed his briefing, the telephone began ringing incessantly with news reporters demanding some comment on the police announcement. Sawahiko and Takuo took charge of manning the telephone, replying repeatedly with the statement, "It is inconceivable that this was an inside job. Surely the police are under some sort of misapprehension." As a result of these repeated inquiries, the Wada family learned all the details of the press conference before they were reported in the news media.

Sawahiko's features had soured to a frown and his gaze fastened on Takuo's face when a television reporter said, "The main reason they gave for considering it an inside job, according to the superintendent, is that they found a pair of gym shoes concealed in a large canister of wheat flour in a basement storage room." On the morning after the murder, the delivery truck from the Kohan Restaurant had arrived suddenly and Sawahiko and Shohei had taken advantage of its arrival to get a ride to the Fuji Five Lakes precinct station to report the killing, so they had not heard what happened with the shoes.

"We've all been careless in this matter of disposing of the shoes." Takuo's response was intended to show that he alone did not want to take responsibility for the discovery of the shoes. Everyone had looked on as Takuo had made the round trip through the snow and cut the telephone line. When he returned to the house they were all relieved and appreciative. After walking on the carpet with the shoes on, he had taken them off and everyone had heaved a sigh of relief. But they had forgotten to dispose of the shoes, which were an important piece of evidence.

"Just as you two professors set out to inform the police of the murder, Jane noticed the shoes." Although Sawahiko and Shohei were both professors, Takuo usually called them by their first names. The sarcasm inherent in the use of their titles now was apparent. "We were all worried and discussed what we should do with them. It was Aunt Kazue who finally suggested the can of flour."

Takuo had merely been the one to actually hide the shoes in the flour, but in all the uproar caused by the investigation, he had not had a chance to make this clear to Sawahiko and Shohei.

"Well, never mind whose idea it was, the question is how were they able to find the shoes so quickly? I suppose some of the flour spilled while you were hiding them."

"No, I don't think that was it, I was very careful about that," said Takuo, pinching his lip.

"Well, it happened and it can't be helped now. I think that detective is just extremely observant," added Jane somewhat hesitantly. Takuo had buried the shoes in the flour, but Jane had accompanied him down to the basement to help. She was quite certain that Takuo was right; they had made no silly mistakes like spilling the flour.

Mine spoke up in an excited voice saying, "But Takuo had flour packed under his fingernails. I should have noticed it sooner and said something about it, but by then the detective had probably also noticed, and that made him think of the flour bin in the basement."

"Don't you think he would've had to have been awfully observant to have noticed something like that?" said Takuo, looking at his now clean nails. Yesterday afternoon, just after he had been called into the dining room for questioning, Mine had pointed out that he had flour under his nails and he had gone to scrub them with a brush. This morning when Nakazato had come to search the bedrooms, Takuo had had the feeling that the detective was surreptitiously looking at his hands.

"Well, I think everything is going to turn out all right," said

115

Shigeru, looking around at them all. "And besides, there is nothing we can do about it now, it has already been discovered."

"Actually, there's one more thing I've been concerned about." Everyone turned to Shohei who had spoken these words, and surprisingly there was a troubled look on his face. "We used a rubber stomach tube to make it appear that Mr. Wada had eaten some of the gratin along with the rest of us. Usually when you use such a tube to wash out a person's stomach or to feed them, the fluid comes from a bottle hanging above the bed, so the tube has to be more than a yard long. But for our purposes we didn't need such a long tube, and I remember cutting off a bit of it with scissors. Does anyone know what happened to the excess scrap I cut off?"

"Don't you have it?" asked Takuo incredulously.

"The piece of tube I used I washed as carefully as I could and put back in my medical bag. This morning when they were searching my personal effects, the detective opened my bag, and that was the first thing he noticed. He tried to be very casual about it, but I could tell he was excited."

"If you didn't remember that other piece until now, it means you must have dropped it somewhere," said Sawahiko.

"If it fell on the carpet and none of us bothered to pick it up, then the police must have found it when they searched the room, and they will have taken it for evidence. The other possibility is that it fell among Mr. Wada's clothing and dropped out when we moved the body to the veranda. I thought of that a little while ago and checked on the balcony, but there was nothing there."

For a time they all sat cloaked in silence. None of them were certain how significant the loss of this tubing might be.

"Even if the police did find it, that alone would not be enough of a clue for them to unravel our conspiracy, I think," said Sawahiko, but his voice was hoarse with anxiety.

"When you stop to think about it, the police must've known since yesterday evening that it was an inside job," murmured Kazue in a low voice as she cut a slice of brandy fruit cake for Shigeru.

Shigeru turned to Shohei and remarked, "You were right when you told us that the Fuji Five Lakes police would be a formidable adversary."

116

"I would like to say that the police are generally quite good in solving cases," said Takuo. No doubt he had been impressed by the way they were handling this one.

"They used the excuse that the intruder may have gotten into something else in order to search the whole house. That means they were convinced that the knife and the stolen items were still hidden somewhere here in the house."

"But after searching the whole house, they were unable to find those things, so that should put an end to their theory." Takuo had a cheerful, optimistic expression as he said this, but at the same time everyone's eyes naturally turned to Chiyo. She was sitting quietly in a chair next to Kazue beside the fireplace. She had a melancholy look, and had not even touched her tea.

"Chiyo, did you dispose of the fruit knife and the briefcase the way we told you to?" asked Sawahiko gently. "No one saw you do it, did they?"

"When I left the house, Elf wanted to come with me, so I had to chain him up, but after I got outside, I didn't meet anyone."

"Umm. Well, in that case I don't think we have anything to worry about," said Sawahiko with a nod. It was evident that he had much sympathy and concern for his stepdaughter.

"As long as the knife and the stolen objects, and the bloody clothing are not found, we can relax. It may be true that the enemy has broken through our first line of defense and suspects an insider did it, but I don't think they will get any further than that," said Takuo in an effort to encourage the others.

"Perhaps, but things may yet get more difficult for us," said Mine in her singsong voice. She looked around at each of them in turn with her gray, wrinkled face. "Now that the police have begun to suspect that it was one of us, we must all be careful not to say anything to belittle Grandpa. As I requested earlier when this all began, we must think first of protecting the Wada family name. I am convinced that this is the best way to protect those of us who remain."

"From now on we have to maintain that we know nothing. If we can just stonewall the investigation, the police won't be able to do anything," reaffirmed Sawahiko. "If any one of us has a weak moment or makes a careless move, they will be onto us right away.

And if that happens, we will all fall. Originally this was Chiyo's problem, and we can't thank all of you enough for what you've done, but at the same time, to the extent that we've become involved in this, it is now a problem for all of us. None of us must forget that." Sawahiko stiffened somewhat and made a formal bow.

"Your burden, Chiyo, will be greater than ours, so you will have to be strong." Kazue's hand was on Chiyo's knee and she gave a firm squeeze of encouragement. "No matter what happens, your alibi will stand. You can count on the rest of us to see to that. Cheer up . . ." As she said this, Kazue began weeping. Chiyo simply turned away and nodded her head in silence. Jane's heart went out to the girl and she shared her agony. With their plan to persuade the police that the murderer had been an intruder largely unsuccessful, Chiyo's safety depended more than ever on the cooperation of the other seven people. Would Chiyo be able to withstand the pressure? Jane shuddered at the thought.

"Well, why don't we have a drink. Maybe that will help," said Shigeru in a faint voice while stroking his mustache.

Nakazato and his men returned to headquarters and called in the nearly twenty investigators who had fanned out from the villa throughout the Asahi Hills region to interview people. At 4:30 all the investigators gathered for a conference.

Unfortunately, the day-long investigation had not produced much in the way of results. They had thoroughly searched the villa, its grounds, and the personal belongings of the occupants, but had failed to find any trace of the murder weapon, nor of the briefcase, nor of the jewelry, nor of any bloodstained clothing. After questioning the residents of Asahi Hills, they had turned up no reports of any suspicious people. This was one of those remarkable cases that produced no eyewitnesses. But after all, it had happened in the middle of a snowy, winter night. The absence, however, of any proof that a thief had fled the house on the night in question suggested that there had never been a thief, and that it was all an elaborate deception. The problem remained of finding out how the murder weapon and the stolen articles had been disposed of.

"I am beginning to suspect that the murderer might have had an accomplice on the outside," said Inspector Tsurumi after the reports had been made. "The way I see it, the murderer was one of the members of the household. When he left the house to make the false set of footprints in the back garden, he took the evidence with him and gave it to his accomplice, who was waiting out in the street."

But since it was impossible to identify any footprints belonging to an accomplice, they were unable to follow up this theory.

"And yet, we have spent all this time and have searched everywhere without turning up a single thing. I think we have to conclude that there is nothing hidden in the villa," interjected Nakazato emphatically.

"In that case," said Tsurumi, "it means that someone took the stuff away. The only one who left the villa that night was Chiyo Wada, so the most obvious thing is to assume that she took it with her."

Apparently Nakazato had already given this idea some serious thought, for he replied very deliberately. "The problem with that supposition is that the girl left the villa at eleven o'clock. The driver of the hired car testified to that. And the story we have from the family is that Yohei ate the gratin at eleven-thirty and then retired to his room. The delivery boy from the restaurant says he is positive he delivered the food at eleven-thirty."

All the investigators in the room were silent as they leaned forward to catch the exchange taking place between Tsurumi and Nakazato.

"All right, we definitely have to accept the fact that at eleven-thirty the delivery boy delivered eight servings of gratin. The fact remains that he did not actually see Yohei eat it. He said that when he arrived, the other members of the family were playing poker in the living room, but Yohei had gone for his bath."

"So? What are you getting at?"

"Shigeru told us it was Yohei's custom to take a bath before going to bed. Now you would normally expect that after a bath a person would change into pajamas, so doesn't it seem unnatural that Yohei was still wearing his shirt and trousers?"

119

Typically, it was Tsurumi who first grasped the point of what Nakazato was saying. "You mean the whole business about Yohei taking a bath and eating gratin may all be a lie cooked up and agreed to by the other seven people? Are you saying that Yohei was already dead by that time?"

"I think that is one way we can look at it. The medical examiner estimated the time of death to have been between nine o'clock and midnight. That gives us a lot of leeway."

"Does that mean that all the other members of the household were accomplices in this?"

"No, I don't think that necessarily follows. The real murderer was one of those seven people, but we cannot yet know if it was only one person, or if it was several, but while we don't know the exact details yet, it is quite likely that everything is based on a conspiracy of lies among them."

As was his custom, Nakazato rested one hand on his ample stomach and drew out a cigarette with the other hand. It appeared as though he had been concentrating his thoughts for a long time and was now ready to take a break.

"In that case," said Tsurumi hesitantly, "you are suggesting that Yohei was killed before Chiyo left the villa, and that she took the knife and the stolen articles back to Tokyo with her."

Superintendent Aiura, who had been listening to all this with a look of utter amazement, suddenly burst out loudly, "We still don't know that for sure since we have no evidence to prove it. We can't say that unless we check her movements from the time she arrived in Tokyo, or else find some way to substantiate the idea that she had those items on her person."

At the last press conference he had stated categorically that the murderer was one of the seven people who had spent the night at the villa. If it turned out that Chiyo was the one, he would have to reverse himself yet a second time.

At that point the telephone on the desk rang. The young detective who answered it said one or two words and held the receiver out to Tsurumi. "It's from Tokyo. They've just finished checking on Chiyo's movements there."

Every eye in the room was on Tsurumi as he took the receiver, and every ear listened to his responses. "Umm. . . . Um. . . . What?" Tsurumi's voice was steadily rising. Several minutes later he finished the conversation and looked over at Superintendent Aiura with an expression that was an odd mixture of sympathy and regret. When he spoke, however, he shifted his gaze to Nakazato. "I'm sure Chiyo told you she didn't go anywhere from the time she arrived home in Tokyo until the car picked her up to bring her back here?"

"Right."

"I'll bet she said she was in the house the whole time?"

For some reason the desperate features of Chiyo's face as she responded to his questioning were etched upon Nakazato's memory.

"Well, if you believe what she said, you're wrong," said Tsurumi. "Chiyo left the house secretly in the early hours of the morning. Not only that, she was carrying a large, cloth-wrapped bundle, large enough to contain a briefcase." There followed a summary of the report the detective had just telephoned in.

At 1:30 on the morning of January 4 Chiyo had arrived in the hired car. The family had a fifty-year-old maid who usually commuted to work, but who was house-sitting along with her daughter while the family was away.

Saying she was exhausted, Chiyo quickly retired to her room. She told the maid she wanted to sleep late the next morning and did not want to be awakened. But at around six o'clock the next morning the maid was awakened by the sound of the dog's chain being rattled in the garden. When she peeked out through a crack in the shutters, it was still dark outside, but the outdoor light was on beside the service entrance, and in its light she could see Chiyo chaining up the dog. It was a shepherd-like dog named Elf, and it usually roamed free in the garden at night. Having chained Elf, Chiyo opened the gate, and slipped out. She was wearing a black coat and slacks, and was swallowed up immediately by the darkness. She was carrying a square, cloth-wrapped bundle in her arms, clutching it as though it was something very important.

The maid could not get back to sleep, and sometime later she heard the gate open and the sound of the dog's chain being unfastened. Chiyo returned empty-handed shortly after seven o'clock, and stealthily climbed the stairs to her room on the second floor.

Chiyo did not come down for breakfast until 10:45 that morning. She made no mention of having left the house earlier, and the maid gave no indication that she knew what had happened. The matter weighed on her mind, however, and she finally took her daughter into her confidence.

At one o'clock they received a telephone call from the company informing them of Yohei's death, and at 1:30 a car came to pick Chiyo up and return her to the villa.

That evening and again today when the detectives had called to question her about the murder, the maid had kept her mouth shut and said nothing about Chiyo's mysterious movements. Perhaps she realized intuitively that if she revealed this it would mean trouble for Chiyo. Next the detectives went after the maid's daughter, and after questioning her relentlessly, the girl finally told what her mother had seen.

"We still don't know where Chiyo went while she was away from the house, but the situation seems pretty clear when you think about it. There's little doubt that the girl took the briefcase into which she put all the evidence: the money, the stocks, the jewelry, and the knife, and hid it somewhere."

"That makes Chiyo an accomplice to murder," murmured Aiura, his features drawn in a troubled frown.

"An accomplice . . . well, yes, there is every reason to believe that at the very least she is an accomplice," said Tsurumi, giving Nakazato a knowing look. "We also asked Tokyo to investigate one other point for us concerning Chiyo."

Nakazato nodded his head in silent agreement, and a smile of satisfaction bloomed on Tsurumi's face. "When Chiyo reached home in the hired car, she was already wearing a bandage on her left wrist. She kept trying to conceal that fact and merely drew people's attention to it. The bandage was seen by both the maid and the daughter."

"In other words, she did not burn her arm while making coffee the next morning as she claims."

"She was already injured when she left the villa on the evening

122

of the third, which makes it doubtful that the wound is really a burn."

"If she wasn't burned, then how did she get hurt?" asked Aiura angrily.

"She might have been cut by a knife. We might theorize that she was wounded while struggling with Yohei. Look at it the other way around: if the wound had nothing to do with the murder, why would she try to hide it and then lie about it?"

Tsurumi broke in excitedly as he looked over the tension-filled room. "It is just possible that Chiyo herself committed the crime, and that she did it alone."

"That's impossible," scoffed Aiura. "How could a frail, young girl have the strength to stab Yohei, and even if she did, it would have taken a considerable amount of time to make the phony footprints and to cut the telephone line, and she would have had to do it all after the rest of the family had gone to bed." Many voices were raised in support of the superintendent's dissenting view. His fine, intellectual features hardened, as though to emphasize what he had said, and he stared directly at Tsurumi.

"On the other hand," he continued, "we have testimony from all seven occupants of the villa that Mr. Wada ate gratin with them. It's standard procedure, isn't it, to believe testimony when it is unanimous? So as long as he ate the gratin, Chiyo had nothing to do with it."

There was nothing to do but wait for the autopsy report.

At about 5:40 the medical examiner at the Fuji Five Lakes Hospital completed the autopsy and phoned in his report. It would be another day before they filed the official report, but he gave a verbal summary to the waiting policemen. Detective Narumi, who received the telephoned report, repeated its main points to the investigators.

"The results of the autopsy indicate that the cause of death was cardial tamponade resulting from a knife wound piercing the heart. The estimated time of death was some time between nine o'clock and midnight on the night of January the third. This corresponds to what the police medical examiner had earlier estimated. In addition, the autopsy found that the victim's stomach contained a mixture of macaroni, onions, milk, and butter, and a small quantity of shrimp, all of which were virtually undigested. This leads to the conjecture that the victim was murdered shortly after he had eaten a macaroni gratin."

Superintendent Aiura's features began to soften when he heard this news. Tsurumi chewed on his lip and breathed heavily through his nose. Nakazato merely folded his arms and looked out the darkening window at the snow that had once again begun to fall.

By seven o'clock they had finished eating dinner at the villa. Mine and Chiyo had withdrawn to their rooms, so the full household was not present as they had been at teatime. Everyone seemed withdrawn and quiet; there was not much to talk about. In the two days since the murder had been announced, they had been confined to the villa, been interrogated, and had their personal belongings searched, all in an attempt to solve the case. They had continually suffered from stress and uncertainty, were all exhausted, and were now beginning to show the effects. Shigeru had been drinking steadily since teatime. Takuo abruptly threw down his knife and fork and stalked out of the dining room.

Jane helped Kazue clear away the dinner dishes and straighten up. Kazue, who normally loved to chat, was now deep in her own thoughts. She took no notice of Jane, and merely washed the dishes mechanically.

At 7:30 Jane went upstairs. Peering out the hall window she saw the sky beginning to clear and stars appearing. Jane felt as though her very soul was being sucked out of her as she looked at these clear, bright, distant stars that bejeweled the winter sky for the first time in so long. The villa's grounds sloped away to the lakeshore to the north. Through the dark stands of maple and keyaki, she could see the twinkling lamplights along the water. After lingering by the window for a time, Jane went to her room. There the window looked out to the southwest, and when she gazed intently into the darkness, she could make out the lofty, grand silhouette of Mt. Fuji.

Still lying on her desk was the manuscript of Chiyo's graduation thesis. Ever since the evening of the third when she had been interrupted by Kazue calling her to tea, the house had been in such an uproar that she had not had a moment in which to sit down at the desk.

The deadline for submitting the thesis was January 10 and she doubted Chiyo would be able to meet it. Nevertheless, it occurred to Jane that the thesis would have to be finished sooner or later, so she decided to resume work on it. Then she decided that if Chiyo got back to work on it too, it might help take her mind off what was happening.

Suddenly making up her mind to suggest this to Chiyo, Jane rushed out into the hall. She went to Chiyo's room with the intention of getting her to begin revising her thesis again. As she was about to knock on the door, Jane heard Chiyo scream from within. At the same moment there was a loud crash as a body slammed against the door.

"Why do you treat me this way?" came the reproving voice of a man. "I would do anything for you, don't you realize that? Right now I am protecting you from your enemy, the police. I'm doing it for you."

"No!"

"What's the matter? Why are you like this?" The man's voice became broken and pleading. Unable to restrain herself any longer, Jane was about to knock when the door opened from the inside and Chiyo came rushing out. Her hair was disordered and her black blouse had been torn open. She was covering her breasts with her hands. The door opened outward, concealing Jane behind it, so that Chiyo did not see her as she ran down the hall, gasping for breath. Takuo pursued her for two or three steps, but suddenly gave up, and stopped. He too was greatly agitated and breathing heavily, but turning on his heel, he went back into the room. He lit a cigarette and appeared to be making a great effort to get himself under control.

Jane walked past the door, keeping an eye on Takuo's back the whole time. The carpet muffled the sound of her footsteps, and apparently Takuo was unaware of her presence. Jane's thoughts were in turmoil. She walked past the door to her room and descended the stairs. Where might Chiyo have gone? Takuo was a disgusting man. He was obviously trying to take advantage of Chiyo's vulnerability to have his way with her. It was clear that he had assaulted and injured her.

The living room was silent and deserted. The lights were out in the dining room and kitchen as well. Jane went into the living room. A floor lamp was on and the room was warm. She opened a door on the left side of the fireplace. On one side of the corridor was the billiards room, and on the other side was the small conference room. There was no sign of Chiyo in either place.

Crossing the room, Jane found a door that opened onto the north side of the hallway. She heard the sound of voices coming from there. The room Sawahiko and Kazue were using opened onto the north end of this corridor. The sound of sobbing voices was coming from inside.

At first she heard what she thought was Chiyo's voice. No doubt after having been assaulted by Takuo, Chiyo had fled to her parents' side. The voice sounded deeply troubled, almost a moan of desperation.

"It's already too late. Something terrible is bound to happen. We have failed to give Chiyo the protection she needed." The mother's weeping and moaning were low and muffled. Jane crept closer to the door, as though drawn by what she was hearing.

"That's not it at all. If we give up now, we won't be able to save Chiyo at all." Sawahiko's mournful voice was gently trying to comfort Kazue.

"No, it's already too late. The police have already seen through our scheme. Soon they will come and take Chiyo away."

"Oh, come on now, what are you saying? The police haven't seen through anything yet. It was unfortunate that they found the gym shoes. After all, why did you come up with such a stupid hiding place as that, where they were sure to be found right away? But don't worry, they haven't found anything except that. They aren't going to arrest Chiyo on the basis of a single pair of gym shoes."

"But the police are positive it was an inside job. As soon as they are certain the stolen goods aren't in this house, their suspicions will surely fall on Chiyo. The next thing you know, they will find out where Chiyo hid everything."

"You're always worrying about the worst possible thing that could happen. Chiyo has an alibi. The results of the autopsy will make a certainty of that." After all, he thought silently, the autopsy was scheduled for 3:30. The results would soon be known to them.

No matter what Sawahiko did to soothe her, however, there seemed no way of calming Kazue. Instead, she continued to weep in increasingly loud gasps, then stopped suddenly. Jane gave a start. She wondered if perhaps Kazue had suffered a heart attack.

After a strange, uncanny silence, she once again heard Kazue's voice, but it was low, almost like that of another person, and quivering with emotion. "I will surrender myself to the police," she said.

"Surrender yourself? What are you talking about?"

"I'll go to the police and tell them I did it. Now is the time to do it. If I wait until they have arrested Chiyo, it will be too late."

"Please, Kazue, calm down. You can't really intend to do such a thing . . ." but his voice trailed off. In her mind's eye Jane could visualize the subdued Sawahiko as Kazue suddenly began making preparations to carry out her plan.

Holding her breath, Jane withdrew down the hallway. The whole villa seemed pervaded with uneasiness and tension. The living room was still deserted. Jane opened the front door, thinking only to flee this madhouse. Outside there was a peacefulness that shut out the scene she had just witnessed. The cold felt sharp and penetrating on her skin.

The snow had been falling steadily since before noon, so the walks and the garden in front of the house, and the cars parked beside the iron fence, were all once again enveloped in unblemished white.

There was one line of footprints in the snow that appeared to have been made by a large pair of overshoes. Jane put on her own boots and stepped down into the front garden, unconsciously following the other trail. Stars were glittering in the breaks in the clouds, but they were not bright enough to light up the landscape.

The surface of the snow gave off a blue-white reflection from the blue, star-shaped light on the roof. This light alone was an expensive extravagance in the huge northern European-style house. Even though the master of the house was dead, the light continued to burn as if nothing had happened.

Pausing for a moment in the pure, untrampled snow, everything that had happened seemed like a dream. Yet the reality would not go away, and they could not turn the clock back. Jane had no way of knowing that from this point on things would only get worse.

She recalled Sawahiko's words, "Why did you come up with such a stupid hiding place as that, where they were sure to be found right away?" He had stamped his foot in vexation and the sound of his voice still echoed in her ears.

It had been Takuo who had concealed the gym shoes, but Jane had accompanied him, and had stood beside him while he did it. Takuo clearly considered Jane to be a stranger and an outsider, and kept on his guard. Perhaps it was for this reason that he always stayed close to her. When they had gone down to the basement, Jane had taken the lid off the can of flour, and Takuo had buried the shoes. She had paid close attention to every detail, making sure that not even a pinch of the flour spilled out. There was no mistake about that. But in that case, how had the shoes been discovered so quickly and so easily?

A certain dreadful suspicion began to form itself in the back of Jane's mind. Absorbed in thought about these matters, she continued to follow the trail of footsteps across the snow.

She crossed in front of the dining room and came out along the south side of Yohei's room. She turned the corner of the building and followed the footsteps into the back garden.

The balcony thrust out from the east side of the house, its high, iron railing forming a medieval-looking pattern. Since the star-shaped light on the roof did not cast its glow onto this part of the garden, the whole northeast side of the house was in darkness. There was, however, a little light coming from the outdoor gaslight.

Suddenly Jane realized that a dark shadow had emerged at the far side of the balcony. She was startled. It was the shadow of a large, well-built man. Looking carefully, she could see that the footprints in the snow led in his direction.

Jane held her breath and stared intently at the figure. Gradually through the darkness she was able to make out the figure of a man in profile. Shohei was gripping the railing of the balcony with both hands, and was trying to peer through the glass door although the curtains had been closed inside the room. He stayed there, immobile, frozen like a statue. The silence continued. It was so still, Jane thought she could even hear the sound of his breathing.

What in the world was he doing out here?

What was he thinking about?

His gaze was fixed on the balcony, on the place where Yohei had been laid out. Placed in the cold air, the body had stiffened, and surely it was here that Yohei's immortal soul had departed this earth and flown up to heaven.

Like an electric shock, the realization went through Jane that at this very moment Shohei was also thinking about Yohei's death. He was clearly worried and seemed about to break under the strain. No, perhaps he would not break, but his brawny shoulders and arms, and his rough-hewn features seemed to waver a bit.

Jane was suddenly aware of a violent and inexplicible feeling that rose up in her breast. Her entire body was wracked by it and she felt smothered by an emotion she could not name. She felt an impulse to cry out, and very nearly did, but just as the cry rose to her lips, a second shadow detached itself from the darkness of the back garden and stealthily approached Shohei.

The slim, shadowy figure came to a halt a few steps from Shohei and said something to him in a low voice.

Startled, Shohei whirled around. "Oh! Chiyo, it's you." He had been caught at an unguarded moment and could only mumble, "Why, what are you doing here?"

"On the contrary, I believe the question is what are you doing in a place like this, Doctor?"

Shohei turned toward Chiyo and moved away from the balcony.

Chiyo started to back silently away, then stopped resolutely and asked, "Tell me Dr. Mazaki, what did you really think of Grandpa?"

He seemed surprised by the question and made no reply. A heavy, agonizing silence passed between them.

"Did you respect Grandpa?"

"Well . . ."

"Did you hate him?"

"No, of course not."

Why on earth was Chiyo asking questions like these? Jane was puzzled and surprised at what she was overhearing. No doubt the reason Chiyo did not insist on having Shohei answer her questions was that no matter what reply he gave, it would not keep her questions from sounding like accusations. He was clearly moved by what she was saying, and Chiyo herself seemed to be revealing her true emotions. Why?

"Tell me, Chiyo, about Grandpa. How did he . . ."

Finding himself cornered, Shohei tried to take the initiative and ask a question of his own, but perhaps because he realized the brutality of what he was asking, he broke off in mid-sentence.

"Grandpa was a fine man." The firmness of Chiyo's voice as she made this declaration confused Jane. Meanwhile, Chiyo took a deep breath and continued, as though to reemphasize what she had just said. "Grandpa was definitely a fine man and a warm person. He loved me more than anyone, and there is no excuse for what I have done. I loved and respected Grandpa with all my heart." Chiyo blurted out this statement with such frankness and truthfulness that it seemed that only now, for the first time, was she able to say what she really felt.

Chiyo saying she could make no excuses for what she had done? Chiyo saying she loved and respected Grandpa with all her heart? Jane turned these statements over in her mind. She did not understand what moved Chiyo to say these things, nor did she know why these statements made such an impression on her. Perhaps it was just the normal stress of this sort of situation that was beginning to tell on all of them.

Shohei, too, was astonished.

At that moment a beam of light swept across the grounds of the villa and they could hear the sound of a car approaching. It was traveling at high speed, and as they watched, it approached the villa, swinging around the curve by the corner of the back garden. The headlights swept across the snow, illuminating Shohei and Chiyo, and reflected a powerful glare off the window of Yohei's room.

Rounding the north side of the building, the car pulled into the front yard moments later and came to a stop by the front door. Because of his ample figure and large head, Detective Nakazato could be immediately recognized as he emerged from the passenger's seat. Nakazato's eyes opened wider than usual when he noticed Jane approaching, but even under his bushy eyebrows there was a look of respect and amiability.

"Thanks for helping us out earlier with your cooperation," boomed Nakazato in greeting. "I hope everyone hasn't gone to bed yet, have they?" His tone was a mildly sarcastic reference to last night when everyone had retired so early.

"Oh, it's quite all right. I'm sure everyone is still up."

"In that case, may I ask you to spread the word that everyone is to assemble in the living room."

"Did you get the results of the autopsy yet?"

"Yes indeed," Nakazato replied emphatically and gave a deep nod. For a long moment Jane and the detective held each other's gaze.

In fact the main purpose of Nakazato's visit was to convey the results of the autopsy. But there was more to it than that. Jane felt he knew something that he was keeping to himself. She wondered if what he knew would enable him to break through the last of the Wada family's desperate defenses.

Jane remained standing in front of the detective, blocking his way. It almost seemed as though she was ready to physically block his assault on the Wada family. Of course this came from her desire to protect Chiyo. At the same time, her mind was in a turmoil. He knows something. I'm sure he knows something, we must have blown it somewhere, she thought.

Without articulating this thought, she gave Nakazato a long, searching look. At that moment her mind suddenly resurrected the memory of a piercing sound. It was the harsh screech of rusty

131

metal scraping against rusty metal. When they had opened the door to put Yohei's body outside, it had made that terrible racket. And later, when she had collapsed in bed after they had completed the preparations for the cover-up, that same sound had once again broken the stillness of the night. Only that time she was not supposed to have heard it.

7

The Stonewall
Collapses

It was after 9:30 that evening when all eight members of the household found themselves facing one another in the living room. There were Mine, Shigeru, Sawahiko, Kazue, Chiyo, and Takuo, in addition to Shohei Mazaki and Jane Prescott. Confronting these eight was Detective Nakazato of the Fuji Five Lakes police precinct with his enormous head and protruding belly. He was sitting in a heap in an armchair at some distance from the others.

A pleasant level of warmth had been maintained in the living room, and the electric heater in the fireplace, which was designed to look like a real fire, twinkled and flickered beautifully. In some ways the scene was much the same as it had been two days earlier, only now Yohei was gone and his place was taken by Nakazato, and the faces of the family members now had an unhealthy pallor due to the strain of the past two days. More than that, however, was a certain evasive nervousness that could be seen in their expressions.

After slowly looking around at everyone with his shrewd, but understanding eyes, Nakazato began to speak deliberately. "I am sorry to have gathered you all here like this at a time when I know you are tired. As you are all well aware, two days have now elapsed since the murder was committed, and at last the investigators have pretty well figured out how it was done. Before we make this public, however, we would like your cooperation in clearing up a few ambiguous points. Since I believe you are all anxious to draw this matter to a close as quickly as possible, I would like to ask just a few more questions."

As Nakazato rambled on, everyone in the group gave an involuntary shudder. They had thought that he had gathered everyone in the living room to announce the results of the autopsy, not to question them further.

"When we first began this investigation yesterday morning," he began, "we came to the conclusion that the killing was committed by an outside intruder. This was because the telephone line had been cut and because of the two trails of footprints found in the back garden. Later, as I believe you all know, we discovered that the footprints were actually made so as to appear that an intruder had entered the house, which led us to the conclusion that the culprit was an insider."

Nakazato continued to outline the progress of the case in precise, fluent terms. "The principal reason we know it was an inside job is because we found a pair of gym shoes in the basement that corresponds exactly to the footprints that were left in the back garden. But even before we found the shoes, we had actually discovered that the footprints approaching the house were superimposed over the footprints leaving the house. On that evidence alone we could assume that the footprints were nothing but a decoy. No matter how flustered the culprit might have been, if he was an outside intruder, there is no possible way his incoming footprints could be superimposed over his outgoing footprints."

Everyone in the room gasped, and all eyes turned on Takuo. His face, which normally appeared sharp and alert behind the metal frame glasses, now looked blank and slack. His mouth hung half open and he mumbled stupidly, "Of all the dumb things to do."

This reaction was enough to convince Nakazato that he was correct in his conjecture that Takuo had made the footprints in the garden.

"All of you are pretty sharp and I am sure you realized long ago that the real objective of the search we made yesterday and today was to find the murder weapon and the articles that were stolen."

"But you didn't find them, did you?" said Takuo, almost tauntingly, probably a reaction to the unspoken pressure being directed toward him by the others.

"You're right. We were unable to turn up a single thing."

"That means it couldn't possibly have been an inside job, doesn't it?"

"If no one had left the premises after the murder occurred, we would be faced with an irreconcilable contradiction, and the investigation would probably have to be dropped. As it turns out, however, one young lady left the villa and returned to Tokyo that night."

"But . . . but you promised you wouldn't bring her into this!" Sawahiko began blustering and stammering. Nakazato ignored him and suddenly directed his gaze at Chiyo. Again tonight she was clad in black, and her slim figure was partially hidden between Kazue and Sawahiko. When the detective directed his penetrating gaze on her, she seemed to shrivel.

"I want you to understand, Chiyo, that we are not trying to persecute you, and I wish we did not have to do this. Nevertheless, when we questioned you this morning, you told some very big lies. At around one-thirty on the morning of January fourth you arrived at your home in Tokyo in a hired car, and you insisted that until one-thirty the next afternoon when you returned here by car, that you went nowhere. You said you were in the house for the entire twelve-hour period. That is false. At around six that morning you slipped out the back door under the cover of darkness, wearing a black coat and slacks. You returned to the house shortly after seven and slipped quietly back to your room on the second floor. We have eyewitness testimony to this from the maid. Where did you go that morning?"

For a time Chiyo merely sat trembling.

"She just went out for a walk," said Sawahiko with some agitation.

"That's right. She often goes out at that hour to take our dog Elf for his walk."

"I'm afraid that won't do. You see, she made a special point of chaining up the dog before she went out. In fact it was the sound of the chain that woke the maid up. So that explanation just won't work unless you want to insist that yesterday, for a change, you went for a walk by yourself."

As Nakazato watched the girl, she moved her head inconclusively, indicating no clear response to his assertion.

"You realize, of course," he said gently, "that what you told us this morning can be shown to be a lie. But never mind that. Tell me why you were carrying a large, cloth-wrapped bundle in your arms? And where did you leave it? We have already established the fact that you returned from your walk empty-handed."

"This has nothing to do with the murder! No connection at all," responded Sawahiko, his voice rising in anger. As the others watched, his face flushed deep red.

"Really," raged Kazue, glaring daggers at the detective, "we must insist that you stop investigating personal matters that are irrelevant to the case!" She was breathing hard and her ample bosom heaved wildly.

"In any case, Chiyo was not even at the villa when the murder happened. You ought to know that from having talked to the driver of the car."

"All the driver knows for certain is that at eleven on the evening of the third he picked up Chiyo here at the villa and they set out together. That does not necessarily prove that he picked her up before Yohei was murdered."

"That's not so. It should be obvious that Grandpa ate some of the gratin after Chiyo left." Shigeru spoke up spiritedly to point out the obvious, but his fingers shook as he stroked his mustache, revealing his uncertainty.

"The gratin was delivered at eleven-thirty. That is clear from the testimony of the delivery boy from the Kohan Restaurant, but no one from the restaurant saw Mr. Wada eat any of the gratin."

"That's only because Grandpa happened to be in the bath when the delivery boy arrived. He ate after he finished his bath."

"I wish there were some way to prove that."

"We all saw him eat, didn't we?"

"Unfortunately we cannot give much weight to assertions for which there is no objective proof. It is possible, for example, that all of you might be lying to protect Chiyo."

Mine, who had been silent up to this point, now began speaking in her high, singsong voice. "Why would I be trying to protect Chiyo? If I thought she had murdered my husband, I would turn her over to the police myself." She laughed as though Nakazato's suggestion was the most ludicrous thing she had ever heard. Mine's speech at this point was probably the most effective rebuttal that had been made.

"If we accept what the detective says, we have to ask how frail, little Chiyo could have killed a healthy man like Grandpa," said Takuo spiritedly. "I can't think why she would do such a thing in the first place, but according to your theory she stabbed Grandpa to death, then single-handedly cut the telephone line in the back garden, made footprints to look as though an outside intruder had entered the house, then hid the shoes in the basement, concealed the murder weapon and the stolen goods on her person, and fled to Tokyo. Do you really believe all that?"

"Oh no. I never suggested that Chiyo acted alone in the matter. This could only have happened if someone helped her, and all of you conspired to cover it up. There is no question about that."

"Conspired to cover up! You may be a police officer, but this is libel. Do you have any proof to support the assertion you have just made?"

"The facts speak for themselves."

As the room broke into an uproar, Nakazato raised his voice above the clamor. "The fact that the footprints in the snow were superimposed on each other and that the shoes that made those tracks were concealed in the basement tells us clearly that the culprit was an insider. On the other hand, the murder weapon and the stolen goods were not turned up anywhere, and all of you shake your heads and insist you know nothing. You may feel reassured as long as we don't find any of the missing items, but unfortunately a contradiction never points to the truth. Since we can't find those things here in the villa, and since you've told us they're not concealed anywhere, then the only remaining possibility is to assume Chiyo took the evidence away with her. So it comes down to this, for some reason as yet unknown to us, Chiyo stabbed Yohei, and the rest of you, finding out about it, sent Chiyo off with the evidence. Later you made it appear as though the crime had been committed by an outside intruder. That's the real truth, isn't it?"

"But my husband ate with us later, after Chiyo had left," said Mine.

Shizuko Natsuki

"There is no proof of that. Let me repeat myself by saying that you are all in on a conspiracy to claim that he ate with you."

"That's not so," said Shohei suddenly in a loud voice. All along he had been standing next to Jane, arms folded, unmoving. Now his voice burst out in the room like a stone dropped in a puddle of water. "What do you mean there is no proof of that?" He glared fiercely at Nakazato and spoke as though he intended to force the detective into submission. "You said you came here this evening to tell us the results of the autopsy that was performed on Mr. Wada this afternoon. You already know the results, so tell us what they are. We will have to accept those results as incontrovertible proof." Nakazato gave the doctor a puzzled look. Shohei was speaking loudly and angrily. "Listen officer, when they did the autopsy on Mr. Wada they surely found the remains of the gratin in his stomach. Are you saying that is not adequate proof that he ate with us?"

For a time the two men faced each other, neither one breathing nor blinking. Shohei's look was one of supreme self-confidence, while Nakazato gazed at his adversary shrewdly, as though trying to make out what was going on inside his mind. In the end, it was Nakazato who breathed first.

"Don't get me wrong now. I agree one hundred percent with what you've just said," he murmured with an amiable smile, but suddenly it seemed there was a smirk of triumph in that smile.

Nakazato drew a brown paper envelope from the inside pocket of his suit; from it he produced a bit of thin, brownish-orange rubber tubing. "When we made our search yesterday evening we found this on the balcony of Yohei's room. At first I thought it was a worm, but on closer inspection, it turns out to be a rubber tube. It has gradation marks every five centimeters. When we found it, the problem was that no one seemed to know whether it had anything to do with the murder or not. But then, this morning, quite unexpectedly, I found the same thing in quite another place. I found a tube just like it in Dr. Mazaki's black bag."

Nakazato once again turned his unrelenting gaze on Shohei. "I asked him what it's used for, and he explained that it's used to pump a person's stomach, or to clear the stomach in order to ad-

138

minister an emergency anesthetic. But the medical examiner at the police station added another detail that Dr. Mazaki had omitted. He told me such tubing is also used to pump fluids or foods into a patient's stomach. So you see, it can be used to put food into the stomach, as well as to take it out. It suddenly occurred to me that you could have used this to put the gratin into Yohei's stomach after he was dead, but I thought perhaps I was becoming too imaginative. Still, when I heard Dr. Mazaki's statement just now, I suddenly found myself returning to that possibility. If he had actually put the gratin into Yohei's stomach, then he would be the one who would be most liable to pick out this particular detail and challenge me with it and be confident about doing so."

Shohei had a blank, stunned look on his face as he listened to Nakazato's words.

"One more thing. There was some white residue in the stomach tube I found in Dr. Mazaki's bag. Since the tube is only five millimeters in diameter, I wondered if those weren't traces of gratin that he had been unable to wash away. In order to confirm this one way or the other, I thought I would borrow your tube this evening and take it around to the lab for tests. But for the present, I have shown that it is possible for Mr. Wada to have ingested some of the gratin after he was dead, and to that extent the results of the autopsy cannot be considered conclusive in determining the time of death."

This time no one put forth an opposing argument when Nakazato finished speaking. All eight members of the household had anticipated defeat the moment he produced the bit of stomach tube. Suddenly they were faced with the prospect that their very last line of defense had been penetrated. An agonizing silence filled the room, punctuated only by ragged breathing as each member of the household unconsciously hung their head.

"There is one thing I would like to draw to your attention," said Nakazato with a keen look on his face. Taking a deep breath, he drew a cigarette from his pocket, but merely held it in his fingers and looked at it for a moment before he began speaking. After observing the havoc he had wreaked on the family members, he felt it was time to make his final thrust.

"Pardon me for bringing up a personal matter, but I understand that the late Mr. Wada's personal wealth was somewhere on the order of two billion yen. Much of it is in the form of villas, art objects, and company holdings. Since he also retained the majority of the stock in Wada Pharmaceuticals, he left behind a great deal of wealth. It may surprise you to learn that everyone who is entitled to inherit a part of that wealth is right here in this room."

Mine was watching the detective closely.

"Apparently Mr. Wada did not leave a will, and since he did not have any children of his own, legally his estate will go to his wife and to his brothers and sisters. In the case of deceased siblings, if they had children, those children will inherit their parent's share of the estate. But, of course, you all know this. In this case it means that those who stand to inherit something are Mine, his wife; Shigeru, his brother; Kazue, his deceased sister's daughter; and Takuo, his deceased brother's son. According to the standard legal formula, the wife will receive three-fourths of the total, and the remaining one-fourth will be divided among the other three. Since the amount of the legacy is so enormous, you all stand to receive quite a lot of money."

One by one the members of the household raised their heads and watched Nakazato, trying to figure out what point he was driving at.

"The legal code, however, also has provisions for disqualifying inheritors. To put the matter briefly, anyone who tries to inherit money unfairly is disqualified. Paragraph one of Article Eight Ninety-One of the *Comprehensive Legal Code* clearly states that any-one who kills another for the purpose of inheriting his wealth will be disqualified. This is simple common sense. But paragraph two goes on to say that anyone who knows of someone who was mur-dered, and does not report it, will also be disqualified from inherit-ing any of the money."

Listening to Nakazato's explanation, it occurred to Jane that American law had no such provisions. Meanwhile, Nakazato, aware that the tension in the room was increasing, tried to keep his voice calm.

"Probably all of you knew that Chiyo killed Mr. Wada. Knowing that, you wanted to protect her, so you did not report it. Instead you engaged in an elaborate conspiracy to obstruct the investigation. But once the police have enough evidence to arrest Chiyo and prove that she is guilty, the rest of you potential inheritors will probably lose all claim to Mr. Wada's estate. I simply want to make clear to you what the situation is."

It was Shigeru whose eyebrows shot up in surprise and who looked around quickly. There was a clear look of shock in his crescent-shaped eyes that were so reminiscent of Yohei's. He had clearly not expected this news and began to shake his head and blink his eyes. At the same time Mine and Takuo looked at each other, and seemed to be reading something in one another's faces. But it was not just the potential inheritors—everyone's inner turmoil could be read on their faces.

The tension in the room increased still further and the silence continued. Sawahiko thrust out his jaw and was about to say something, but faltered, and remained silent. Nakazato had the impression that Sawahiko would have liked to have called to the others in order to regain their unity.

At last Nakazato lit his cigarette and leaned back in the armchair to relax. "Personally, of course, I wouldn't quibble about anyone's right of inheritance, but this is a different matter. If we apprehend the murderer under these circumstances, there would be strong evidence pointing to the fact that the rest of you aided and abetted a criminal and manufactured false evidence. We have to suppose that all of you had a very natural urge to try to protect Chiyo, but the fact is that we almost have all the evidence we need to convict her. Why don't you cooperate with us to find a clear solution to this case before we have to have any more unpleasantness? Wouldn't that really be the best memorial you could provide for Mr. Wada?"

Following Nakazato's lead, two or three of the other men also lit cigarettes. They blew out long streams of smoke and watched with tired eyes as the smoke spiraled upward. No one was in the mood for talking. If only one person gave in to this pressure, the others would no doubt follow one by one with their confessions. Nakazato finished his cigarette, stubbed it out, and continued to

141

wait. Only after he had pulled out another cigarette did he remember that he had yet again forgotten the filter his wife and been so insistent about. This was an odd time to be thinking about something like that. He put the cigarette back in the pack and looked at his watch. It was after ten.

Taking a deep breath he raised himself out of the armchair. Getting his short legs in motion, he propelled his large bulk toward Chiyo. Even as he looked at the frail girl, Nakazato felt an inexpressible pain in his heart. Tonight she was wearing a black dress with a high collar that hid her slim, curved neck. The flesh was stretched across her cheeks, and her pale skin had lost its luster. Her usually graceful Japanese features had lost all trace of vitality, and her bloodshot eyes were glassy and unfocused, like those of a deranged person. It was clearly the expression of one who was weighed down with a terrible preoccupation.

"Chiyo, no one is able to help you with this matter. I'll have to ask you to tell me about it yourself." Nakazato's voice was so gentle and careful it surprised even him. "We know now that you are the one who stabbed Mr. Wada. I'm sure you only did it because you had to. Then the rest of the family sympathized with you, and they all worked together to protect you. That's what really happened, isn't it?"

Chiyo remained silent.

"You realize, of course, that as I have just explained, the longer you continue to deny it, the more you will be creating a terrible problem for everyone else. Legal inheritors lose their rights of inheritance by protecting a criminal. Even people who had no part in the actual crime can be charged with aiding and abetting a criminal. You are asking these seven people to sacrifice their own well-being and even their reputations so that you can avoid the consequences of what you have done."

Both Sawahiko and Kazue threw their arms around Chiyo, one on each side.

"Stop it! It's unfair of you to pick on the weakest member of the family."

"Can't you understand what we've been telling you all along? Chiyo is not involved in this."

"I see."

Nakazato suddenly grasped Chiyo's left hand. Pulling back the sleeve, he exposed her wrist wrapped in its white bandage. With deft motions he removed the bandage, revealing the fresh wound on the inside of the wrist.

"You told us you burned your hand yesterday morning while making coffee. But this wound was obviously made by a knife, don't try to deny it. We know that you were already bandaged when you arrived at your home in Tokyo; both the maid and her daughter are eyewitnesses. Tell me the truth now, when and where did you receive that wound?"

"She did it with a knife while sharpening a pencil," blurted Jane. "I know because I was there helping her with her graduation thesis. It was right after dinner on the evening of the third. She was sharpening a pencil."

"That's a lie," said Nakazato simply. "I checked Chiyo's room and her personal effects this morning. There was a plastic pencil sharpener on the desk by the window. I saw no sign of a knife used for that purpose. Come now, Chiyo, are you going to insist on being stubborn?"

"No! It's not Chiyo, my daughter wouldn't . . ." Kazue continued to protest and snatched Chiyo's hand away from the detective's grasp while Chiyo let slip a small cry of pain. Automatically both Takuo and Shohei took a step forward, and suddenly everyone was talking at once. All were moved by an impulse to block the detective's assault, and at the same time to keep Chiyo from answering.

But it was too late, the victory had already been determined. When Nakazato released Chiyo's hand, she collapsed on her mother's breast and burst into tears. Beneath the weeping her words could clearly be heard: "I killed Grandpa."

Ukyo Nakazato nodded once silently, then went into the foyer, instructing his assistant to call in a report of what had happened to headquarters. Certainly Superintendent Aiura and Inspector Tsurumi were waiting there for further word. Then he went over to Chiyo and said, "I would like to talk to you privately in the other room and ask a few questions."

Excusing himself from the group, he helped Chiyo to her feet and took her to the small conference room. A formal questioning would take place at headquarters, but Nakazato thought it would be a good idea to get a preliminary confession that would establish the order of events.

Although Chiyo was still sobbing fitfully, she seemed to have lost all sense of defiance, and answered questions regarding everything that had happened from the beginning of that fateful evening.

After dinner on the evening of January 3, Yohei had whispered in Chiyo's ear that he would like her to come to his room later. When she arrived there at about 8:15 or 8:20, Yohei appeared to be very drunk. He locked the door and tried to assault her. Dazed, Chiyo snatched up the fruit knife from the bedside table and tried to tell him that if he attempted violence, she would kill herself. By this time, however, Yohei had gone completely berserk and once again lunged at Chiyo. In the struggle that ensued Yohei was stabbed in the left side of the chest.

Chiyo had made up her mind on the spot to commit suicide, and used the same knife to slash her left wrist, but the next thing she knew, Kazue was coming down the corridor calling for her. At the sound of her mother's voice, Chiyo opened the door, and fled the room.

When the other seven heard what had happened, they decided to get Chiyo away from the villa, and to make it look as though a burglar had broken in as a way of protecting Yohei's name from the scandal that would develop if the truth were known.

Chiyo took her bloody clothes, the knife, and the briefcase, and stuffed them all in her overnight case. At 11:00 she had gotten into the hired car that had been summoned from Asahi Hills, and set out for Tokyo.

The above was Chiyo's account of what had happened at the villa. In response to the question of where she had gone when she left the house early the next morning, she said, "There is a temple with a cemetery about twenty minutes away from our house; my father is buried there. In fact, members of our family have been buried there for generations, so we have a mausoleum with a rather large vault. I hid the evidence I brought back from the villa in the

144

vault. It was very unpleasant to have to go there by myself in the dark, but my stepfather told me I could be assured that no one would ever find the evidence there."

When Chiyo had finished making her confession, Nakazato escorted her back to the living room. He seated her in a chair in the corner and asked her to relax. He thought there was a slight chance that she might try to kill herself or run away, so he did not want to leave her alone.

He then went to confront the other seven about the conspiracy they had carried out after the crime had been committed. It was at this point that Inspector Tsurumi and several of his aides arrived to help with the questioning.

Of the seven, Kazue was as distraught as Chiyo, and did nothing but weep. Mine sat with her shoulders slumped pitifully. The men held up better, however, and answered the questions that were put to them.

After Chiyo had left in the hired car, the delivery boy arrived from the Kohan Restaurant at 11:30. Shohei, using the stomach tube, had fed some of the gratin into Yohei's stomach, and then they had laid the body out on the balcony so the process of decay would be slowed by the cold outdoor temperature. They had hoped in this way to make it appear that the time of death was somewhat later than it actually was. They calculated that Chiyo had killed Yohei at about 9:00 and it was necessary for them to make it appear that he had died sometime after 11:30, after Chiyo was long gone, and after Yohei had eaten the gratin.

Next they had made the tracks suggesting an outside intruder. Takuo had put on an old pair of gym shoes and made the round-trip tracks in the snow of the back garden, and had also cut the telephone line. After that, the seven members of the household had played poker in the living room for a couple of hours. When the police had questioned them, their story was that a burglar must have entered sometime during the night while they were engrossed in their game, and no one had heard any suspicious sounds.

They finished playing poker at 3:40 on the morning of the fourth, and after settling up their debts, they brought in Yohei's body, which had been out on the balcony for nearly four hours, and placed it on the bed and closed the French doors.

It had been 4:00 A.M. when the seven conspirators retired to their own bedrooms. They had all gotten up at 9:00 on the morning of the fourth. Their plan was that Mine would discover the body right after she got up, and then Shohei and Sawahiko would go to the Fuji Five Lakes police station. Just as they were about to leave, the van from the Kohan Restaurant arrived to pick up the dishes, so they got a ride with the delivery boy.

Just after the van had left for the police station, Jane realized that they had completely forgotten about the gym shoes used to manufacture the footprints. They decided to follow Kazue's suggestion and hide them in the can of flour, so Takuo and Jane had gone to the basement storeroom and done that.

This was the story the seven had agreed upon, and there was virtually no discrepancy in their individual testimonies. Even Nakazato was amazed at their ability to think together and to act in concert, to be able to pull off such an audacious plan.

"You even went so far as to actually play poker for two hours, eh? You did that just so there would be no uncertainties in case you were questioned about the details of the game."

During the first questioning, Tsurumi had gotten each of them to talk about the game; who had won and how, and so forth, and he had remarked at the time that their comments hung together very well.

"But the trade-off for covering that detail was that you did not get to sleep until four o'clock in the morning. None of you got enough sleep because you all looked very tired the next morning." Nakazato spoke with a bitter smile on his lips and sarcasm in his voice. That morning he had noticed that everyone at the villa had bloodshot eyes and that they were all stifling yawns. This alone had aroused his suspicion.

"At least we carried out our plan very systematically," said Sawahiko with a sigh and a resigned look on his face. "It was all because some of the flour was spilled that the gym shoes were discovered so easily. After that the whole thing came unravelled." He ground his teeth and pounded on his knee with disgust.

146

With a hurt look Takuo turned to Jane and pleaded, "But I am sure I was careful not to spill any of the flour. Isn't that right, Jane?"

"Yes, you're right," she said gloomily. It would not do any good to start blaming each other now for what had gone wrong. There was no hope now of saving Chiyo from the clutches of the police. As she thought about this Jane felt a sense of deep sadness, but also a feeling of profound uneasiness. She was sure there was something not quite right in all this.

Takuo seemed unhappy about taking all the blame himself. He pushed his glasses up on his nose and looked over at Shohei. "That was rather careless of you to cut the end off the stomach tube and leave it lying around on the balcony. That's what ruined Chiyo's perfect alibi."

"I wonder about that. When I thought about it later, I definitely remember bringing that other piece back here to the living room, but . . ." Apparently Shohei realized the pointlessness of what he was saying and broke off abruptly.

"In any case, in order to persuade the medical examiner that the time of death was later than it really was, you had a pretty good plan as far as it went, but, of course, it wasn't perfect. By putting the body out on the balcony, for example, you were successful in slowing down the process of deterioration, but at the same time you made the internal body temperature suspiciously low. Even the police department's medical examiner noticed this unusual fact right away. Actually it was a pretty risky plan to put the body outside for four hours. Even a profesional would have a hard time predicting how that would alter the estimated time of death." Tsurumi's assured voice seemed to emphasize the success of the police investigation. "The changes that take place in the condition of a body and the judgment of the medical examiner are very complicated and idiosyncratic. In this case the official estimate put the time of death between nine and midnight on January third. Even though you were able to push back the possible time of death till midnight as you had hoped, it was still possible that he had been dead by nine. On top of that, as a routine matter of investigation, we generally assume another hour at either end of the spectrum just to be sure. That way we can take every circumstance into account in the investigation of a crime."

It was decided to take Chiyo into custody immediately, and to transport her to the police station. Sawahiko and Kazue went upstairs to help her get ready. Tsurumi expressed the opinion that the other seven would also be investigated individually about their roles in the murder.

A short while later Chiyo came downstairs wearing a black fur coat. She paused in the doorway of the living room and briefly nodded acknowledgment to the other five members of the household. Clearly this was intended as an expression of her thanks to them for doing all they could to protect her. She had not repaired the damage her tears had done to her makeup, and there was evident grief in her clear, youthful features. Nevertheless, she had regained her composure and seemed admirably in control of herself. Kazue, who followed her daughter at a distance, was still sobbing uncontrollably. She kept her face half-hidden in a handkerchief while her bosom and shoulders heaved with sobs.

Chiyo looked at each of the others in turn, bidding them a silent farewell. Mine, Shigeru, Takuo, but when her gaze met Shohei's, her features suddenly began to crumple. Her lip trembled and fresh tears started streaming down her cheeks. Jane had never before seen Chiyo with such a pained feminine expression. And even on Shohei's rugged face there appeared a look of inexpressible grief.

At last Chiyo turned her gaze to Jane, who was standing beside her. Jane was also in tears and could say nothing, though she wanted to say something, anything, to comfort her friend.

Suddenly Chiyo was whispering in her ear a last, determined farewell. "Jane, don't blame Grandpa for what happened. I still think he was a wonderful man. Please don't hold him responsible."

The largest conference room at the Fuji Five Lakes precinct was jammed with thirty reporters and cameramen. The room hummed with excitement and anticipation as they awaited a late-night news conference. The clock on the wall said 11:15, and despite the late hour, a short time earlier Superintendent Aiura had issued word that he would give a statement. Although the various papers around the country had different deadlines, Aiura was aware that his news would be in time for Tokyo's morning editions.

The reporters also knew that right after the announcement of the news conference, police detectives had escorted a young woman into one of the rooms set aside as the investigation headquarters. Someone recognized her as being a member of the Wada family. Following close behind was a red-eyed woman who appeared to be the girl's mother. From this the reporters had guessed that new developments had taken place in the case.

A set of glass doors marked with large letters saying SPECIAL INVESTIGATION HEADQUARTERS FOR THE MURDER OF YOHEI WADA swung open and the always energetic figure of Superintendent Aiura appeared. It was public knowledge that after he retired from the police force he was going to run for mayor. Even now his public appearances seemed more like rehearsals for a political campaign than police work. With quietly assured movements he strode forward to face reporters. After surveying them quickly, he promptly began his briefing. "I want you all to know that thanks to good fortune we now have this case wrapped up. This evening our special investigative unit has taken into custody the person who murdered Yohei Wada."

Pandemonium erupted among the reporters. Some sprang to their feet, flashbulbs popped constantly and were accompanied by the whirr of advancing film.

Since he was in plenty of time to make the morning editions, Aiura began speaking again. "The person being charged with the murder is Chiyo Wada. She is a twenty-two-year-old senior at Japan Women's University in Tokyo. She is the daughter of the victim's niece. On the night in question, Mr. Wada was drunk and called Chiyo to his room. When he tried to assault her, she picked up a fruit knife, and in the midst of a struggle with Mr. Wada, she stabbed him fatally in the left side of the chest."

The press conference had only been called to announce that a suspect had been taken into custody, but as usual Aiura had allowed his sense of the dramatic to get the better of him.

The questions began to fly. "But we had understood that Ms. Wada had returned to Tokyo before the murder took place."

"No. That was just a clever ruse on the part of the others to make us think that. They took the murder weapon and all the other evidence and sent it back to Tokyo with Chiyo, then took steps to make it appear that Mr. Wada had died at a later time. They also made an elaborate set of footprints to suggest the presence of an outside intruder. At first we were misled by this, but our investigative team broke through layer after layer of deception and finally got to the truth."

Apparently he wanted to explain in detail how the family had contrived this hoax, and how his men had seen through it.

"Does this mean that Ms. Wada alone is responsible for the murder?"

"Yes. At the time the murder was committed she alone was entirely responsible. We have already confirmed with the Tokyo police that she took the murder weapon, the bloodstained clothing, and the items that had been stolen from Mr. Wada's room, and hid them in a cemetery near her home.

"Does that mean the other seven people are accessories to murder?"

"They may be charged with obstruction of justice for tampering with the body."

"So the murderer was not one of the seven people staying at the house on the night of the murder as you said earlier."

"That's right. The real murderer is Chiyo Wada. We actually figured this out early on and proceeded to prove it through a careful investigation."

Aiura did not turn a hair over the fact that at the press conference earlier that day he had stated categorically that the murderer was one of the seven people staying at the villa. Nor, for that matter, was he concerned that at the first press conference he had clearly stated that the crime had been committed by an outside intruder. He seemed capable of conveniently forgetting these discrepancies. Instead, he went out of his way to emphasize the fact that his men had solved the crime and arrested the murderer within forty-eight hours of the murder. He had completely forgotten his earlier reversals and misstatements and all his attention was now devoted to the dramatic fact that they had taken a prisoner into custody.

150

8

A Phantom
Emerges

During the night the temperature plummeted and the following morning dawned as the finest day of the new year. Brilliant sunlight flooded the landscape as the sun rode across a transparent blue sky. The golden rays of sunlight reflected off the pure white snow. On the grounds of the villa the mounds of snow that had accumulated on the branches of silver fir and white birch began falling silently to the ground. Each drop of water that fell glittered and shown like a jewel.

Only four people showed up in the dining room for breakfast at shortly after eight that morning—Mine, Shigeru, Shohei, and Jane. Chiyo had been detained at the police station. Kazue had accompanied her, but had been brought back to the villa by a police officer at about two in the morning. She had not felt like talking to anyone and Sawahiko had taken her straight to her bedroom. She had not reappeared. After Chiyo was taken away, Sawahiko had repeatedly telephoned a close friend who was a lawyer in Tokyo, but the friend was out of town for the holidays and could not be reached. Sawahiko was in a foul mood. No doubt he was in his room this morning, still trying to get through on the telephone. Takuo had been in the living room earlier, but was now nowhere to be seen. No one knew where he had gone.

Jane had awakened before six, and getting up quickly, set about preparing breakfast for everyone. It was simple enough to fix eggs, toast, and coffee, and she joined the others at the table, but no one talked very much.

The first thing Shigeru did was take a long swallow of coffee, and when he finally put his cup back on the saucer, said, "It's really a shame. I'll bet Chiyo didn't get a wink of sleep last night."

He spoke in a voice that expressed the depth of sympathy he felt for her. One could see the deep lines of fatigue etched on his face as he looked out at the dazzling garden. The crow's feet at the corners of his eyes suddenly seemed more pronounced than before. His was the sort of face that seemed unsuited for greeting the morning sun; perhaps this was due to his dissolute youth.

"It was pretty cold last night, I wonder if he's coming down with the flu," murmured Jane to herself. At the same time she felt a pang of regret as she wondered how Chiyo might be feeling this morning. Chiyo had never been able to stand the cold. "Today I'll take some blankets and clothes and ask that they be given to her," she said to no one in particular.

Shigeru turned to Jane and asked, "Did you happen to see the seven o'clock news this morning?"

"No."

"I caught a bit of it and I felt they really did not say much of anything about the murder. Maybe the newspapers will report things in greater detail. My brother was known to the world as a man devoted to his work, but in the end he showed his true character. The press will make a big deal out of that for a while, but all we can do is try to ignore them."

He seemed to be directing his comments toward Mine. She, however, seemed to pay no attention to him and merely sat at the table without eating. The skin of her face was streaked by countless wrinkles and was uniformly gray in color, but there was no expression on it at all, causing Jane to feel some concern about the anguish and despair she was keeping bottled up within her. If Yohei's indiscretions became public knowledge, Mine would be hurt more than anyone.

"In a way perhaps it was appropriate for Yohei to have died like this; it all seems very human," said Shigeru. "It appears that all the Wada men have a fatal streak of lechery, and if they don't give in to this very human excess, they'd be missing some essential part of their characters."

Mine's face went rigid as she heard this, and she was just about to respond when the accordion doors of the dining room opened. In came Takuo wearing a dark blue suit and a conservative tie. He

152

took a seat next to Jane and placed the heavy book he was carrying on the table. "Have you got a cup of coffee for me?"

Jane nodded and brought over his breakfast from the nearby tea cart. She also poured him a cup of coffee. Meanwhile Takuo had opened the book and was intently scrutinizing a certain page. The others were naturally curious to see what he was reading.

"Yes, here it is. It's all spelled out here quite clearly," said Takuo in a flippant voice. "You remember what Detective Nakazato said yesterday about how if we knowingly help conceal the identity of a murderer, we could lose our right of inheritance? He is obviously trying to threaten us with that, so I checked the legal code, and it is quite clear on the subject."

He showed the others the title of the book he had. On the spine in gold letters were the words *Comprehensive Legal Code*. Jane supposed he must have found the book in the conference room along with the books on the company's history and the like.

"Shall I read it out? Article Eight Ninety-One of the legal code: 'The following people are not allowed to stand as inheritors: when a prospective inheritor knows that murder is involved and does not bring charges or make accusations. This stipulation does not apply, however, to a person who is mentally incapable of distinguishing right and wrong, nor does it apply when the criminal is a spouse or an immediate family member related by blood.' These two provisions apply to us. Even though we knew that Grandpa had been murdered, we did not charge or accuse Chiyo with being the murderer."

Even Jane recalled what Detective Nakazato had said the previous evening about the laws of inheritance. These laws were apparently quite different from those in America. Americans generally made out wills at a relatively young age, but if they happened to die without one, a man's wife would inherit all his property. Also, there was no provision saying that a person lost his right of inheritance if he didn't bring charges or accusations against a murderer. Jane supposed the Japanese legal provisions were based on the Oriental idea of the retribution of karma.

"That's right, you studied law at the university, didn't you?" murmured Shigeru. "But this still doesn't alter the fact that Chiyo

Shizuko Natsuki

committed murder." He rambled on, talking to himself in a dejected voice. He busily stroked his mustache and wiped his forehead. He could not conceal his despair at the thought of losing his right to a potentially vast inheritance.

No doubt Mine felt the same sort of regret and remorse in her heart. Indeed, since Mine was to inherit three-fourths of the total, the blow of Nakazato's insinuation must have been even more painful for her than for the others. But she merely pursed her lips together determinedly and made no reference to the matter. She did seem angry, however, at the irresponsible comments Shigeru was making, and began to question the others in her usual forthright way. "What do the rest of you plan to do now? Shigeru and I will be leaving at nine. They are sending a car for us."

Having completed the autopsy on Yohei the previous afternoon, the authorities were going to turn the body over to the bereaved family this morning. Mine and Shigeru would go to the hospital where they would be joined by senior staff members of Wada Pharmaceuticals, and together they would take the body back to Tokyo in a hearse. With the exception of Chiyo, who was in custody, the police wanted the other seven to remain available for possible questioning later, but in the meantime, out of respect for the Wada family's prestige, the police put no restraint on their movements.

"I'll go with you," replied Takuo. "After all, I was Grandpa's nephew and also an employee in his company. It would be appropriate for me to accompany the body back to Tokyo and to attend the wake."

Having said that, he left the room, presumably to change into a black suit. Although he insisted that Yohei had intended that he marry Chiyo, once it was clear that Chiyo had murdered Yohei, Takuo began moving quickly to maintain his position in the company and to put as much distance as he could between himself and Chiyo.

"Last night I called the chief of medicine at the hospital and got permission to extend my vacation for a while longer, so if no one objects . . ." said Shohei in a deep voice.

"I would like to stay a while longer, also, if I won't be in the way," said Jane. "At least until we know what is going to happen to Chiyo."

Mine nodded her approval of both these requests, saying, "On the contrary, you will be doing us a favor by staying. Of course Kazue and Sawahiko will be staying on, and if you can stay too, just your presence here will give Chiyo some support." Mine then seemed to straighten in her chair and face them all. "No matter where each of us goes, from now on we will be under constant scrutiny by the police and by the press. Please never forget the request I made on the night of the murder. We must try not to cut each other down, and we must never say anything ill of Grandpa. I personally don't believe it is too late to hide the shame of the Wada family from the world at large. In the present instance, Grandpa committed a small indiscretion, and when it turned out to have tragic results, suddenly the whole world wants to know about it. If we go out now and talk about his shortcomings, the Wada family will never regain its good name. I hope all of you will make every effort not only to preserve Grandpa's reputation, but my own as well."

When she spoke of her own reputation, she quietly bowed her head, and for the first time a light shone in the large, round eyes. Jane felt sure the woman's high-pitched voice would echo in her ears for some time to come.

"There is one question I must ask." Takuo spoke up. "Last night while Chiyo was getting ready, I took Detective Nakazato aside and asked how they had managed to discover the gym shoes so quickly. He explained briefly that while the first news conference was being held here in the dining room, he went by himself to investigate the rear garden one more time. That was when he discovered that one of the incoming footprints overlapped the outgoing ones. It was the very first footprint beside the stone step at the door. On the snow beside the footprint he found some flour dust. This suggested to him that he might find the source of the dust in the kitchen pantry. Once he started looking around there, it was just like a well-marked road leading to the basement storeroom. When he got downstairs, he found a small quantity of flour that had been spilled. This naturally led him to open the can of flour.

But I am absolutely certain that I did not make the mistake of stepping on my outbound footprints when I returned to the house."

Takuo clenched his fist on the table and repeated the words, "I am absolutely certain of it." Then, turning to Shohei, he said, "You remember how careful we were. While I was out there making the footprints, Dr. Mazaki warned me to be careful not to step on my outbound tracks, and I told him that I wouldn't make a dumb mistake like that."

"Ah, yes . . ." said Shohei, staring off into the middle distance and nodding.

"Besides that, and I have said this over and over again, I don't remember spilling any of the flour while I was hiding the shoes. Jane will confirm that."

"Yes. I have no recollection of him spilling any of the flour."

At this point Shohei broke in sharply, "Yes, but the simple fact is that the flour was there and they found it and the shoes and they knew that the murder was an inside job."

"Not necessarily. The detective may be lying. It may just have been a lucky guess, and he's making all the rest of this up. I guess what I really want to believe is that the whole thing did not fall apart because of a mistake I made. I want Chiyo to know that it was not my fault." There was remorse in Takuo's voice and he bit his lower lip.

Jane turned these thoughts over in her mind, wondering what had really led the police to discover the shoes. Somehow it all didn't make sense.

This morning Fuji's white peak shone brilliantly in the sun and seemed to pierce the very blue of the sky itself. Even the leafless forests of larch on the lower slopes shone brightly in the sunlight, making a blinding glare that caused one to squint.

In buoyant spirits, Ukyo Nakazato was sitting by the second-floor window of the Fuji Five Lakes police station gazing at the scene. Finally turning away from the window, he fished a cigarette from his pocket. Along with the blue pack of cigarettes came the little plastic filter his wife was always nagging him to use. He merely placed it on his desk and took a cigarette from the pack as usual. Absentmindedly he lit the cigarette and ignored the filter.

The same morning sunlight was also streaming through the high window of the jail cell where Chiyo, wrapped in a blanket, was lying on a bed in the corner. Since there was no one else in custody at the moment, Chiyo was alone and she was so quiet that one could not even hear her breathing. Because the blanket was thin and offered little protection from the cold, she wrapped it tightly about her. The guard on duty reported that last night the girl had seemed exhausted and upon returning to the cell had immediately collapsed on the bed. At 7:00 when he had called out that it was time for breakfast, she had merely rolled over and gone back to sleep.

They had questioned her until midnight the previous night, and then sent her to bed. At the police station Chiyo had been cooperative and replied readily to all questions, and showed no sign of trying to hide anything.

"All the others joined together in an effort to protect me, and I shamelessly accepted what they did for me. Now I am prepared to accept my punishment, whatever it may be." Chiyo had spoken these words in a tearful voice, but held her head up with great determination, and this had impressed Nakazato.

What Chiyo did not know was that not all of the other seven had joined together to protect her. Though it appeared that they had all decided to carry out a cover-up to help her get away, the fact was that one of them had tipped off the police by sabotaging the cover-up and ensuring that she would be arrested by the police.

Nakazato stubbed out his cigarette and, stroking his jaw, gazed once again at Mt. Fuji.

Several things had happened that had helped the police investigation. First of all, there were the superimposed footprints in the garden. Takuo had spoken to him last night and had insisted that such an error was inconceivable. Thinking about it now, Takuo's story was rather curious, and his manner of speaking had been urgent. Whether he believed Takuo or not, the footprints raised some questions. If they had been superimposed from the beginning, it had escaped the notice of two police searches. The first search had been conducted by Detectice Narumi and an assistant shortly after they were notified of the murder. An hour later they had been joined by detectives from the prefectural police bureau, and had conducted another complete search of the site. Narumi was a meticulous detective who always paid close attention to details, but for Inspector Tsurumi to cover the same ground a second time and still fail to notice the overlapping footprints seemed inconceivable to Nakazato.

The footprints must have been altered after the initial investigation while the police were questioning members of the household, or while Superintendent Aiura was holding the first press conference. During that time someone must have taken the gym shoes and altered the footprints. Since the altered prints were right next to the doorway, a person could have done it easily without leaving the house.

Nakazato had noticed the footprints right away. If he had failed to notice this, of course, the phantom would no doubt have done something to draw them to his attention.

Beside the altered footprints he had found traces of flour on the snow. This, too, was probably a clue designed to lead Nakazato to the storeroom. Once there, the discovery of the shoes was all but inevitable. Certainly after seeing the flour spilled on the floor there could be no question about it.

Gazing at the slopes of Mt. Fuji had tired Nakazato's eyes and he massaged them lightly. Then, still seated at his desk, he opened the drawer and took out the plastic bag containing the bit of brown rubber tubing that had been discovered the previous morning on the balcony of Yohei's room. In Shohei's medical bag he had found the longer tube from which the piece in front of him had been cut. He had taken it as evidence and sent it to the police lab, asking them to confirm that the white residue in the tube was the same substance as the gratin in Yohei's stomach. He did not have to wait for the lab reports, though, because the confessions he had obtained already confirmed the point.

Nevertheless, the idea of putting food into a dead person's stomach as a way of pushing back the estimated time of death was an original one requiring some technical expertise. If it had not been for the discovery of this bit of tubing, the deception might have worked. As long as the police had not been able to dispute the "fact" that Yohei had eaten the gratin, Chiyo's alibi was unshakable.

Here too the phantom's kindness worked in the police's favor, for it seemed unlikely that the taciturn surgeon would have carelessly dropped such a crucial piece of evidence. In fact, he had said he remembered quite clearly having carried the extra piece of tubing back into the living room. No doubt the phantom had picked it up there and planted it on the balcony before the police search was conducted on the morning of the fifth.

"That must be how it happened, and yet . . ." murmured Nakazato to himself. If either Takuo or Shohei was the phantom, it would mean he was implicating himself in order to draw the suspicion of murder away from himself, but the question remained why either of them would have wanted to sabotage the cover-up. Was the phantom covering up his own crime while pretending to protect Chiyo?

"What about Kazue?" Nakazato caught himself speaking the name aloud. He toyed with the idea for a moment, then rejected it. Nevertheless, he thought, we cannot just assume the phantom is a man.

Just then Narumi poked his pale, boyish face into the room. "Kazue Wada is waiting downstairs. She came to see her daughter and has brought some things she wants to give her."

"They are not allowed to see each other. We have not finished the questioning yet, but if she wants to arrange to have Chiyo's meals sent in, we will order them from whatever place she designates. If she has anything else, she can leave it and we will give it to Chiyo after we have examined it."

Narumi nodded and was about to leave when Nakazato caught his eye and said, "Hold on, I want you to consider something for a moment. Of the seven people at the villa, who is the one who would most likely want to see Chiyo arrested?"

Narumi looked surprised, but gave the matter some thought. Presently he licked his lower lip and said, "Everyone seems to be quite fond of Chiyo, and it appears they have all tried to protect her. Those who stand to inherit something from Yohei's estate are now in danger of losing their right of inheritance because of their part in the conspiracy. And even those who won't inherit anything could be punished for aiding and abetting a criminal, so I don't see why any of them would want to see her arrested."

"But there is someone who wanted to see Chiyo charged with this murder."

"Well, if I had to name someone, I would say Mine."

"Mine?" repeated Nakazato in surprise.

"Yes. In the first place she is no blood relation to Chiyo. Also, she had been married to Yohei for more than forty years. She was very unhappy, of course, about Yohei's womanizing ways, but she must have felt a great deal of affection for him as only a wife of long standing can know. Maybe she gave in at first to the family's pressure to help protect Chiyo, but perhaps her real feelings got the best of her later on and she took steps to see that Chiyo was charged with the crime."

"Yes, I see. Well, that's one way of looking at it." In his mind Nakazato called up Mine's features, and her expression that seemed aloof from all ordinary emotions.

The snow-clad, forested slopes of Mt. Fuji could also be seen from the second floor of the Wada villa at Asahi Hills. Since the villa was situated on the top of a hill, they could see here and there the roofs of a few other villas among the trees. But mostly it was the vast, uninterrupted slope of Fuji that dominated the view. To the east one could also see Kagosaka Pass.

"Most of the villas at Asahi Hills face southwest because Mt. Fuji is in that direction." Jane suddenly recalled having heard Chiyo say that, and felt a pang of grief for her friend. Chiyo explained that to her on the evening she had arrived at the villa. Now as she recalled seeing the beautiful villa for the first time in the twilight and recalled the excited feeling she had experienced, it all seemed a long time ago. And when she thought of all that had transpired in the three days since then, it was as though the time had passed in a dream.

Jane cocked her head to one side and her gaze traveled back to the desk in front of her. Continuing work on the thesis now would surely serve no useful purpose. And yet her heart and mind were filled with thoughts of Chiyo and she wished she could do something to help her friend.

The hired car arrived on schedule at nine, and Mine, Shigeru, and Takuo left the villa. From there they would go to the Fuji Five Lakes Hospital to pick up Yohei's body and then, together with representatives from the company, would return to Yohei's home in Tokyo for the wake.

After Sawahiko and Shohei had seen the others off, Jane began thinking about taking some clothes and personal effects to Chiyo. She was concerned that Chiyo had not taken enough things with her when she left the previous evening. But before Jane could begin making preparations, Kazue had gotten up, hurriedly gathered a few essentials, and asked Shohei to drive her to the police station. Kazue had no makeup on her haggard face, and her hair, which she ordinarily kept swept up in a neat bun, hung loosely down her back. Her eyes shone with a strange intensity, and it was clear that she could think of nothing but her daughter. Jane had wanted to accompany Kazue and talk to Chiyo, if only for just a moment, but before she could say anything, the car had roared away.

Sawahiko had gone into the living room and picked up the telephone. He had finally been able to reach his lawyer in Tokyo, who was planning to come to Asahi Hills that afternoon. But Sawahiko was still worried and could be heard talking to someone in the law department of his university to get another opinion of what the outlook might be for his daughter.

Jane returned to her room on the second floor. She sat down at the desk with the idea of continuing the work on Chiyo's graduation thesis. She sat at the desk and looked at the sheets of report paper, her eyes merely skimming over the words. Inside her head thoughts whirled chaotically. Jane found that reading Chiyo's English sentences was the best way to concentrate all her attention and feeling on Chiyo herself.

Before long she recalled something else Chiyo had said: "Don't blame Grandpa for what happened. I think he was a wonderful man. Please don't hold him responsible." Last night, before the police had taken her away, Chiyo had stood in the living room and given each of them a parting look, but to Jane she had suddenly muttered these words in a low, husky voice that seemed to come from the bottom of her heart. Though this parting statement seemed spontaneous, it also reminded Jane of what she had overheard Chiyo say to Shohei out in the garden.

"Grandpa was a wonderful person. He was a great man and a warm human being. I loved him more than anyone, and there is no excuse for what I have done. I truly respected Grandpa."

They were almost the same words she had spoken to Jane. But why?

If Yohei had been drunk and had violently assaulted Chiyo, a member of his own family and a blood relative, then why did she apologize for what she had done to defend herself, and why did she say that she had great respect for Yohei? And yet there was a sincerity in her voice as she said these words. It was almost as though she was desperately trying to tell Shohei and Jane her true feelings. Could it be that Yohei had really not done anything improper, and that she secretly wanted to hint at this? People could think what they would, but perhaps this was Chiyo's way of saying, "As far as I am concerned, he was a good man."

This speculation brought with it a whole string of questions. It suggested that Yohei had not assaulted Chiyo, and that she had not stabbed him. Was she taking the blame for someone else and covering up someone else's crime? Could it be that the real cause of Yohei's death was not the sort of foul play they had all supposed? Such speculations seemed farfetched and yet . . .

Jane was conscious of the rapid beating of her heart. She looked up at the sky, then turned her gaze to the L-shaped roof of the first floor. She had a good view of the east wing of the house, which did not have a second story. Beneath the snow-covered roof of the east wing was the dining room, and across the corridor from it, Yohei and Mine's rooms.

Then there was that sound she had heard. There was no question that it had come from the corner of the east wing. She had heard the sound of rusty metal screeching. The first time Jane heard that sound was in Yohei's room on the night of the murder.

After they had fed the gratin into Yohei's stomach and had decided to put the body outside on the balcony for a time, it had taken both Sawahiko and Takuo to force open the rusty, glass door. It had hardly ever been used and the rusty hinges made a frightful sound. After laying the body out on the tablecloth, they had closed the door again, and even though they were careful about it, they could not avoid making that noise.

When they were done playing poker, Mine and Shigeru had gone to bed while the other five returned once more to Yohei's room. It was nearly 4:00 when they brought the stiff body back into the bedroom and laid it on the bed. At that time they had to open and close the door again, so altogether Jane had heard the harsh sound four times, and it was firmly imprinted on her mind. But that should have been the last of it. There was no reason for the door to be opened again before the police began their investigation at about 10:00 that morning. There was no reason to suppose that she had heard that sound again before the police arrived. And yet she was positive she had heard it a fifth time—it must have been around 5:00 or 5:30 in the morning. To the best of her recollection they had completed the preparations for the cover-up and retired to their bedrooms at about 4:15. Jane's mind had been numb and she was exhausted, so she had simply washed her face and gone to bed in her underwear. She had fallen asleep right away, but later, somewhere deep in her consciousness, she had heard that sound again. The shriek of metal against metal had, for an instant, awakened a part of her mind. At the time she had tried to identify the sound, but being unable to, she had once again fallen into a deep sleep.

There was only one conclusion to be reached, namely, that while everyone else was asleep, someone had opened the glass door to the balcony one more time. It could only have been for the purpose of cooling Yohei's room to the same temperature as outdoors in order to further retard the body's process of deterioration.

At this point Jane assumed the existence of a phantom person. A person who for some reason had murdered Yohei and persuaded Chiyo to take the blame. Chiyo had consented and at 9:00 on the evening of the third she had pretended that she had stabbed Yohei and had confessed as much to the rest of the household. At that time, of course, the real murderer pretended to learn about the killing for the first time.

After discussing the matter excitedly, they had decided to send Chiyo off to Tokyo right away, and had tried to arrange things so it appeared that the murder had happened later. In short, everyone except Chiyo and the phantom believed that the murder had actually occurred around 9:00, and had worked furiously to make it appear to the police medical examiner that it had not happened until nearly midnight.

Jane, of course, had fully believed Chiyo's story, and that that night had indeed been the opening scene of a tragedy. And yet, it seemed that even before then, the real killer and Chiyo and Yohei had mounted the stage for a performance of their own, a shadowy drama with no spectators.

Yohei had probably been killed even earlier than 9:00, which Chiyo had confessed to as the time of the murder. The real killer would have known that, and would have taken steps to see that the deterioration of the body was even slower than that arranged by the others, so that it would still appear that he had died around midnight. Consequently, after the others had gone to bed, the phantom once again entered Yohei's room and opened the balcony door in order to chill the room. The sound Jane had heard in her sleep was definitely the sound of the door being opened by the phantom. Since the balcony door was closed when they had all gotten up at 9:00, the real killer must have closed it again. No doubt it had again made a noise, but by then Jane was fast asleep, and probably none of the others had heard it either.

Jane nodded slightly to herself. She decided there could be no other explanation for what had happened. The question was, who was the phantom? And what had that person said to Chiyo to persuade her to take the blame for a murder she had not committed? Jane was livid with anger and impatience as she began to understand the unseen phantom's clever scheme.

Who could it be?

Regardless of anything else, it was certain that Chiyo must be deeply in love with that person. So much in love that if that person were in danger of being arrested, she would be willing to take the blame herself. One by one Jane sifted through the names until, finally, only two lingered in her mind.

Shortly after 11:00 the telephone at police headquarters began to ring again. It was the second report from the three teams that had been dispatched to Tokyo. The Tokyo investigators already knew, of course, that Chiyo had been taken into custody. Nevertheless, Inspector Tsurumi had ordered them to continue to pursue their investigation. Chiyo's crime was probably linked to circumstances within the family. For one thing, they could not simply dispose of the case by assuming that Chiyo had acted alone. The suspicion that there was a more subtle and complex set of circumstances at work was one that Tsurumi was beginning to share with Nakazato.

The detectives in Tokyo reported the progress they had made in investigating Yohei's personal life. "Just as we expected, it turns out that he was keeping other women. Two of them are prostitutes, and the third is the widow of an office worker who died young. They all live in apartments or homes he bought for them. The rest of the family knows about them and the relationships were long-standing ones. Each woman has the house or apartment in her own name, so they are pretty well off and there was never any suggestion of intrigue to claim part of Yohei's estate."

The detective who relayed this report was a veteran of the force. "None of the three women have any children; apparently Yohei was not a particularly potent man. I did hear of an interesting, but old episode from a maid who has been with the family for forty years or more. She told me of something that happened thirty years ago when the old president was still in good health and before Yohei took over. One night a woman with an infant in her arms came to the house asking Yohei for support.

"She appeared to be a rural girl in her early twenties who might have been a geisha at one time. The maid met her at the door and she asked to see Yohei. It was about nine o'clock in the evening and Yohei had just returned home. At first he told the maid to send the woman away, but the girl made a big row in the entry hall and

Shizuko Natsuki

Yohei finally agreed to see her. The maid says they talked for nearly an hour before the woman left in tears.

"Mine, of course, overheard the whole thing as the girl insisted that the child in her arms was Yohei's. Yohei, however, denied having any responsibility, and sent the woman away."

"I see. So what happened after that?" asked Tsurumi.

"Well, that's something neither the maid nor anyone else knows. The woman only came to the house that one time."

"You say this happened thirty years ago?" muttered Tsurumi thoughtfully to himself.

The detectives had also learned that the bachelor Shigeru was also keeping a couple of women.

The team that investigated Sawahiko, Kazue, and Chiyo had made no progress that previous day, but had turned up some new information today. "All reports are unanimous that these three make a happy, harmonious family, but there are hints that relations may not have been so good between Sawahiko and Yohei." The officer in charge of this team was the plodding, middle-aged detective.

"I learned this from a colleague of Yohei's at the same university. This man acted as go-between when Sawahiko and Kazue were married, so he knows them quite well. As you know, Sawahiko does research in medical microbiology. Specifically his field of research is, ah . . . let me see here . . ."

The sound of rustling paper could be heard on the telephone as he consulted his notes. "Sawahiko's research team is doing studies on production through genetic engineering. They are developing ways to massively increase production by tinkering with miniscule bits of genetic material. If their work is successful, they will be able to manufacture specific medicinal remedies for cancer and other serious diseases."

"Is the man who told you all this also a genetic engineer?"

"Yes. Yes, that's right. I'm sure you know that this genetic engineering has unlimited potential for producing large quantities of medicine or unlimited sources of energy without using fossil fuels, and for producing huge quantities of food stuffs without using fertilizer. It is an enormous field that is threatening to bring about a

166

second industrial revolution. On the other hand, they can also use the results of this sort of research to clone human beings and to produce all sorts of organisms that are unknown in nature. They can even create bacteria and toxins for which there is no known cure. Some scholars say that this is a dangerous field, an evil science, that will lead to the destruction of mankind. But whatever else it is, it is a field that is receiving worldwide attention." The detective was apparently quoting the professor verbatim.

"I see," said Tsurumi, "but what has all this got to do with the fact that there may have been hard feelings between Sawahiko and Yohei?"

"Yes. Well, it appears that Yohei was opposed to the sort of research Sawahiko was doing. In Japan, as in other countries, private research facilities are being established on a commercial basis, and some are even getting into the area of production, but at Wada Pharmaceuticals, Yohei was adamantly opposed to these developments, and refused to spend any money on them."

"What do you mean?"

"Sawahiko's research requires a great deal of money. For one thing there is considerable danger involved in doing experiments in genetics, and they follow the American safety guidelines for ensuring that bacteria do not get out of the laboratory. In Japan the government has established ratings for such experiments, ranking them from P-One to P-Four depending on what they involve. The research and experiments being done by Sawahiko and his team are classified as P-Three and require special facilities, expensive facilities. The university has no budget to provide the sort of laboratory he needs, so they have to find outside sources of funding."

"Then what you are saying is that Sawahiko asked Yohei for the money, and Yohei refused."

"His colleague did not hear it stated quite that baldly, but he did suggest that it's quite possible to suppose that this was the source of the animosity between the two men. He also said he thought Kazue had intervened with Yohei on Sawahiko's behalf. Anyway, there is one more thing: Sawahiko also has a lover who runs a bar in Roppongi. Apparently she has been after him for some time to set her up in a bar of her own. I learned this at the bar where he often goes drinking with his students and research associates. Naturally he has kept this secret from Kazue."

Tsurumi revised his opinion of Sawahiko, who always appeared so serious and sincere on the outside, but who was turning out to be profligate and philandering just like the rest of the Wada men. Indeed, the fact that he had problems with women was further evidence that he was right at home with his in-laws. It was clear that the traits of the Wada men were shared even by those who had only married into the family.

The previous day Tsurumi had also ordered investigations of Shohei Mazaki and Jane Prescott, but that assignment had gone to a different investigative team. Twenty minutes later they phoned in their report. This was a team of young detectives who had met with Yohei's attorney the previous day.

"You asked us to look into the fact that Shohei Mazaki was relatively young to be acting as Yohei's attending physician, and to see if there was any unusual reason for the appointment. I think we've really got some big news for you," said the young detective triumphantly. "Shohei was born in a hot springs resort in the remote northeast and was raised by his mother in a single-parent household. His mother was a hot springs resort geisha, but she died of illness the year he entered junior high school, and he was taken in by his aunt. She was a stepmother to him, but later her husband went to Tokyo to find work and abandoned the family. The aunt set out for Tokyo to look for her husband and took along her own two children as well as Shohei. They never located her husband and the poor woman suffered great hardships trying to raise the three of them. She died six years ago."

All this information had been gleaned from Shohei's stepbrother, a thirty-six-year-old businessman who was two years older than Shohei.

"At the time Shohei was taken in by his aunt, he already knew who his father was, and hated the man."

"So who was Shohei's father?"

"Yohei Wada. He had met this hot springs geisha while on a trip to the area, and after meeting her several times, she became pregnant. The woman believed Yohei loved her, so she decided to go ahead and have the child, but once Yohei found out about it, he dropped her. At the time all this was happening, Yohei's father was president of the company and was still in good health. Apparently Yohei was afraid that if his father found out about this indiscretion, he would not be allowed to take over his father's position. The woman did go to Tokyo once to see him, but he insisted that the child was not his, and said the whole thing was an attempt at extortion. He drove the woman away. The woman was determined to raise the child on her own, but she used every possible opportunity to speak ill of Yohei. Apparently the mother's anger left an indelible impression on the child."

Tsurumi had had a hunch the child he had heard about earlier might have been Shohei.

"Shohei always performed well, even as a child, and eventually went on to Tokyo University Medical School and became a doctor. It turns out that despite his ill feelings toward his father, somewhere in the bottom of his heart he always maintained a desire to meet the man.

"When Yohei was a junior in high school and had made up his mind to go to the university and study medicine, his elder stepbrother was already at the university and the family just could not afford to send Shohei as well. After giving the matter much thought, his aunt decided to bring it to Yohei's attention. First she wrote a letter to him explaining the circumstances of Shohei's birth and upbringing. In the letter she wrote, 'In the end you turned your back on my younger sister, but as Shohei has grown older, he has come to resemble you a great deal. If you wish to see him, I will arrange a meeting where you can see him from a distance. The fact is that Shohei's mother suffered greatly trying to raise him, and as a result he continues to feel some resentment toward you. Still, if you would like to see him, I think something can be arranged.'

"Yohei responded to this letter by saying he would by all means like to see the boy. By this time, of course, Yohei was president of Wada Pharmaceuticals and had no children of his own. To rediscover now a child who was already a high school student was something he had never imagined.

"The aunt carried out her plan by taking Shohei to a hotel lobby on some pretext or another and Yohei was able to observe the boy from a distance. After only a glimpse he was convinced that this was his own son. From that time onward Yohei discreetly sent money to the aunt to cover Shohei's school and living expenses."

"I suppose Shohei's aunt explained all this to him before she died?"

"Yes. His stepbrother was present the whole time and said that Shohei was greatly shocked to learn all this. But after all, I guess this sort of thing does happen sometimes. He had hated Yohei from the time he was a young child, and he had worked very hard and was determined to succeed despite the fact that he had been rejected by his father. Now he found that he had become a doctor only because of Yohei's help. No doubt when Shohei's aunt explained all this to him, she did so in the hope that someday he and Yohei would be reconciled as father and son."

Shohei was twenty-eight at the time his aunt died and was already working at the university medical school. The following year Yohei entered the hospital for gallstone surgery and Shohei was put in charge of his ward. After being released from the hospital, Yohei called Shohei to his home for advice on health matters, and he naturally ended up becoming Yohei's attending physician.

"So they had a special relationship in that even though they knew they were father and son, they couldn't act that way or admit it publicly."

"Perhaps they were both trying to reach out, trying to find each other?"

"Of course."

Yohei did not have any children of his own and it may have been that he was examining Shohei's character and feelings with the thought of someday openly recognizing him as his son. But the question still remained of how Shohei felt about his father. Not only had Yohei originally rejected the boy and his mother, it was possible that Shohei hated him even more for his secret patronage.

While Tsurumi was listening to the reports from Tokyo, Nakazato was on another telephone exchanging views on the case with the district prosecutor. Nakazato had a copy of the

Comprehensive Legal Code open in front of him. He was discussing with the prosecutor the details of Article 891 on the disqualification of inheritance claims and the implications it had for this case. When at last he put the telephone down, Tsurumi summarized for him the results of the reports from Tokyo.

"So, Shohei Mazaki is really a bastard child of Yohei's."

Suddenly Nakazato recalled Shohei's features and realized that he really did have the same long, crescent-shaped eyes that both Yohei and Shigeru had. "Well I suppose society at large would consider him a bastard child, but there are other circumstances involved here as well."

"When we put all this together with the reports we got yesterday, it is clear that many people had motives for killing Yohei." Tsurumi perused his list of the nine people at the villa on the night of the murder. The list had their names and family relationships, and so far, Yohei's was the only name that had been eliminated as a suspect.

"Mine has the accumulated anger of a long neglected wife. Shigeru has financial problems and was going to be relieved of his position as director in the company. Takuo may have wanted to get rid of Yohei before the old man found out about the bar-girl mistress, and thus make sure he got Chiyo for his wife. Sawahiko was angry with Yohei for not funding his research project, and I have just explained Shohei's situation. So far, the only ones who do not have an obvious motive for killing Yohei are Kazue, Chiyo, and Jane Prescott. Certainly at this point it seems most unlikely that Chiyo killed him."

"Nevertheless, the fact that they were willing to try and protect Chiyo suggests that some of them believed she had done it." Nakazato told Tsurumi of his suspicion that someone had carefully arranged things so that Chiyo would be arrested.

"So even though there are many people who would be glad to see Yohei dead, the real question is, who wanted to see Chiyo arrested?" murmured Tsurumi, folding his arms across his chest.

"It is not out of the question to suppose that Mine might have exposed Chiyo's crime as a way of getting revenge on her husband, but that would mean that Mine would have to expose her own shame to the world. This is too much to expect from a woman whose whole life was devoted to protecting the good name of the Wada family. In fact, I have just been discussing the matter with the prosecuting attorney, and it looks more and more as though the murder is part of a larger plan to deny someone their right of inheritance. We have to consider the fact that everyone who is legally eligible to inherit something of Yohei's estate was gathered at the villa at the time of the murder."

"So the provisions of Article Eight Ninety-One of the *Comprehensive Legal Code* really do apply in this case," said Tsurumi, pointing to the two paragraphs with his finger.

"I think it is safe to say that is a good possibility. According to clear legal precedent, it applies to anyone who 'conceals a crime or who obstructs justice.' The prosecuting attorney says that in a legal sense bringing charges means making an accusation at the time the case is actually being investigated. All that is involved is simply saying who committed the crime, where, and how. The people at the villa did notify the police that Yohei had been killed, but they omitted the crucial point of saying who killed him. In that sense they cannot be said to have 'brought charges.' In fact, it is the prosecuting attorney's opinion that by creating a fictitious intruder and intentionally misleading the investigation, they collectively committed the serious crime of obstruction of justice, and by applying these two paragraphs of the law, they clearly forfeit their legal rights of inheritance."

"But doesn't it also say that an exception is made in the case of the victim's spouse or a direct blood relative?"

"That's right. It's a matter of recognizing human nature. It would be hard for a person to bring charges against a spouse or a relative. But the court has wide latitude in interpreting this law and can disregard it if it chooses to."

"And if the court wishes to apply the law?"

"In that case they all worked together to conceal Chiyo's misdeed, but they were found out and she confessed, at least that is where the case is at this point. So the question we have to ask now is, who profits most from having Chiyo arrested?"

"Ummm." Tsurumi once again reviewed the list of family members. "In that case, I would bet my money on this one," he said pointing his finger at one of the names.

"I disagree. I don't believe that person would contrive to have Chiyo charged with murder; it's not in character."

"Yes, but what if there were another person in the background who was able to manipulate Chiyo?"

"All right," nodded Nakazato. "It's a possibility I've been mulling over in my mind since last night. If there is such a person in the background, someone who ultimately contrived to have things work out for his or her personal gain, it would have to have been a very subtle and ingenious plan. It's hard to believe that this person could have implemented such a complex scheme on the spur of the moment once Chiyo happened to stab Yohei."

Suddenly Tsurumi looked up. "But what if the murder itself was a part of the plan?"

The two detectives stared at one another in silence, each immersed in his own thoughts. Neither of them noticed when Superintendent Aiura came in and sat down.

"Well, you may be right, but I am not entirely convinced."

After expelling a long breath, Nakazato continued the discussion in an animated voice. "Someone murdered Yohei in a premeditated way, then drew Chiyo into the affair and she decided to take responsibility for the crime and confessed in front of the others. Since everyone is so fond of Chiyo they decided to join together to protect her, but the real murderer was all the time working behind the scenes to make Chiyo's crime known and leading us to the arrest. The whole process could have been carefully planned from the beginning."

"There are only a limited number of people for whom Chiyo would accept a charge of murder."

"The first one who comes to mind, of course, is her mother, Kazue."

"How about Takuo? I heard they were engaged to be married."

"I don't know. She has always been somewhat aloof from Takuo whenever I have seen them together. On the other hand, I have the impression that she is quite fond of Shohei. But you may be right.

Even if she makes an outward show of being indifferent toward Takuo, it may just be a deception."

Aiura had a puzzled look on his face as he tried to follow the conversation between the two detectives. Finally unable to endure it any longer, he cleared his throat loudly. When the two detectives looked at him, he said, "It is nearly twelve-thirty. The press is waiting for a news update in time to make the evening news. I thought I would go ahead and announce what we have learned since this morning."

There had been a news conference the previous night after Chiyo was arrested, but it had simply been to announce that fact. Aiura had assumed that she had committed the murder and that the subsequent investigation would prove it, so today he was planning to discuss the details of her confession. But now as he listened to the discussion between Nakazato and Tsurumi, there was a perplexed look on his face, and he found it hard to follow what they were saying.

Tsurumi gave Nakazato a knowing look, and letting slip a long sigh, said, "Maybe you should revise your announcement about its being a simple case of murder."

"What?"

"Well, last night you told the press that Chiyo alone was responsible for the murder and said it was clear that the others were only involved in the cover-up after the murder was committed. It doesn't look like it's going to be that simple and clear-cut after all."

"Do you mean I'm going to have to go out there and make another retraction?" Aiura raised his eyebrows and his nostrils flared as he glared at Nakazato. There was a look of disbelief and disappointment on his face, and in his eyes they could see a momentary look of silent, desperate entreaty. "If I have to make another retraction, this will be the third one. Do you realize what that will do to my reputation? Besides, I thought it was all settled. Chiyo committed the murder, didn't she? She confessed."

"I'm afraid that whole theory may be overturned." Nakazato stroked his protruding stomach with the palms of his hands and gazed into the distance as he replied. "I think it would be in our best interests if our announcements to the press were more low-keyed. In fact, it would probably be best to say nothing of these new findings for the time being."

When Superintendent Aiura appeared before the assembled press corps ten minutes later, the expression on his face had none of the cheerful enthusiasm he had exhibited the previous day when he had announced that the murderer had been apprehended. He was aware of his changed attitude, and his mouth turned down and his forehead wrinkled in a frown. Distress was evident in all his delicate and intellectual features, and his voice was weighed down with fatigue as he spoke. "This case has become more complex and mysterious the further we progress in our investigation. Last night and today we spent our time here at headquarters obtaining a detailed confession from Ms. Chiyo Wada. Nevertheless, it now seems likely that there was some sort of mystery person behind her, someone manipulating her actions."

"You say someone was manipulating her. What does that mean? Can you be more specific?"

"I am saying that she confessed to the murder, but we're not sure she actually committed the murder."

The response to this statement swept the room like a tidal wave. Since the official version had changed once again, the reporters were not able to grasp all the new implications at once.

"What are you saying? Did Chiyo act alone as the murderer, or is the real murderer someone else?" a veteran reporter sharply questioned.

"Yes. Well, you see that all depends . . ."

"Have you found out who the real murderer is?"

"Well, uh, not exactly."

"Is it a member of the Wada family?"

"Can you give us a name?"

"Is it a man or a woman?"

The questions came flying from all quarters. Aiura was stunned and closed his eyes for a moment. Once he had caught his breath, however, he regained his composure. He knew that if he mishandled this situation now, it would stain his image and jeopardize his political opportunities later.

Quickly and confidently words spilled from his lips. "The principal suspect is a woman. If our investigator's theory is correct, this has been an extremely subtle and ingenious case of one person taking the blame for another person's crime." Superintendent Aiura decided to end his briefing on a positive note. "There is only one true set of facts in this case, and we are prepared to pursue our investigation until we uncover those facts."

9

The Tragedy of W

Sawahiko drove to Gotemba Station to meet Chiyo's lawyer, who was arriving from Tokyo.

Kazue retired to her room after returning from the police station. She reported that she had not been allowed to see Chiyo, and had only left the things she had brought for her with the officer on duty. Kazue seemed to have given herself up to despair, and had to be helped into the house by Shohei. He took her to her room, and she did not appear again even when Sawahiko set out for the station. This was unusual since at home it was always her custom to accompany her husband to the front gate whenever he went out, making sure he had his overcoat and such. The fact that she did not see him off today was a clear indication of her physical and emotional condition. Shohei also retired to his room on the second floor and did not come down again, nor even make a sound.

For some time Jane was alone on the sofa in the living room, which was flooded with bright, winter sunlight. Presently she stood up and began to pace back and forth on the carpeted floor. Not only was the weather clear, it had gotten warmer since noon and the snow in the garden was beginning to melt. Jane watched the drops of water dripping steadily from the eaves of the house and the branches of the trees. They caught the sun and shone like diamonds.

From time to time she could see figures of men wearing anoraks or jackets moving about in the shrubbery near the front gate. Most of them had cameras around their necks and occasionally one of them would approach the house and ring the doorbell. They were reporters hanging around in hopes of having a chance to talk to some member of the Wada family. Each time one of them ap-

peared, Jane ducked behind the curtains, and when no one answered the door, the reporter would go away again.

Jane had begun prowling about the room thinking some move-
ment would be a relief, but there was still a knot of tension in the
pit of her stomach. Well, I guess I have done everything I could, so
far, she thought. Now is the time to do something really drastic to
help Chiyo.

She crossed the living room and opened the door on the left of
the fireplace. Coming into the north wing between the billiards
room and the conference room, she approached the door to the
room Kazue and Sawahiko were using. Jane steadied her breathing
and knocked twice, lightly. Hearing no response, she knocked
again.

"Who is it?" called Kazue, at last, in a faint voice.

"It's Jane. I'd like to talk to you for a moment."

After a pause Kazue said, "Perhaps we can talk later, I'm just
exhausted right now."

"I understand how you feel, but there is no one else around just
now. I'm afraid that if we miss the chance to talk now, it may
never come again." Jane tried to keep her tone of voice reasonable,
and above all not to sound threatening.

There was no reply to this last statement, but after an interval the
door opened a crack from the inside. Kazue's hair was hanging loose,
and she had a dressing gown thrown over her shoulders. After
ushering Jane into the room, she closed the door and latched it.

"I am terribly sorry to be bothering you like this."

Kazue's manner remained rigid, and without acknowledging
Jane's apology, she invited her to take a seat on the three-piece sofa
set. "Please sit down here."

Seated opposite Kazue, Jane made a shrewd assessment of the
older woman and quickly looked away. There were dark circles
under Kazue's eyes, and deep wrinkles at the corners of her eyes
that had not been there before. She looked as though she had suddenly aged ten years. Kazue was just forty-five years old, and she
ought to have been in the prime of her womanhood with a sleek,
well cared for complexion, spending her days devoted to her happy
family, but now . . .

Jane looked down at her hands and suddenly found herself unable to speak. The desperate aura of fear she saw in Kazue's eyes made her hesitate, but suddenly she realized that if she did not speak now, she never would.

"It may be impertinent of me to say this, but I want to talk to you about the real facts of this case as far as Chiyo is concerned. I have thought the matter over and reached the conclusion that Chiyo is taking the blame for someone else. Isn't that right?"

Kazue's breast shuddered as she sucked in her breath.

"A number of factors have led me to this conclusion, but the one thing that moved me most was something Chiyo said shortly before she was taken away by the police. She's a good person and even when she was willing to be charged with a crime in order to protect someone else, she was concerned that in doing so she cast her great-uncle in a bad light." Jane went on to repeat for Kazue the words Chiyo had uttered about not wanting any blame to fall on Yohei for what had happened.

"I saw the look in Chiyo's eyes as she said that, and I am convinced of her innocence. The only question is, who is she trying to protect? At first I thought it might be either you or Shohei. There was some rumor that she was to be engaged to Takuo, but I saw the way she treated him and knew she was not acting. On the other hand, it is clear that she is very fond of Shohei, but I can't believe he is brutal enough to force Chiyo to protect him by taking the blame on herself."

Jane did not realize that as she spoke, her innermost feelings were being reflected in her words. She looked directly at Kazue and this time it was Kazue who looked away.

"So of course that left only you. Chiyo would willingly take the blame for something like this in order to protect you. Please don't get me wrong. I don't suppose for a moment that you would willingly sacrifice your daughter in order to protect yourself. What probably happened that night was just as Chiyo told it, only it was you Mr. Wada assaulted, not Chiyo, and after you had stabbed him, you naturally took Chiyo into your confidence before telling anyone else. After all, she's your own daughter and the one you would most likely rely on in a crisis. Once Chiyo learned what had happened, she was afraid you would be arrested, more afraid of this than you were. She thought it would be better to take the blame herself than to see her own mother arrested for murder. And you, of course, understood her feelings in this matter. I believe you chose this course of action because it was the only one that would allow Chiyo to do something to lessen her own pain and sorrow."

Kazue's eyes were wide with astonishment, her face paled, and her lips began to quiver.

"Besides, if everyone thought Chiyo had committed the murder, there was a good chance that the other members of the family would join together to try to protect her. And even if she was arrested for murder, she's young and there were plenty of extenuating circumstances, so there would be no doubt she would get off lightly. Not only did you take all this into consideration, you foisted your secret plan off onto the rest of us as well. It has all been a big charade in which you have used Chiyo to protect yourself. I suppose Mr. Wada was dead for some time before Chiyo came running and weeping from the room."

Kazue was speechless.

"It must have been at that time that Chiyo slashed her wrist. You and she may not even have planned that together. She may really have wanted to die once she found herself in such a cruel position."

"Stop it! That's enough!" screamed Kazue hysterically. Breathing heavily she turned on Jane and cried out, "Stop it! Please, you don't know what you're talking about."

"Please. I'm not trying to blame you, but I cannot stand by and allow this sort of deception to continue. I'm only thinking of Chiyo and what's best for her. Please get hold of yourself and try to think of Chiyo's future and what this means."

"Stop it. Stop it, I said." Kazue suddenly seemed to lose her senses and began mumbling incoherently. She stood up and stumbled across the room, collapsing limply on the bed, but her body continued to be wracked with sobs.

Thirty or forty minutes later Jane left Kazue's room, her face lined with fatigue and uncertainty. "I hope I'm doing the right

180

thing," she said to herself. The determination and confidence she had felt earlier had dissipated. Clearly Kazue had been deeply shaken by Jane's harsh assertions. Indeed, she had quite literally been wracked with spasms of emotion. Kazue had lain on the bed and wept, unconscious of herself or of her surroundings. And yet, there was something deep in Kazue's soul that remained undaunted. Waiting for Kazue to regain her composure, it occurred to Jane that the older woman had not answered any of her questions. She had merely closed her eyes tightly in an expression of misery, but had resolutely refused to speak.

Once again Jane walked through the deserted living room and went into the foyer. She opened the door to the entry hall, determined to escape the grim silence of the house. Outside, the cold air enveloped her, and the dazzling sunlight reflected off the snow and lit up her face, but Jane was not aware of any of this. She was preoccupied with her thoughts. Is there a flaw in my thinking? she wondered. No, there is definitely something about Kazue; I am sure she is involved in this somehow.

Suddenly noticing a shadow on the snow, she stopped and looked up. A small cry escaped her lips and she gasped. Blocking her way was the burly figure of Detective Nakazato, who was wearing an anorak and overshoes. His large head was bare, covered only with coarse hair, and his face had bushy eyebrows to match, but there was an amiable look in his narrow eyes. When she looked up at him, Nakazato was standing in his usual stance, stroking his protruding belly. Jane regained her voice and said, "I was just thinking of coming to the police station to see you."

Nakazato's eyes crinkled with a smile and he said, "Yes, of course. I would love to have a leisurely chat with you, my dear, but first I have to ask Kazue a few questions."

"Oh, I see. Well, that may be impossible just now."

"Why is that?" asked Nakazato, looking sharply at Jane.

"I just finished a very unpleasant interview with her. I'm afraid I said some rather rude things."

Nakazato said nothing but gazed for a time at the house as though trying to see through the living room curtains. Slowly his gaze returned to Jane. "You did, eh? Maybe I should wait a while before I try to see her." He took a cigarette from the pocket of his anorak.

"How is Chiyo holding up?"

"Oh she seems to be doing surprisingly well. She was very calm in answering all the questions we put to her." His voice was gentle as he spoke, but there seemed to be some sort of insinuation in his words.

Jane nodded and asked, "Do you think I would be able to see her, even if it is only for just a few moments?"

"Surely. I don't see any reason why you can't see her now that we've finished questioning her," said Nakazato thoughtfully as he lit his cigarette and turned to look out at the garden. "My car is parked at the bottom of the hill. I didn't want the reporters to get excited at seeing me drive up here."

Jane walked beside Nakazato and they passed among the silver firs and white birches. The detective stopped when they reached the yard light and turned to her. "Earlier when you talked to Kazue, how did she respond? Was she antagonistic?"

It was nearly 5:00 when Jane returned again to the villa, and the broad lower slopes of Mt. Fuji were wrapped in the chilly blue-black of a winter evening. The red beacon of the setting sun shone only on the bare larch grove at the extreme western edge of the mountain. The bleak, bare trees formed a striped pattern across the landscape.

Only the Mercedes sports car was parked in the front yard of the villa. Apparently Sawahiko had not yet returned with his car. He had gone to Gotemba Station to meet the lawyer coming from Tokyo, and from there they had gone directly to the Fuji Five Lakes police station to see Chiyo. The lawyer had heard the details of the case and the charges from Inspector Tsurumi.

By the time Jane and Nakazato had arrived at the police station, Sawahiko and the distinguished, middle-aged lawyer were just leaving. When Sawahiko saw Jane, he gave her a suspicious look, but seemed satisfied when she explained that she had come to visit Chiyo. "Please try to cheer her up," he said.

From the police station Sawahiko had taken the lawyer to a hotel on the lakeshore, where they discussed what sort of case they could make for Chiyo's defense. No one was at the villa to greet Jane when she arrived, so she supposed the others were still in their rooms.

The only lights burning in the house were in the foyer, the living room, and in Shohei's room on the second floor. As Jane approached the front door, she could see a shadow moving at the window of Shohei's room. The first floor of the house was silent and deserted. Kazue and Shohei were the only other people in the house at the moment.

Jane crossed the carpeted floor and went upstairs. She flipped on the light in her room and sat down on the edge of the bed. Her body relaxed in the warmth and it felt pleasant after having walked through the snowy evening without a coat. Her nerves, however, were still taut. Indeed, even as she sat there she became increasingly aware of the uneasiness she felt.

Jane held her breath and listened intently. Surely she hadn't heard any sound from Shohei's room, especially since it was separated from hers by the rooms Chiyo and Takuo had been using. Still, there was something suspicious in the air. There was some sort of invisible, yet definitely mysterious tension in the air, and somehow she felt strangely alert to it.

She suddenly stood up as she heard a door bang open. Footsteps were approaching along the carpeted hallway. She pressed her ear to the door and heard the footsteps stealthily approach Shohei's room. There came the sound of heavy breathing and a woman's whispered voice. "Please doctor, let's do it now. There is no one else here right now, just the two of us." It was Kazue's voice, no doubt about it. "Please, for my sake, hold me in your arms. My nerves are so frazzled I feel they will snap at any moment."

"Kazue . . ." The voice was definitely Shohei's.

"Please, hold me in your arms. Look! See how I'm trembling?"

Hearing the rustle of clothing, Jane closed her eyes and imagined Kazue's full-figured body beneath her clothing.

"You haven't forgotten, have you? I have done everything for you. I have given up everything, all for you."

"Kazue . . . You . . ."

183

"Don't say anything, just hold me in your arms. That's right. Don't ever try to leave me, I won't permit it. I have done everything for this, if you abandon me now, I'll . . . I'll . . ."

"You'll what? Are you trying to blackmail me or something? Be careful what you say. Even the walls have ears."

"It's all right. No one can hear us now. All I need is you. Just hold me close. Please don't ever leave me." Kazue's soft voice dissolved into tears.

Jane stood transfixed at her door, unable to believe her ears. The image of Kazue's folly that flashed before her eyes now was vastly different from the image she had had earlier, the image of a woman who loved her family and who was devoted to her younger husband.

"Earlier when you talked to Kazue, how did she respond? Was she antagonistic?" Jane recalled the words spoken by Detective Nakazato.

During the first few days of the New Year's holiday, a few people came to Lake Yamanaka, but as the days passed, these people left and the typical off-season winter solitude once again descended on the area.

It was 9:30 on the evening of January 6.

Jane was wearing her fur-lined Burberry coat and Indian boots as she walked down the hill, away from the villa. The outdoor lights were on as they had been on the third, but the only sound that came from the dark, lonely villas she passed was the hum of yard lights.

The snow that had melted during the day had frozen again, and as she walked along the icy street, her footsteps made a squeaking sound on the ice. The clear sky was filled with stars, and the air was clean and cold. There were so few lights burning at the lakeshore hotel that one could easily count them.

Jane turned up the collar of her coat and took care not to slip on the ice. She crossed the pedestrian bridge at Asahi Hills intersection. It was dark enough to be midnight and the streets were deserted as she walked along. To her left was the sloping land going down to the lakeshore. She quickly checked to make sure no one was watching, then headed toward the water.

184

The shore was built up with a number of boathouses, and in between were countless boats used for catching freshwater smelt. The shore curved and she saw a special kind of boat designed to travel over the ice, but on such a cold night there was no one who wanted to fish.

Jane walked along the frozen beach to one of the small boathouses. There was no wind, but the shore of the frozen lake was icy. Even though she wore winter boots, Jane had already lost all feeling in her toes.

She stopped beside the last boathouse on the shore. In the light that came from the street she looked at her wristwatch. It was 9:43. She had arrived at the rendezvous early. Although she had hoped to retain her composure, she could feel her heart beating and was quite excited.

The surrounding area was mysteriously silent. There was no sound of waves from the frozen lake, and no sound from anywhere else. Occasionally, she could hear the muted sound of snow chains from a car driving along the street above. Each time a car passed she could hear the sound steadily approach and then recede into the distance.

Jane looked up at the pale, glittering stars in the night sky. She took a deep breath to steady herself, but the icy air penetrated her lungs and seemed to freeze her entire body. Because of the cold and probably also because of the strain, she had lost all feeling in her body; even her brain felt numb. Above in the faint darkness of the sky were the winter stars, her only companions. She wondered what she was doing here, and began to question the wisdom of her actions. Her only emotion was an indescribable sense of loneliness that came welling up within her heart.

Why did all of this have to happen?

Be brave now, there is really nothing to be afraid of.

Surely no one will appear in the next ten minutes, so there's nothing to worry about for at least that long.

Suddenly she saw a medium-size car on the slope above her, the one she had just walked down. The car came down the slope toward the lakeshore at a fast clip. As Jane pulled back in alarm, the car slid to a stop in front of her.

The door on the driver's side opened and a large, shadowy figure emerged. He walked around the front of the car and came toward her. Jane was paralyzed with fear and unable to move as the figure approached; she still could not see who it was. All she could tell was that it was a large man wearing heavy shoes and a work jacket. The headlights of the car cast a dim light on the man's profile.

The rough shoes and jacket don't really suit this man, thought Jane irrelevantly.

"That must have been quite a discussion you had with Kazue," he said guardedly, his cool gaze searching Jane's face. She tried to say something but her tongue was paralyzed and no sound came out.

"It's cold out here; why don't we talk in the car?"

"No . . . I prefer to stay right here."

"Get in the car." He opened the door on the passenger side and pushed Jane on the shoulder. It was not really a violent shove, but there was a determined force behind it.

Keep calm now, she said to herself. You have to talk to him. Jane allowed herself to be pushed into the passenger's seat, but her impulse was to bolt from the car.

The man quickly slid into the driver's seat.

Jane told herself, It doesn't really matter that I got into the car as long as I can keep him occupied. Before she could open her mouth to say anything, however, the man had put the car in gear and begun driving. They sped up the slope toward the street at a furious speed and turned east. Jane had no time to look back.

"Where are you taking me?"

"There is a bluff on the far side of the lake; there is a nice view from there," he said in a harsh voice. His attention was now occupied by driving and his gaze alternated between the front windshield and the rearview mirror. Jane's first panicky thought was that she was being taken away from the arranged meeting place. She was frightened now and her heart was beating like a drum.

"Why did you come? I wanted to talk to Kazue."

"She is too tired, and wanted to rest. She got your letter, but did not know what to make of it. She asked me to talk to you instead and explain things to her later."

As the car sped around the eastern end of the lake, his tone of voice became more normal and relaxed.

"That's not true. Kazue is at the police station now visiting Chiyo. She must have shown you my letter before she left. She must have asked you what to do about it."

Earlier in the evening, Jane had written a letter to Kazue:

On the morning after the murder I heard the balcony door of Yohei's room being opened, and the sound woke me up. Thinking it strange, I went to the top of the stairs and peeked down. I saw someone hurrying out of Yohei's room. At the time I did not know what to make of it, and still don't for that matter. I had only been half awake and was not sure whether I had really heard the sound or just dreamed it.

This afternoon when I saw you in such a miserable state, the truth suddenly dawned on me. You had not asked Chiyo to take the blame for the murder simply to protect yourself. You too were protecting someone. You pretended that you had murdered Yohei so you could persuade Chiyo to take the blame, but at the same time, someone else had already persuaded you to take the blame. The person I saw coming out of Yohei's room was the one who actually committed the murder and who talked you into getting Chiyo to take responsibility for it.

I still don't know who that phantom person is. I want to have a chance to meet privately with you once more since you are the only one who really knows the truth. Together perhaps we can decide what to do.

She had gone on to suggest a meeting at the boathouse on the lakeshore at ten o'clock that evening. It was a secluded place where they could talk without danger of being overheard.

"I don't think Kazue was acting alone in this. Surely there was someone else helping her. I suppose that must have been you. This afternoon I overheard a conversation between Kazue and Shohei. At first I was shaken by what I heard, but then I realized it was all just a charade performed for my benefit. It was your last, desperate attempt to make your scheme work. Kazue was even willing to go that far to keep your identity a secret. Chiyo truly believes her mother was the murderer, and was willing to take the blame for her. You have been successful in cleverly manipulating both these women's feelings in order to carry out your own vicious scheme."

Sawahiko Wada made no reply to this charge. The car turned north along the lake and continued to speed along. In front of them now loomed the black hulk of the mountains. Occasionally they met the lights of a car heading in the opposite direction. The more Jane talked, the more angry and outraged she became.

"Chiyo always said that your research was the most important thing in your life, and it turns out she was tragically right. It is clear now that you are obsessed by a desire to continue your research in genetic engineering, and at the same time, to gain control of Wada Pharmaceuticals so you can commercialize your research in a big way. Yohei opposed what you were doing, so you decided to kill him and grab all his wealth for yourself. I've figured out your plan. If Yohei died, Mine would inherit three-fourths of his estate, the remainder would be divided evenly among the others, so Kazue's share would be one-twelfth of the total. But she did not have any aspirations for gaining control of the company. You probably discussed the matter with a lawyer, and came up with this elaborate plan. You saw your opportunity when all those who were in line for the inheritance were gathered together for the holidays. First of all, you stabbed Yohei yourself. You probably left the knife in the wound so as not to spill too much blood. Then you called Kazue and asked her to help you. It was probably apparent to her that if she were accused of being the murderer instead of you, the punishment would not be as severe. But you took it one step further, insisting that Chiyo take the blame. If Chiyo claimed to have done it and appealed to the others, they would all feel sorry for her and help protect her. If everyone got together and agreed to a cover-up and insisted that it had been done by an outside intruder, there was no reason to suppose that the police would see through the ruse. That meant it was unlikely that Chiyo would be arrested. But in order to get the others to cooperate, it was essential to make them believe that Chiyo had committed the murder, and in order to get Chiyo to go along with the plan, it was crucial that she believe her mother was the real murderer. So you suggested that Chiyo take the blame in place of her mother.

"Kazue is deeply in love with both you and Chiyo, but she realized that if Chiyo assumed responsibility for the murder, she would probably not be caught, and if she were caught, she would surely get off with a suspended sentence. That was preferable to having you arrested and charged with murder. No doubt you explained all this to Kazue when you suggested your plan. No doubt you presented it to her in a very clever way, taking advantage of both Kazue's love for you and her desperate wish to protect the well-being of the family.

"At that point you withdrew and Kazue called Chiyo to Yohei's room. Kazue confessed to Chiyo that Yohei had assaulted her and she had stabbed him. Chiyo believed her mother's story and offered to put herself in her mother's place. She pulled the knife from Yohei's body, allowing some of the blood to get on her clothing.

"At this point the drama was ready to be performed for an audience. Chiyo and Kazue came running from Yohei's room, and Chiyo collapsed on the floor saying, 'I killed Grandpa.' Naturally, we all believed that this was the very beginning of the drama that was about to involve all of us. In reality, however, you had already briefed Kazue on what to do, and she had already deceived Chiyo, so at that point a two-act drama had already been completed."

Sawahiko gripped the steering wheel in silence. Jane was too busy talking to look at his face, but his narrow eyes burned with fierce intensity. The road followed the north side of the lake and was now rising along the slope of the mountains. No other car lights could be seen either in front of them or behind, only the impenetrable darkness of the mountains at night. Assailed by fear and despair, Jane was nevertheless animated by a desire to verify that things had happened the way she thought they had.

"It was all part of your plan that once Chiyo had confessed to the murder, the rest of us would try to make it look as though it was the work of an intruder. At the same time, you had another secret scenario you planned to put into effect. You secretly sabotaged each step of the cover-up we worked so carefully to create. You altered the footprints in the garden and spilled some of the flour in the basement so the police would surely find the gym shoes. You also made off with the scrap of stomach tube and planted it so that the police would see through our cleverest trick. Bit by bit you forced Chiyo into a corner and your ultimate goal was to get her to confess to the murder publicly because that was the only way to disqualify the other inheritors and make it possible for you to get your hands on all of Yohei's money."

189

A sigh suddenly escaped Sawahiko's lips. He could no longer conceal the fact that what she was saying had struck home.

"Remember how Detective Nakazato explained to us the provisions by which a person is disqualified from inheriting money, and how Takuo showed up the next morning with a copy of the *Comprehensive Legal Code* and read it to us? If I had studied those provisions more carefully at the time, I might have figured out what was going on sooner. It is all very clear to me now. Article Eight Ninety-One specifies who is disqualified from being eligible to inherit money. The second paragraph says quite clearly that a person is disqualified if he knows murder has been committed and does not inform the authorities or bring charges. This does not apply, however, if the murderer is a direct blood relative. So, if the cover-up failed and Chiyo was arrested, the circumstances put forward in the second paragraph would be invoked and three of the inheritors, namely, Mine, Shigeru, and Takuo would be disqualified. They would lose their right of inheritance because they knew that Chiyo was the murderer and did not bring charges against her. Of the four who stood to inherit from Yohei's estate, only Kazue fit the second provision of being a blood relative of Chiyo's, the supposed murderer. So once the cover-up failed, Kazue was the only one who would be exempted from the statute's disqualification of inheritors.

"So you first had to get everyone to join the conspiracy, and then make sure it failed and that Chiyo was charged with the murder. Once that happened, Kazue would become the sole inheritor of Yohei's estate. And of course once Kazue got the money, it would be the same as giving it to you.

"The only problem was that you planned to perform this little drama in front of your family because you could count on them to be sympathetic to Chiyo's situation. But unexpectedly I joined the group, and as an outsider, I surely made you nervous. That first night when I met you in the living room at the villa, there was an anxious look on your face that you were unable to conceal. You tried to cast yourself as a simple naïve scholarly type whose feelings can clearly be read on his face, and maybe that's the way you were originally, but . . ." Suddenly Jane stopped talking and the inside of the car was enveloped in a deathly silence.

After a while Jane took her hands off the dashboard and pressed them to her cheeks as she saw a flickering of light in front of them. It appeared to be a farmhouse situated on the shore of the lake. Gradually she was able to make out that it was hidden among the trees. Directly in front of them was a thick forest. The lake must be below the house. The car turned off the highway and came to an abrupt halt at the edge of a small promontory. Once the headlights were shut off, they were in total darkness, but as Jane's eyes became accustomed to the dark, she could make out the dim outlines of things.

"Get out of the car," ordered Sawahiko in a low voice. Jane did not move.

"I said, get out." This time the tone was menacing.

Jane slowly opened the door. Once again her heart began to pound wildly. Now more than ever I have to keep calm, she reminded herself.

Once she was standing on the ground, she realized that the slope fell away abruptly, and that there were some trees lower down between her and the shore of the lake. She could not see the surface of the water, but could estimate where it was by the slope of the land and the way the trees were growing.

Once again Sawahiko's shadowy figure came around the front of the car and approached her. The car was parked sideways facing the lake.

Sawahiko stopped about six feet away from Jane. Though it was too dark to make out the expression on his face, she could see his silhouette and hear his ragged breathing.

"That was quite a story you gave me in the car. Have you said everything you intend to say?"

"Why don't you give yourself up to the police," she said, fighting down the scream of desperation that rose in her throat. She was afraid of what might happen once the talking stopped. "They already know that you committed the murder; there is no way you can escape now. The best thing you can do is give yourself up."

Sawahiko chuckled softly. "I have a way to escape." His shadow loomed over Jane.

"You . . . you have nothing to gain by killing me. Detective Nakazato knows that I was coming here tonight."

"Is that so? All the detective knows is that you were supposed to go to the boathouse. He thinks that's where you are, but you see, I got there first and took you away. I didn't see any sign of the police, or of their cars when I went there to get you. What sort of arrangement did you have with the police anyway?"

"The plan was to lure Kazue out and get the phantom to follow so he would reveal himself." Jane struggled to keep her voice steady. She had stalled for time, but now everything had come to nothing. The plan was in a shambles. "I sent her a letter asking that she meet me at the boathouse. After she received it, the police came and took her to headquarters saying that Chiyo wanted to see her urgently. We figured she would have no choice but to turn to the phantom and ask him to come to the boathouse in her place, and we would be able to find out who it was."

According to the plan Jane was to meet the phantom alone and urge him to give himself up. Nakazato and his men would be observing all this from a distance, ready to move in and arrest him on the spot if there was any sign that Jane was in danger. But Jane had arrived at the boathouse fifteen minutes early and had suddenly fallen into Sawahiko's hands.

"So you had a net spread to catch me. You thought that if you could get Kazue into a corner, the person who was manipulating her would have to put in an appearance."

"That's right, and you fell for it."

This time Sawahiko laughed aloud. "Don't you realize that in telling me this you have made the biggest mistake of your life. You wrote in your letter that on the morning after the murder you saw a person coming out of Yohei's room. But if you knew that person's identity, you would have already known who Kazue's phantom partner was. You could have arrested me right away without having had to have set up this elaborate scheme to trap me. You may have heard the French doors open and close that night, but you had no way of knowing who opened them. And if you didn't know who it was until tonight, then surely the police don't know either. In fact that was the only reason I allowed myself to be lured out here in the first place; to find out whether or not you really knew my identity. I'm satisfied now. You didn't and the police don't either."

Sawahiko moved closer. The only thing behind Jane was the steep slope and the scattered trees. Even the highway was completely dark. It was like being inside a cave.

"Wait! It's already too late. If you kill me, they will know right away who did it."

"No they won't. There is a spring at the bottom of this cliff that keeps the water moving so it doesn't freeze. If you fall into that, you will drown and your body will be trapped under the ice. It will be months before anyone finds you. And even when they do, there will be no proof that you were murdered."

"No. Please. You're wrong. They'll know for sure."

"Well, let's give it a try and see. I'm afraid that at this point it's the only choice I have." Sawahiko braced himself and his dry voice rasped against Jane's ear. "My work is too important to be left undone. I have a responsibility to do whatever has to be done to see that my research is completed."

Suddenly a beam of light sliced across the landscape. It approached through the trees; a car was coming in the opposite direction from the one in which Jane and Sawahiko had come. The white Mercedes sports car pulled up beside Sawahiko's and its headlights illuminated them.

Everything seemed to happen at once. Sawahiko lunged at Jane and at the same moment Shohei leaped from the driver's seat of the Mercedes. With the strength born of fear, Jane thrust Sawahiko aside and felt herself tumbling down the slope. She bounced off several trees before she finally managed to stop herself. Shohei and Sawahiko grappled briefly, then separated. Gasping for breath the two men stood facing each other.

"This is the end of the line for you. I figured out your plan when Kazue tried to seduce me. She said she wanted to deceive you and asked me to protect her from the police investigation. But that was so contrary to her character that I realized that you were just using her to protect yourself."

Sawahiko stood facing Shohei. He was about to say something in reply when suddenly his gaze turned toward the highway. Another car had pulled in beside Shohei's, and Nakazato and Kazue leaped out.

"Now at last I think you understand," said Nakazato in a

mournful voice to Kazue. "Now you see the real nature of this man you trusted and devoted yourself to so completely."

Kazue wore a long coat, and a black shawl covered her head. She turned her haggard face to look directly at her husband. For a long moment she stared at him intently without blinking, then with terrifying calmness she approached him. "You," she cried, her voice overflowing with the love and affection she still felt for him. "You. You called me to Grandpa's room at eight o'clock that night. Grandpa was already dead, stabbed in the chest with a fruit knife. You told me you had been discussing your research project with him when he became agitated and attacked you with the fruit knife. You said that in the ensuing struggle, Grandpa was accidently stabbed in the chest. You said you were afraid no one would believe that's how it happened, and I trusted you. I told Chiyo I had done it and she agreed to take the blame instead of me. There was only one thing you said in this whole thing that was true, and that was that you were in trouble because you had stabbed Grandpa. You must have planned to kill him all along."

Sawahiko returned his wife's stare without blinking. His sharply chisled features gave him the look of an honest, open man. Although there was still an enigmatic look in his eyes, there was also a glint of surprise. Presently his mouth began to move and he uttered a strange laugh. "Doesn't it all make sense?" His voice was a mixture of regret and laughter. "I had such an ingenious plan, don't you see, it was more than just a game."

"Yes . . . yes, I see. I understand." Kazue nodded her head quietly. Her final statement also sounded like a reply to Nakazato's earlier query.

In a gesture that revealed her continuing love for her husband, she suddenly stepped up next to him and threw her coat around his shoulders to protect him from the cold.

Their embrace lasted for some time, and when at last they separated, Sawahiko's body slowly crumpled to the ground. As he fell to the frozen earth, a stream of blood spurted from the wound on his chest, and they saw that Kazue was grasping a thin knife in her right hand.

*   *   *

By the time all the questioning had been completed, it was 1:30 on the morning of January 7.

Ironically, Sawahiko had died from a single stab wound to the chest just as Yohei had died. Kazue was taken into custody as the murderer, and cars dispatched by radio took both Sawahiko's body and Kazue to the Fuji Five Lakes police station. Shohei and Jane were also taken to the station for questioning.

Jane reported in detail to Nakazato and Tsurumi all that had happened since she was picked up in front of the boathouse by Sawahiko.

"It didn't go as we planned, and we lost your trail. It took us a while to find you." Nakazato paused during the questioning and apologized to Jane. "Even though you got to the rendezvous early, it was a mistake on our part not to have had better surveillance."

"No. It was my fault for getting there too early."

As it turned out, she thought, it was Shohei who saved me rather than the police. It had been Shohei who had helped her up the slope from where she had fallen, stunned, against the trees. She had regained her senses in Shohei's warm, strong embrace. She had felt a delicious tingling in her breast.

"You must be very tired after all that has happened tonight. You should go back to the villa and go to bed," said Nakazato to Jane and Shohei, thanking them for their trouble after the questioning had been completed. "I still have to explain all of this to Superintendent Aiura, and then arrange for Chiyo to be released." Apparently he had still not told Aiura the latest developments. "After I get all the details cleared up, I will give you a call and maybe you can come down and pick up Chiyo. She will probably be in a pretty bad way once she finds out what has happened, so someone should be here to give her some support."

After helping Jane into Shohei's car, Nakazato stood for a time and watched the red taillights disappear into the distance. Without realizing it he murmured aloud, "Jane is quite a remarkable woman." As he turned around he saw that Tsurumi was standing behind him and their eyes met. Each man had a weary smile.

"Well, we still have one tough problem to deal with."

"I'm afraid so. How do you suggest we explain all this to the superintendent?"

"He will have to make a fourth retraction when he holds the next news conference."

Stroking his protruding stomach, Nakazato once again murmured, "I'm afraid so," and they walked back to the police station.

The white Mercedes sped through the night along the highway and entered Asahi Hills from the west shore of Lake Yamanaka. With the lake behind them, they ascended the hill toward the villa. The snow that still clung to the tree branches was bathed in ghostly light and glittered brightly as Jane looked over the landscape.

She wondered what Shohei was thinking as he drove in silence with his thick lips tightly compressed and a frown on his face. Jane had a million things she wanted to say, but somehow she felt that at the moment it was better not to say anything. She wished this quiet drive would go on forever.

As the outdoor light in the corner of the back garden came into view, Shohei began to slow down. He turned into the drive lined by the snow-capped fence and the car approached the iron gate of the villa.

The large capital W of the brass name plate fitted into the stone pillar was bathed in the pale light of the yard lamp.

Suddenly it occurred to Jane that the W in Wada could just as well stand for Women—for Mine, and Kazue, and Chiyo. For years Mine had endured Yohei's infidelities and put up with his contempt, and had sacrificed herself to protect the family's reputation. There was Kazue, who had seen two marriages crumble and who was nevertheless able to give everything in her devotion to her third husband. Hadn't these women suffered the tragic circumstances of traditional Japanese women? And then there was Chiyo, who was just beginning to know the misery of being a woman bereft of the protection of her family. Jane had the feeling that human lives lingered in the dim shadows of this silvery light.

"In mathematics W stands for the fourth unknown," murmured Shohei. Had he also been thinking of the W? "When the three unknowns of X, Y, and Z are not enough, it is customary to go on and use U, V, and W."

"Now that you mention it, perhaps in this case as well the fourth

196

suspect was the one. I guess we will have to notify Tokyo of these new developments," she said as an afterthought.

"I've already called. I used the telephone at the police station," said Shohei. "I explained to Mine and Shigeru what had happened and both of them could hardly believe it."

"At any rate, the case has finally been solved."

"At least everyone will have their right of inheritance restored."

"That's right, since Chiyo was not the murderer."

Eventually the conversation trailed off. The silence was uncomfortable.

"How much longer do you plan to stay in Japan?" Shohei suddenly asked in English.

"I don't know, maybe six months or a year."

"And after that?"

"I'll return to the United States and teach Japanese literature at some university."

"Then you definitely plan to return to the United States?"

"Well, it doesn't seem likely I can find a permanent job in Japan. How about you? Do you have any plans for going to America?"

"I spent two years working at a hospital in Chicago. I'll probably have a chance to go there again someday. Who knows?"

"If you do then perhaps we'll see each other in America."

Shohei made no response to this.

As they approached the European-style house, the star-shaped light on the roof sent out its melancholy greeting. There were still lights burning in several rooms in the villa and the radiators were still warm. But now there was not the cheerful bustle of nine people as there had been on the evening when Jane had first arrived. Now there was only Jane and Shohei.

As they walked across the carpeted foyer, they both sighed unconsciously. With heavy steps they climbed the stairs and were reminded of the fatigue they had felt in the early hours of January 4 when they had climbed these same stairs after completing the preparations for their cover-up. Jane felt a lump in her throat as she thought back to that night.

They stopped in front of Jane's door. Shohei opened it for her and she said, "Good-night."

"Good-night."

Even after the words had died away neither of them moved. Then Shohei's right hand went to Jane's shoulder, and his left arm circled her waist. He held her in his strong embrace and his lips sought hers.

It was past seven the following morning when the telephone in the foyer rang. Jane ran down the stairs to answer it. Picking up the receiver, she heard Nakazato's amiable voice. "Thank you for all you did last night. Did you have a good rest?"

"Uh, yes . . . Yes, I did."

"Actually I got all the details cleared up for Chiyo's release some time ago, but she didn't get any sleep last night and was tired, and I figured you would be pretty tired too, so I decided to just leave things as they were until morning. Chiyo has just woken up, and I'm going to tell her what happened. I would appreciate it if you could come down here soon to pick her up and be with her."

It was clear that he considered it Jane's duty to give Chiyo some encouragement after she learned that her stepfather was dead and her mother had been arrested.

Before hanging up Nakazato added, "Last night Kazue confessed to everything. Sawahiko had asked her to persuade Chiyo to take the blame for the murder, explaining that even in the remote chance that she were arrested, she would certainly not be charged with any crime. The plan was for Chiyo to confess that Yohei had assaulted her and she, threatening to commit suicide, had put the knife to her throat. Yohei had lunged at her, and in the ensuing struggle he had been stabbed in the chest. Under those circumstances Chiyo would not be charged with premeditated murder, and it would be a case of self-defense. This plan seemed ideal. Believing this to be the case, Kazue had gone ahead and persuaded Chiyo to take the blame for the murder."

"He certainly didn't say anything to the rest of us about Chiyo's actual innocence." Even now Jane was angered at the thought that Sawahiko's plan had two or three levels of intrigue and deception.

"Later, when Chiyo slashed her wrist and pretended to attempt suicide, Kazue was as surprised as everyone else. If Chiyo had actually succeeded in killing herself, Kazue would probably have committed suicide too. Kazue went on to explain that last night when she realized what had really happened, she made up her mind to kill Sawahiko as a way of getting even for what he had put Chiyo through." Nakazato concluded in a sympathetic voice, saying, "It was a terrible choice for Kazue to have to make. She was torn between being a woman and being a mother."

It occurred to Jane that Chiyo would surely understand the anguish her mother had experienced. Halfway up the stairs Jane paused, the long, narrow window on the landing framing a full view of Mt. Fuji as neatly as if it were a painting. The morning mist shrouded the mountain in pale blue and the unscathed white peak of the majestic mountain soared up into the winter sky. Jane wept softly to herself as she stood looking at the mountain.

Jane and Shohei left the house at 7:30. She wore her fur-lined Burberry coat and Indian boots, the same ones she had worn when she had first arrived at the villa. She carried her bag on a shoulder strap. As the car descended the slope, they could catch glimpses of the lake between the trees. The surface of the water was a cold, deep, dark blue covered with blocks of broken ice. Jane wondered how long it would be before the lake thawed.

"I'll get out at the Asahi Hills intersection," said Jane softly as they came out onto the highway along the lakeshore. Shohei stopped the car and looked at her, but she said, "It would be better if you go alone to pick up Chiyo. Will you tell her, though, that I finished going over her graduation thesis yesterday. I think she still has time to finish it before the deadline."

Shohei looked at Jane and then out at the lake. A frown appeared on his face, perhaps because of the glare of the sunlight, and a faint chuckle came to his lips. "Well, in that case I will take you to Gotemba Station."

"Thank you, but I'll take the bus from here."

Jane got out of the car in front of the pedestrian crosswalk. The road was wet and shiny with the melting snow as she walked toward the bus stop.